HALLOWEEN
PARTY
MURDER

Books by Leslie Meier

MISTLETOE MURDER
TIPPY TOE MURDER
TRICK OR TREAT MURDER
BACK TO SCHOOL
  MURDER
VALENTINE MURDER
CHRISTMAS COOKIE
  MURDER
TURKEY DAY MURDER
WEDDING DAY MURDER
BIRTHDAY PARTY MURDER
FATHER'S DAY MURDER
STAR SPANGLED MURDER
NEW YEAR'S EVE MURDER
BAKE SALE MURDER
CANDY CANE MURDER
ST. PATRICK'S DAY
  MURDER
MOTHER'S DAY MURDER
WICKED WITCH MURDER
GINGERBREAD COOKIE
  MURDER
ENGLISH TEA MURDER
CHOCOLATE COVERED
  MURDER
EASTER BUNNY MURDER
CHRISTMAS CAROL
  MURDER
FRENCH PASTRY MURDER
CANDY CORN MURDER
BRITISH MANOR MURDER
TURKEY TROT MURDER
SILVER ANNIVERSARY
  MURDER
INVITATION ONLY
  MURDER
CHRISTMAS SWEETS

IRISH PARADE MURDER
CHRISTMAS CARD MURDER
(with Lee Hollis and Peggy
Ehrhart)

Books by Lee Hollis

Hayley Powell Mysteries
DEATH OF A KITCHEN DIVA
DEATH OF A COUNTRY
  FRIED REDNECK
DEATH OF A COUPON
  CLIPPER
DEATH OF A CHOCOHOLIC
DEATH OF A CHRISTMAS
  CATERER
DEATH OF A CUPCAKE
  QUEEN
DEATH OF A BACON
  HEIRESS
DEATH OF A PUMPKIN
  CARVER
DEATH OF A LOBSTER
  LOVER
DEATH OF A COOKBOOK
  AUTHOR
DEATH OF A WEDDING
  CAKE BAKER
DEATH OF A BLUEBERRY
  TART
DEATH OF A WICKED
  WITCH
DEATH OF AN ITALIAN
  CHEF
CHRISTMAS CARD MURDER
(with Leslie Meier and Peggy
Ehrhart

Poppy Harmon Mysteries
POPPY HARMON
   INVESTIGATES
POPPY HARMON AND THE
   HUNG JURY
POPPY HARMON AND THE
   PILLOW TALK KILLER

Maya & Sandra Mysteries
MURDER AT THE PTA
MURDER AT THE BAKE
   SALE

Books by Barbara Ross

Maine Clambake Mysteries
CLAMMED UP
BOILED OVER
MUSSELED OUT
FOGGED INN
ICED UNDER

STOWED AWAY
STEAMED OPEN
SEALED OFF
SHUCKED APART

Jane Darrowfield Mysteries
JANE DARROWFIELD,
   PROFESSIONAL
   BUSYBODY
JANE DARROWFIELD AND
   THE MADWOMAN NEXT
   DOOR

*Collections with Leslie Meier,
Lee Hollis and Barbara Ross*
EGGNOG MURDER
YULE LOG MURDER
HAUNTED HOUSE MURDER
HALLOWEEN PARTY
   MURDER

Published by Kensington Publishing Corp.

HALLOWEEN PARTY MURDER

Leslie Meier
Lee Hollis
Barbara Ross

KENSINGTON
PUBLISHING CORP.

www.kensingtonbooks.com

KENSINGTON BOOKS are published by

Kensington Publishing Corp.
119 West 40th Street
New York, NY 10018

All Kensington titles, imprints, and distributed lines are available at special quantity discounts for bulk purchases for sales promotion, premiums, fundraising, educational, or institutional use. Special book excerpts or customized printings can also be created to fit specific needs. For details, write or phone the office of the Kensington Special Sales Manager: Attn. Special Sales Department. Kensington Publishing Corp, 119 West 40th Street, New York, NY 10018. Phone: 1-800-221-2647.

Library of Congress Card Catalogue Number: 2021935336

The K logo is a trademark of Kensington Publishing Corp.

ISBN-13: 978-1-4967-3382-5
ISBN-10: 1-4967-3382-7
First Kensington Hardcover Edition: September 2021

ISBN-13: 978-1-4967-3384-9 (ebook)
ISBN-10: 1-4967-3384-3 (ebook)

10 9 8 7 6 5 4 3 2 1

Printed in the United States of America

Contents

HALLOWEEN PARTY MURDER

Leslie Meier

For Stella Rose Levitt
and
Abigail Meldrim Meier,
because they know everything!

Chapter One

"Lucy, you were really wrong about Ty Moon," said Bill, stepping into the kitchen and taking off the barn coat that was his autumn uniform. "He's a really nice guy," he continued, hanging the tan jacket on one of the hooks beside the kitchen door. He crossed the kitchen to the fridge and took out a beer, then joined his wife at the round golden-oak table.

Lucy, who had been doing a crossword puzzle, looked up and smiled at her husband, even though she felt the slightest bit defensive. "I wasn't the only one who suspected he was up to no good," she said, remembering how most people in town had reacted to the strange noises and flashing lights emanating from the old Victorian house Ty and his wife, Heather, had bought a year or so ago. "I admit I may have overreacted," she continued, thinking back to the frightening afternoon when her grandson Patrick disappeared inside the Moons' house, a once-grand Victorian that had become so derelict that townsfolk suspected it was haunted. "But it wasn't all my fault. Things kind of spiraled out of control."

"You can say that again," said Bill, popping the top on his can of beer. "It's a miracle nobody got shot once the SWAT team arrived."

Lucy put down her pencil. "All's well that ends well," she said. "If Ty hadn't been so unfriendly and downright secretive about his work, people wouldn't have been so suspicious."

"He's been real successful; he told me he's got a huge job coming up that's gonna make him a lot of money."

Lucy knew that Ty created computer-generated special effects for TV and movies, and was able to work from home in the quaint seaside town of Tinker's Cove, Maine. "And I think I was entirely justified in thinking he was abusing Heather," she said, warming to her subject. "How could we know she was undergoing chemo for cancer?"

"Well, she's in remission now, and they're ready to start a family," said Bill. "And they've hired me to renovate that old monstrosity of a house and restore it to its former grandeur." He took a long swallow. "With some modern improvements."

Lucy was definitely interested. She and Bill had recently expanded their former bedroom into a luxurious master suite, and she was nurturing plans for a kitchen reno, obsessively watching the home improvement shows on TV. "What have they got in mind?" she asked.

"Well, they want to keep all the old moldings, the doors and fireplaces, all the stuff that gives the place character. The rooms are big and have high ceilings, which is great. We can't go all-out open plan, but there are double doorways between the two living rooms and also from the hall into the dining room. I'm thinking of moving the kitchen into one of the living rooms, making the dining room a living room, and turning the old kitchen into a solarium." He paused. "What do you think?"

"I'm jealous," said Lucy, glancing around at their antique farmhouse, with its small rooms, cramped staircases, and dormered bedrooms where they had raised their four children, who were now grown. "I love our house, I always have, but it would be nice to have a kitchen island, and a laundry room instead of having to go down to the basement, and," she looked at the messy collection of coats and boots by the kitchen door, "a real mud room, with plenty of storage."

"Well," said Bill, shrugging philosophically, "if the Moons go ahead with this reno, maybe all your champagne dreams will come true." He fingered his beer can. "They're talking big, and that means a big paycheck for me."

"When will you know?" asked Lucy.

"Soon, I hope. I've got to draw up a plan and give them an estimate, but I don't anticipate any problems. They were very clear about what they want, which makes it easy for me." He drained his beer. "And, oh, you'll love this, Lucy. Before we start demo, they want to have a big Halloween party. They said everybody thought the house was haunted, so why not throw a big bash? Heather said it could even be a fundraiser for your Hat and Mitten Fund."

Lucy was definitely revising her opinion of the Moons. "That's a great idea." She and three friends had created the fund years ago to provide warm winter clothing for the town's less-fortunate kids, collecting outgrown clothing and distributing it to those in need. Through the years, the fund had grown, and it now provided back-to-school backpacks, holiday parties, and even summer-camp scholarships, in addition to its original mission of providing gently used jackets, boots, hats, and mittens.

"Yeah, Heather said you should give her a call, see what you can work out."

"Will do," said Lucy, reaching for her phone. She was still talking to Heather, inviting her to the next Hat and Mitten Fund meeting, when her youngest child, and the only one still living at home, arrived. Zoe was finally finishing up her degree at nearby Winchester College, ending a protracted higher-education career in which she'd sampled practically every major the small liberal-arts institution offered, finally settling on communications. She dropped her backpack on the floor and shrugged out of her bright pink Winchester hoodie, hanging it on the hook beside her father's jacket.

"What was that all about?" she asked, extracting a yogurt from the fridge and leaning against the kitchen counter to eat it. "I didn't know you were friends with Queen Heather."

"I don't know what you mean," said Lucy. "As it happens, your father got a job fixing up the Moons' old Victorian, and they want to have a big Halloween party there before the demo starts. A haunted house in the haunted house! It should be really popular, and it's going to be a fundraiser for the Hat and Mitten Fund; that's why I called her."

"Wow, Mom, I guess your suspicions about Ty Moon were way wrong," she said, causing Bill to chuckle as he beat a hasty retreat to the family room.

Lucy took a deep breath. "As I told your father, I was not the only person who had doubts about Ty Moon. If you remember, everybody thought he was abusing Heather and probably conducting all sorts of ungodly goings-on in that spooky house."

"Yeah, well, now he and Heather are the most popular couple in town," said Zoe, licking the last of the yogurt off her spoon and tossing the cup into the trash.

"Really?"

"Yeah. They're part of this young crowd of smart, hip creative types."

This was news to Lucy, who thought she and her friends were the smart, young crowd. After all, the population in Tinker's Cove definitely skewed upward, with a large percentage of elderly citizens in their eighties and even nineties, which allowed Lucy and her friends to think of themselves as comparative youngsters. "Who are these people?" she asked.

"Oh, you know. There's Matt and Luisa Rodriguez, from the Cali Kitchen restaurant. That's where they all hang out, especially for Sunday brunch. The Moons are regulars, and Juliette Duff shows up if she's in town."

Lucy knew the Rodriguezes, a brother and sister who ran the restaurant created by their father, renowned chef Rey Rodriguez. Juliette Duff was a supermodel who had inherited her extremely wealthy grandmother's estate on Shore Road, where it occupied a spectacular piece of property overlooking the ocean. "Who else?"

"Well, Rosie Capshaw, she's always there."

Lucy, who was a reporter for the *Courier* weekly newspaper, had interviewed Rosie, a recent arrival who was distantly related to Juliette and was living on the estate, where she created spectacular puppets in a disused barn.

"What about Brendan Coyle?" Lucy knew the director of the local food pantry was a good friend of Rosie's.

"Yup, he's there a lot, and so is Kevin Kenneally. They give the place a real happening vibe; you'd almost think you were in Portland or Boston."

"Kevin doesn't seem to fit in with the others; they're all creatives, and he's pretty conservative, being the assistant DA and all," said Lucy, trying to picture the group.

"They love teasing him, and he's a really good sport about it all."

Lucy suddenly wondered how her cash-strapped student daughter had come by this knowledge. She certainly couldn't afford to frequent the expensive Cali Kitchen Sunday brunch. "How do you know all this?" she asked. "Since when have you been eating brunch?"

"I wish," said Zoe, sighing and rolling her eyes. "Don't you remember? I filled in at Cali Kitchen for my friend Catie a couple of weeks ago. It was brutal hard work; that bunch had me running my feet off getting them mimosas and Bloody Marys, but they were generous tippers. Especially Ty."

"Well, I better get supper started," said Lucy, pressing her hands on the table and pushing herself up off her chair. She had to admit it; she wasn't as young as she used to be, what with her aching back and diminished energy. "I could use some help," she suggested, hopefully.

"Sorry, Mom, I've got a paper due," said Zoe, zipping up the back stairs and leaving Lucy to peel the potatoes.

Lucy and her Hat and Mitten Fund friends had been meeting at Jake's Donut Shack on Thursday mornings for years, beginning when their kids had gone off to college and they no longer ran into each other at sports practices and school events. The four women had shared advice and offered emotional support as their kids entered their tricky twenties and launched their own careers and families. But now, as she glanced around the table, she realized they were no longer the young, hip bunch she'd always considered them to be.

Nowadays, they were on the far side of middle age, and it was beginning to show. There were streaks of gray in Rachel Goodman's shoulder-length black hair; Pam Stillings still wore her reddish hair in a ponytail, but bags had begun to appear under her eyes. Sue Finch, always the most stylish member of the group, worked hard to maintain her slim figure, but Lucy had noticed the slightest beginnings of a muffin top around her waist, and one day her chic ballet shoe slipped off, revealing an orthotic arch support. As for herself, Lucy knew she was fighting a losing battle when she smoothed on her drugstore moisturizer every morning and faithfully applied night cream before going to bed.

The years were definitely taking a toll, but they'd also given the four friends the gift of friendship. They formed a tight group, having shared so many experiences, and Rachel was quick to remind them when they gathered at their usual table that Heather might find them a bit intimidating. "She's a newcomer," began Rachel, who had majored in psychology in college and had never gotten over it, "and we need to make her feel welcome. No inside jokes, no references to past events she knows nothing about, that sort of thing. Also, I would imagine she's still dealing with the emotional effects of her cancer diagnosis and treatment, even though she's now in remission and may even be cured."

"I don't know about that," said Lucy, signaling to Norine, the waitress, that she wanted a cup of coffee. "Zoe calls her 'Queen Heather' and says she and Ty are the most popular couple in town. They're part of a group of bright young things that regularly gather for Sunday brunch at Cali Kitchen."

Lucy felt Sue bristle beside her as Norine approached to fill their mugs and take their orders: a sunshine muffin for Rachel, hash and eggs for Lucy, granola and yogurt for Pam, and black coffee for Sue. When Norine went off to the kitchen, Sue practically exploded.

"Queen Heather? That's ridiculous!" she exclaimed, tucking a glossy lock of hair behind one ear with a perfectly manicured hand. "And since when did these upstart social climbers—millennials who, I can guarantee, don't know the first thing about writing a thank-you note or a proper letter of sympathy—when did they become the most popular social set in town? And who decided that anyway?"

"Shhh," cautioned Pam, nodding toward the door, where Heather had paused, checking out the room. "Remember," she whispered, "this fundraiser could mean some big bucks for the fund." Then she lifted her head and made eye contact with Heather, waving her over.

"I'm so glad you could come," she said, as Heather seated herself. "Are you famished? Do you want to order?" she asked, looking for Norine.

"Oh, no. Nothing for me. No food," replied Heather, sounding horrified at the thought. "I wouldn't mind some herbal tea, if they have that here."

Sue snorted. "It's a donut shop. They have coffee."

"I guess then I'll just have a glass of water," said Heather, shrugging out of her stylish fake fur coat to reveal a painfully slim body and tossing back her long, silvery hair. "As you probably all know, I'm Heather Moon, and I live in that big, old haunted house on School Street."

"We're so glad you could come this morning," began Rachel, "and we're so excited about the fundraiser, which is so generous of you." She smiled. "I'm Rachel Goodman, and I know you've met Lucy . . ."

"We've met," said Heather, without much enthusiasm.

"I just want to say that I'm sorry about any misunderstandings in the past," offered Lucy. "I'm looking forward to working with you and publicizing the haunted house. I know Ted is always eager to promote local events, right, Pam?"

"Absolutely," said Pam. "I'm Pam Stillings, I own the *Courier*, along with my husband Ted, and I can guarantee that the paper will provide plenty of free publicity."

"That's great," said Heather, turning to Sue with a questioning expression.

Sue took a sip of coffee, narrowed her eyes, and gave Heather a tiny smile. "I'm Sue Finch," she said, "and it's an absolute pleasure to meet you."

"Same here," said Heather, as Norine arrived with their orders.

"Ohmigosh, I didn't see you," she apologized to Heather, distributing the plates and then pulling her order book out of her apron pocket. "What can I get you, hon?"

"Chamomile tea with lemon," said Heather.

"Oh, sorry. No can do. We've got Tetley."

"I'll just have a glass of water. Thank you."

"Okay." From her tone, it was clear that Norine did not approve of her choice.

Heather pressed her lips together, but whether she was suppressing a smile or a thought wasn't clear. She glanced around the table, then began speaking. "Well, as you know, my husband and I are hosting a grand Halloween party, including a haunted house, before we start modernizing the old place."

"It's the perfect venue for a haunted house," said Pam, enthusiastically.

"That's what we thought," said Heather. "And my husband has the technical skills to provide amazing special effects. You wouldn't believe what he can do with light and sound."

"Oh, I think we have an idea," said Sue, as Norine arrived with a tall glass of water. A clear plastic straw topped with a white paper casing was in the glass.

"Oh, oh. No plastic straws!" exclaimed Heather. "But what can I do with it? It's already been opened, and now it's going to go in the ocean . . ."

"No big deal," said Norine, extracting the offending straw.

"But it is a big deal. Some sea turtle will eat it and die, and they'll all become extinct."

"I'll make sure it doesn't get in the ocean," promised Norine, furrowing her brow.

"But how?" demanded Heather.

"I just will," said Norine, hurrying off to the kitchen.

"Plastics, they're terrible," said Heather. "They last forever."

"So true," agreed Pam. "But we really need to talk about the fundraiser. Do you have a date in mind?"

"Well, I certainly don't want it to conflict with the children's party you ladies always have for the elementary school kids."

"That will be on Halloween, which is a Friday this year," said Pam.

"I think the haunted house party should be on a weekend, but maybe not the weekend just before Halloween. If we hold it a week earlier, it will kind of set the tone and get people in the mood, if you know what I mean."

"I assume you'll need lots of volunteers to help construct the scary effects, and it will take some time to organize, too," said Rachel.

"Absolutely. Maybe Lucy can put out a call for volunteers in this week's paper," said Heather.

"We'll all be glad to help," said Pam.

"Well, I'm not sure how much I can do," said Rachel. "My husband is running for state rep, and I'm pretty busy with his campaign."

"You get a pass," said Sue. "But for the rest of us, it's all hands on deck, right?"

"Righto," said Lucy, as they all nodded their heads. "And don't worry," she told Rachel. "I've been covering the campaign and Bob's a shoo-in, running as an independent. Nobody ever heard of the Democrat, Andi Nardone, and George Armistead, the Republican, is ninety years old if he's a day."

"I hope you're right," said Rachel. "You can't ever be too sure; things can change in a minute in a campaign."

Chapter Two

Lucy decided Rachel's fears were unwarranted when she stood outside the IGA grocery store on Saturday morning, handing out leaflets for Bob. It was a brisk fall morning, and she enjoyed being out in the fresh air and sunshine, which she knew would soon be only a memory, along with the bright yellow and orange leaves that were already starting to fall. The store was busy; many shopping carts were loaded with pumpkins, potted chrysanthemums, and jugs of apple cider. She knew most of the shoppers, who were friends and neighbors, and everybody seemed pleased to learn that Bob was running for state rep.

"It's about time George Armistead took to his rocking chair," said retired kindergarten teacher Lydia Volpe. "He's been a state rep for over forty years, and I don't think he even bothers to attend the sessions, or vote. And when he does vote, it's always against anything that might raise taxes, like improving the schools or health care. I'll gladly vote for Bob; I think he'll be a great state rep."

"That's great. I know he'll appreciate your vote. And while I've got you, Heather and Ty Moon have offered to hold a haunted house fundraiser for the Hat and Mitten Fund, and we're looking for volunteers . . ."

"Say no more," said Lydia. "I'll be happy to help, but

you know I'm already on the committee for the children's party, and I really don't want to go to any more meetings."

Lucy laughed. "Anything you can do would be appreciated. How about taking tickets on the night of the event; that's just a couple of hours."

"Okay, put me down for that," said Lydia, giving her cart a push and heading across the parking lot to her car.

As Lucy watched Lydia's progress, her attention was caught by a young mother struggling with a toddler on one hand and what looked like a four-year-old girl on the other. The toddler kept going limp, impeding their progress, and the mom finally just picked up the tot, telling the little girl to hang on to her jacket.

"Why, Mom?" asked the girl.

"Because I don't have a free hand. I've got to carry Benjy, and I want you to be safe in the parking lot."

"Why does Benjy have to be carried?"

"He's little and gets tired."

"Well, I'm big, and I can take care of myself." With that, the little girl darted away from her mother and ran ahead, just as a zippy sports car rounded the line of parked cars.

Seeing that the little girl was directly in front of the approaching car, Lucy ran into the parking lot, waving her arms and screaming "Stop!" The car braked and stopped mere feet from the girl, who burst into tears and ran back to her mother. She fell to her knees and enfolded the girl into her arms, along with the toddler brother.

"It's okay, you're okay," crooned the mom, smoothing the little girl's hair.

The driver of the car climbed out, and Lucy was surprised to recognize Kevin Kenneally, whom she'd frequently covered at press conferences. Kenneally, who was dressed in freshly ironed jeans and a North Face windbreaker, angrily confronted the little family. "You know, lady, you really ought to keep that kid under control."

"Well, maybe you should drive a little more carefully. If it wasn't for this lady here, we would've had a real tragedy," declared the mom.

"This is a parking lot, not a playground," insisted Kevin, turning to Lucy. "That girl was in no danger. I saw her and was braking."

Lucy was trembling, and her heart was pounding, but she wasn't about to let Kevin have the last word. "Maybe so, but it didn't seem like that to me. There's no excuse for speeding in a parking lot where there are elderly folks and children. If a cop was here, you would've been cited."

"I'm not so sure about that, Lucy," he said, with a knowing smile. On second thought, Lucy figured he was right; it was doubtful that a local cop would cite an assistant district attorney. "And if I were you," he added, "I wouldn't be so quick with the accusations." Having said his piece, he hopped back in his fancy sports car, backed away too fast into a three-point turn, and zoomed out of the parking lot. As she watched him go, Lucy wondered exactly how much assistant district attorneys made these days, and whether his salary would stretch to cover such an expensive car.

"Well, I never . . ." said the shocked mom, picking up the toddler.

"What a reckless driver," said Lucy, rolling her eyes. She took the little girl's hand and began walking to the entrance. "My name's Lucy, what's yours?"

"Stella. Stella Rose Levitt."

"And how old are you, Stella?"

"Four."

"Well, remember to be extra careful in parking lots and to mind your mom, okay?"

Stella scowled. "I'm a big girl."

"Yes, you are, but cars are bigger." Lucy turned to the mom. "By the way, I'm campaigning for my friend Bob Goodman. He's running for state rep. Can I give you a brochure?"

"Sure, thanks," said the woman, who was settling the toddler into the seat of a shopping cart. "And thanks so much for stopping that car and saving Stella. I can't even imagine . . ."

Lucy gave her a big smile. "No problem. And don't forget to vote for Bob."

Lucy recounted the episode that afternoon at a meeting of the Hat and Mitten Fund planning committee at Sue's antique captain's house on Parallel Street. "I'm pretty confident I got at least one sure vote for Bob," she said, ending the tale. All the members of the breakfast group were there, as well as Heather Moon and Rosie Capshaw, who Lucy suspected had come to offer moral support to Heather.

"I should think so," said Heather, in her soft voice. "You saved that little girl's life."

Rosie Capshaw didn't hesitate to express her opinion. "I like Kevin and all, but sometimes he can be a big jerk."

"What kind of car was it?" asked Pam.

"I dunno. Some sort of sports car," answered Lucy, with a shrug.

"It's a second-hand Corvette, and he loves it," said Rosie.

"Men and their toys," sighed Sue.

"Well, I hope that mother will take better care of her children," said Heather, sounding a bit wistful. "They're really a gift from God, you know, and not everyone gets them."

Lucy's ears perked up at this. Bill had told her that Ty and Heather wanted to start a family, and she wondered if they'd run into difficulties. She and the others were seated at Sue's prized wine-tasting table in her breakfast nook, and were nibbling on home-baked madeleines and sipping chamomile tea in Heather's honor.

"Right," added Pam. "I'm sure that near-accident was a real wake-up call for her." She pressed her lips together thoughtfully. "Did you get her name? Maybe she could help with the fundraiser or the kids' party."

"No. Her last name is probably Levitt; that's what Stella said her name was," said Lucy, reaching for another madeleine even though she knew she shouldn't. "And in the poor woman's defense, I have to say she really had her hands full with those kids."

"Families aren't what they used to be," offered Sue. "Lots of women keep their birth names; kids have different fathers and different surnames. It can be hard to keep it all straight."

Sue spoke from experience; she used to be engaged full-time as the part-owner, executive director, and head teacher at Little Prodigies Child Care Center, but was now semi-retired and acted mostly as a silent partner, helping out occasionally.

"Well, let's turn our attention to the matters at hand," urged Rachel, draining her cup and setting it in the saucer. "I think the kids' party is pretty much under control. We've done it so many times, it doesn't require much thought."

"Can you do the fortune-telling?" Pam asked Rachel. "Or will you be too busy with the campaign?"

Rachel traditionally put on a pair of oversized hoop earrings, wrapped herself in colorful scarves and shawls, seated herself in a little tent with a garden globe as a crystal ball, and pretended to tell the future. Her fortunes, really advice for good behavior couched in mystical terms, were terribly popular, especially with the older kids.

"Absolutely, I wouldn't miss it for the world. And the fortunes may include advising the kids to tell their parents to vote for Bob." She furrowed her brow. "Would that be wrong?"

"Actually, we could include his brochures in the treat bags," suggested Lucy.

"You can even get specially wrapped candies. Vote for Bob Bars or something," said Rosie, who admitted skipping breakfast as an excuse for eating most of the madeleines. She was dressed in a plaid shirt and jeans and was much sturdier than her fragile friend, Heather; as a puppeteer, she was used to the hard physical labor that constructing and working her oversized creations required.

"Thanks, Rosie, I'll look into that," said Rachel, impressed with the idea. "So the kids' party is all set?"

"Yup," said Pam. "I've got plenty of refreshments, the DJ is booked, the soccer moms are doing the decorations, the PTA is organizing games, posters are up . . . can anybody think of anything I've missed?"

"Sounds great," said Sue. "Let's move on to the haunted house. Any thoughts?"

"I guess we could have one of those gruesome operating rooms; those are pretty popular," said Lucy.

"Oh, yeah," said Pam, enthusiastically, reaching for one of the rapidly disappearing madeleines. "And surprises. Like a ghost that pops out of a closet, something like that. And I'm sure Ty will come up with lots of eerie noises and spooky lighting effects."

"You can count on him," said Rosie, getting a big smile from Heather.

Heather didn't smile often, thought Lucy, biting into her madeleine, but when she did, she looked even more angelic than usual. Lucy tried to figure out how she did it, what made her look so ethereal, like a fairy or some otherworldly creature. Was it the long, ash-blond hair? Her big blue eyes? The fluttery clothes she chose, always in shades of white and dripping with lace and ruffles. And, of course, she was fine-boned and very thin, really too thin. Somewhat guiltily, she put down the rest of her madeleine on her saucer.

"Actually," continued Heather, speaking rather hesitantly, almost whispering, "Ty and Rosie had some thoughts about the tableaux that would elevate the haunted house above the usual stuff people expect."

Pam wasn't sure she liked the sound of this. "Really? Like what?" she asked, in a challenging tone.

"Oh, it was just an idea," said Heather, shrinking into her lacy tablecloth shawl.

"Don't let Pam put you off," said Sue, patting her hand. "Tell us how you want to do it. It's your house, after all." She stood up. "More tea, anyone?"

Getting a few nods, she refilled the cups and then sat down, tenting her hands expectantly. "Go on, Heather," she invited.

"Well, we thought—" she began, looking to Rosie for approval and getting a nod. "Well, it's really Ty, he's the one with the ideas. He suggested we might base the tableaux on famous books and paintings. For instance," she said, warming to her subject and speaking somewhat less hesitantly, "I thought I could portray Ophelia, but with a twist. You know, there's a famous painting of Ophelia floating in a river by an artist named Millais. He painted the creek *en plein air*, out in the woods, and that's how he got all the beautiful plants and nature in the background. But he had his model for Ophelia pose in a bathtub, so that's what I thought I would do. What do you think?"

"I think that might be rather chilly," offered Pam.

"And damp," said Lucy.

"Oh, I wouldn't use real water. I'm going to use plastic sheeting and bubbles, and Ty will fix the lights, so it will look quite realistic. He says he can create the illusion of rippling water."

"It's easy-peasy with the right equipment," offered Rosie. "And I have some ideas for recycling the plastic in my puppets."

"I suppose someone will portray the artist, Millais?" asked Rachel.

"Yes. Kevin Kenneally has offered to play the artist; he'll wear a smock and a beret, and since he's the assistant DA, I think I'll be in very good hands."

Lucy was tempted to say something like "as long as he's not driving," but bit her tongue. She didn't want to strain her fragile relationship with Heather.

"Right," said Pam, thoughtfully. "You'll be in a rather vulnerable position, and you don't want anybody messing with you."

Heather hadn't considered this and was alarmed. "Do you think they would?"

"I wouldn't put it past some. Teen boys, for example, might try to get a rise out of you just to break the illusion."

"I'm pretty sure Kevin can keep me safe," said Heather.

"One thing I can tell you," said Sue, tucking a stray lock of midnight-black hair behind one ear with her perfectly manicured hand, "is that posing as Ophelia didn't work out very well for Elizabeth Siddall, the model. Millais did have her in a bathtub of water, which he tried to keep warm with oil lamps, but one of the lamps went out, and she caught a chill and was seriously ill for months."

"Really?" asked Heather, sounding doubtful.

"It's true," said Sue, responding to her friends' skeptical expressions.

"How on earth do you know this?" asked Lucy.

"I took art history in college, and the professor told us all about it. He really despised the pre-Raphaelites, of which John Everett Millais was one. He said it was a sad and pathetic attempt to idealize the past when the art world was moving forward into exciting new ways of seeing, like impressionism, and painting speeding trains, trying to capture movement and light, and, well," she grinned naughtily, "that professor made a big impression on me." She took the teapot over to the stove and added some hot water. She was smiling at the memory when she apologized, saying, "I'm sorry. I got carried away down Memory Lane."

"Not at all, that's very interesting," said Heather. "But I won't be chilly. No real water." She smiled. "And I'll wear my long johns."

"Actually, I like this idea of yours," said Pam. "We could reference all sorts of classics. Hamlet and poor Yorick, along with the witches."

"The witches were in *Macbeth*," said Rosie.

Pam was not about to be put off. "Well, just Hamlet and Yorick's skull then, in a graveyard. And how about Dr. Jekyll and Mr. Hyde? Maybe with a mirror and a strobe sort of light that flicks from one to the other? Wouldn't that be cool?" She paused momentarily. "Oh, and what about Van Gogh? Slicing his ear off!"

"Maybe we should leave the choice of scenes to Ty and Rosie," suggested Rachel.

"Right." Pam took a deep breath. "I was letting my imagination run away with me."

"All good ideas," said Heather, politely.

"What else do you have in mind, apart from Ophelia?" asked Lucy. "Is there anything for us?"

Heather smiled, one of those "butter wouldn't melt in her mouth" smiles. "Actually, we do. Don't we, Rosie?"

Rosie was grinning broadly and could hardly contain her excitement. "It's terrific!"

"What is it?" asked Pam, eagerly.

"Well, remember, you don't have to do it," said Heather. "It's just a suggestion."

Sue returned to the table with the fresh pot of tea. "We're all dying to hear," she said, setting it down. "Tell us while it steeps."

"Okay." Heather bit her lip. "It was Ty's idea, really. He thought we could have a guillotine, and the blade would come down and a head would roll." Her eyes had grown quite bright, and her face became animated as she went on to describe the special effects. "He can create the illusion of blood with lights, and he'd add the sound of the blade whooshing and thumping down."

"It would be like that scene from *A Tale of Two Cities*, you know, the book by Dickens," said Rosie.

"'Tis a far, far better thing that I do than I have ever done,'" quoted Lucy, with a dramatic flourish. "I guess I could be that guy."

"Oh, no," said Heather, hastily. "No. We thought you'd make a perfect Madame Defarge, Lucy."

Lucy felt rather deflated. "Madame Defarge?"

"Yes," continued Heather brightly. "And you could all be *tricoteuses,* the women who knitted and chortled gleefully while the guillotine did its grisly work in the French Revolution."

"Well, that would certainly be interesting," said Sue, rather coolly. "More tea?"

Nobody seemed interested in tea. The mood in the room had suddenly changed; the enthusiasm was gone. Silent glances were exchanged, and suddenly, as if with one accord, they were all beginning to gather up their things and preparing to leave. Thank-yous were offered, goodbyes were said, and the women quickly departed.

Rosie and Heather were standing together on the porch when Lucy went outside, but when she tried to say goodbye, they didn't respond, but ignored her and continued their conversation. Walking down the brick path to her car, Lucy had the unnerving sensation that she was becoming invisible. And when Rosie and Heather actually deigned to acknowledge her, she fumed, they thought she would make a perfect Madame Defarge. Settling herself behind the steering wheel, she came to the unwelcome conclusion that it wasn't a compliment.

Chapter Three

Lucy was still fretting about Heather's assertion that she would make a perfect Madame Defarge when she went, along with Bill, on Sunday afternoon to work on setting up the haunted house. As luck would have it, she was assigned to work with Ty on painting the walls in the upstairs hallway black, and she felt uncomfortable, worrying that he might harbor some resentment toward her. She decided to tackle the problem head-on, while he was bent over, stirring the paint.

"Ty," she began, "I want you to know that I'm really sorry about that whole thing with my grandson. I was terrified when I couldn't find him, and when the kids said he'd gone into your house, I called the police, but honestly, I never dreamed they'd bring the SWAT team. I thought one of the officers would knock on your door, that was all."

He looked up at her, a smile playing on his lips. "Listen, that's all water under the bridge. I can understand how terrifying it is to lose track of a kid, and, well, to be honest, that whole situation was a much-needed wake-up call for me and Heather. We were so involved with her treatment and my work that we didn't realize the impression we were making on other people, like our neighbors and the school kids." He put the paint-covered stirring stick down carefully on a sheet of newsprint and stood up, facing her. "That's one reason we want to do the haunted house. We want folks in Tinker's Cove to know that we're really rather nice, and we want to be good neighbors."

Lucy was struck by his sincerity, and if she was honest with herself, his remarkable good looks. Ty was tall and broad-shouldered, with tousled dark hair and dramatic eyebrows, and he wore his ripped jeans and paint-daubed sweatshirt with casual flair. Maybe it was those boat shoes, held together with duct tape, which reminded her of boys she'd been smitten with in college. "You and Heather are not only good neighbors, you're exceptionally generous, and if this haunted house is successful, it will give the Hat and Mitten Fund a much-needed boost."

"That's what we're hoping." He squatted down and poured some of the paint into a roller tray, then unwrapped a roller and stuck it on a holder. "I've recruited some of my special-effects and theater pals, and"—he stood up and shrugged—"well, if it all goes according to plan, this will be like nothing this little town has seen before."

She picked up a roller and smiled at him. "So where do we start?"

"Just pick a spot," he said, grinning broadly. "And remember, you don't have to be too careful. There'll be special lighting, and we want it to look kind of shabby and creepy anyway."

"Hey!" protested Lucy, smiling. "I'm practically a pro. I've painted every room in my house several times over!"

"So you've lived here in Tinker's Cove for quite a while?" he asked, climbing on a step ladder and brushing paint on the crown molding.

Lucy had started in the middle of the opposite wall,

hoping to leave the baseboards to younger and spryer volunteers. "Yup, we were living in New York and hating it. Bill was making a lot of money on Wall Street, but it wasn't what he wanted to do, so we took the plunge and bought an old farmhouse here in Tinker's Cove. He gradually built up his restoration contracting business. We have four kids, but they've pretty much flown the nest now . . ." Lucy was enjoying spreading the black paint on the faded wallpaper that clung to the old cracked plaster surface using the W strokes she'd learned from one of Bill's painter subcontractors.

"So you've become real Mainers?" he asked, moving the stepladder.

"I wouldn't say that," admitted Lucy. "We'll always be washashores. Even our kids, who were all born here, aren't considered natives. You have to have ancestors going back at least a hundred years, maybe longer, to be a real Mainer."

He climbed up on the ladder and extended the line of black. "Wow, Heather and I have our work cut out for us."

"I wouldn't let it bother me," advised Lucy. "You might not be accepted by the old guys in the o-five-hundred club . . ."

"The what?" he asked, stretching as far as he could with the brush.

"The good old boys who gather at the gas station for coffee every morning when it opens at five a.m."

"Trust me, I'm not getting up before seven at the earliest."

"Me, either," said Lucy. "And I doubt you'd have much in common with them anyway. But there are a lot of newcomers, younger people like yourselves, moving into town now." She dabbed her paint roller in the tray. "I really enjoyed interviewing Rosie Capshaw, and Matt and Luisa Rodriguez; they're like a breath of fresh air, if you ask me." She picked up where she left off, rolling the paint onto the wall and obliterating the faded flowers on the wallpaper. "And this town can use some new, young blood."

"I have noticed that there are a lot of old people . . ." he said.

"It's a real problem in these coastal towns," said Lucy, pushing her roller back and forth. "Property values are keeping young people out of the market, so they move away. Pretty soon, we're not going to have any teachers or cops or firemen . . . just a lot of old folks."

"Well, Heather and I hope to stick around and start a family; we're not going anywhere."

"Good for you," said Lucy, putting down her roller and pressing her hands on her behind and arching her back. "How did you two meet?"

Ty hopped down from the stepladder and moved it along once again. "Pretty typical story, I guess. We were both working in an off-Broadway theater in New York, but supporting ourselves by working in restaurants, temporary jobs, anything we could find. We were killing ourselves and not feeling like we were making any progress, so one day we decided to head out to LA, kind of a do-or-die kind of thing. We didn't hit the big time, like we'd hoped, but I discovered I really liked special effects, and Heather got steady work as an assistant to one of the big makeup artists. She was doing great until she got sick. Her doctor recommended a treatment program at Dana-Farber in Boston, so we decided to move back East. Boston was real expensive, but we were able to arrange for her to get her chemo in Portland, so we rented there for a while until we found this house." He climbed back on the ladder and slapped some paint on the molding. "It's been a big adjustment, but, thank God," he said, his voice husky, "she's doing fine now. We did the right thing."

"It must have been hard for you," said Lucy, wishing she'd been a bit more charitable toward Ty and Heather when they moved into town.

"Well, it's all in the past now," said Ty, jumping down from the ladder. "You know what we need? Some music!"

He disappeared, and soon the old house was rocking with upbeat disco tunes that pepped everybody up. Lucy found herself smiling and humming along as she rounded the corner and started on a fresh wall.

The days until the Haunted House flew by in a whirl. October was Lucy's favorite month anyway; she loved the crisp weather, the gorgeous reds and yellows of the changing trees, and the swirling leaves caught by the breeze. Most of all, she enjoyed the relaxed, blowsy look of many gardens and backyards as late bloomers like Montauk daisies and autumn clematis took over and lawns were dotted with colorful fallen leaves. She found the cooler weather energizing and fully enjoyed spending every spare moment working with the other volunteers at the Moon house.

Excitement was palpable when the big day finally arrived and the cast and crew assembled for the fundraiser. Rachel, who frequently directed shows for the town's amateur little-theater group, said it felt just like an opening night. "I'm nervous and excited, all at the same time," she said, with a little shiver, checking her makeup in a little mirror.

She was seated, along with Lucy, Pam, and Sue, behind a fake guillotine in an upstairs bedroom painted a lurid red-orange shade. They were all costumed in long skirts and shawls, and Heather had used her theatrical makeup skills to horrifying effect, giving them sooty eyes and dark parentheses around their mouths. They'd each brought along a knitting project.

"I've been working on this scarf for about six years," confessed Sue, who was working with a lovely shade of lavender angora yarn. "You know how it is, you get the yen to knit when it starts to get chilly, so I dig it out and add a few rows, but then the holidays roll around, and I get too busy, and it gets put away." She sighed. "At this rate, I'll never finish it."

"All I ever make are kids' hats and mittens," confessed Pam, who was working on a few inches of ribbing. "For the fund, of course."

"I'm almost finished with this vest for Bob," said Rachel, holding up a length of navy yarn worked into a cable design.

"Wow, that's beautiful," said Lucy, who was holding her needles awkwardly and trying to remember if she was supposed to go into the stitches from the front of the needle or the back. "I don't really know how to knit," she confessed, setting the tangled mess into her lap.

"Just pretend," advised Rachel, as the masked executioner joined them. The women all gasped at the sight of the hooded man, who was carrying a stuffed cloth dummy under one arm and its head under the other.

"Hi," he said, lifting his hood and revealing a big smile. It was Matt Rodriguez, dressed in blood-stained knee breeches and shirt, with a red scarf around his neck.

"Wow, that's quite a getup," admitted Lucy, when her heart resumed beating.

"Anybody have any idea how this thing works?" he asked, approaching the guillotine and arranging the dummy.

"I think there's a rope that lowers the blade," offered Pam.

"That's right," agreed Pam, putting down her knitting and going into a corner, where she bent down. "And Ty showed me that all we have to do for the special effects is flip this little switch." She looked up. "Everybody ready?"

Matt took his place behind the guillotine, the women nodded, and Rachel turned on the switch. The room immediately became darker, and a stomach-turning thud was heard, followed by a flash of red light that simulated blood gushing from the dummy. "I guess that's the sound of the guillotine," she said, in a tone of professional detachment. "You'll need to coordinate dropping the blade with the sound effect."

Pam, however, had a different reaction. "I think I'm going to be sick," she said.

"Put your head between your knees," advised Rachel. "Trust me, stage fright often has that effect on people."

"It was awfully realistic," said Lucy, patting Pam's back.

Pam's reply was muffled. "I'll be okay in a minute."

An air horn went off, announcing that the doors were opening, and Rachel hurried back to her seat. "It's show time!" she announced, picking up her knitting. "Remember, we're *tricoteuses*, and we're enjoying this! The rich and stuck-up, the oppressors who've been lording it over us, are finally getting what they deserve!"

"I'm just not going to look," whispered Pam, raising her head.

"That's the spirit," said Lucy, encouraging her. "*Aux armes, citoyens!*" she proclaimed, struggling to remember the rest of *La Marseillaise*. Coming up empty, she improvised, saying, "Let the blade fall and the blood flow!"

"Whuh?" moaned Pam, as the waiting crowd could be heard entering the hallway below.

People were soon jostling each other in the doorway to

see the tableau, some in costume and others not, and Lucy was interested to see their reactions as the blade thudded down. Some laughed nervously, some gasped in horror, and others scurried away, eager to see what terrors the next room held, or perhaps hoping for something a bit tamer to show their kids. Lucy wished she had thought to explore a bit before settling in to her assigned role; she was curious about the other tableaux, but from the screams and giggles and moans, it seemed as if the haunted house was a big success.

The four friends found themselves getting into the spirit of the thing, whooping and cheering and muttering insults as the blade fell again and again, even adding some spirited dialogue. "Ah, the marquis! He deserves to lose his head! What about the king? When will it be his turn? And that filthy whore, the queen? That will be the day, eh?" All too soon, it seemed, the air horn sounded again, signaling that the haunted house was over and the party would begin.

They all joined the crowd of revelers streaming downstairs to the living and dining rooms, where the Lobster Claws were already playing covers of rock classics. From the buzz in the room, it was obvious that everyone was having a great time. Some were dancing, others were talking with friends, and everybody seemed to be finding plenty to eat and drink. Lucy was helping herself to the generous buffet, filling a plate with zombie fingers, batty wonton bites, and a mini mummy pepperoni pizza, discovering that she'd built up quite an appetite witnessing all those faux decapitations. She was also thirsty and helped herself to a mad scientist's potion, which appeared to be rum and ginger beer served up in a lab beaker and garnished with a gummy worm.

She stood along the wall while enjoying her refreshments, watching the costumed crowd of partiers and trying to figure out who was who. Some were easy, like her friend Sgt. Barney Culpepper, who was the largest man in town by far and had decided to come as the Michelin Man. Others were harder, like the mummy she suspected was actually Bob Goodman, and a classic ghost in a white sheet, who could have been anybody. She'd just polished off her potion when Bill appeared, costumed as a green-tinted Frankenstein carrying a red plastic cup of draft beer.

"Having a good time?" he asked.

Lucy gave him her last zombie finger. "Yeah. This is fun, and I'm really happy that it's so successful. It was a lot of work, but I think we pulled it off."

He bit into the crunchy baked pastry, helped it down with a gulp of beer, and nodded in agreement. "Have you seen Ty and Heather?" he asked. "I want to congratulate them . . ."

Lucy finished the sentence for him: "And find out when you can start demo?"

"That too," he said, laughing.

She scanned the crowd and spotted a tall, gangly scarecrow from the *Wizard of Oz* movie. "I think that's Ty over there," she said, pointing him out. She continued to search for Heather, who, she was sure, would have remained in her flattering Ophelia costume, but saw no sign of a small woman wearing a long, red wig and a medieval robe. "But I don't see Heather."

"The party was her idea," said Bill. "She wouldn't miss it."

"I didn't see her come downstairs with the rest of us," said Lucy, growing concerned. "I think I better go up and make sure she's all right. That bathtub arrangement's a bit tricky, and she might've fallen trying to get out."

"Okay," said Bill, studying his empty cup. "I'll get a re-fill and go talk to Ty."

Lucy gave him her empty plate and beaker and headed for the stairs, which were now littered with scraps from people's costumes as well as a number of discarded paper plates and cups. She made her way through the mess, clucking with disapproval, and along the dimly lit hall to the bathroom.

Oddly, she thought, the door was shut. Well, maybe somebody was using the toilet, which still worked and was disguised behind a screen. Just in case, she knocked on the door with a few polite taps.

Receiving no reply, she turned the knob and cautiously opened the door, half expecting a voice to say, "Occupied, just a minute, please."

Hearing no such warning, she pushed the door open wider and reached for the string dangling from the old-fashioned ceiling light. Giving it a yank, and blinking from the sudden brightness, she spotted an arm hanging limply over the side of the tub. Dashing across the small room, she found Heather, eyes closed, still lying amid the plastic sheeting, fake bubbles and stringy green reeds. For a moment, she feared the worst, that Heather was dead, but wrapped her hand around that dangling wrist and discovered a pulse. She was alive, but barely. Lucy dashed for the stairs, and help, before it was too late to save her.

Chapter Four

Returning to the party, Lucy searched frantically among the costumed revelers for a first responder and finally spotted Barney helping himself to refreshments. She told him about Heather, and he produced his official walkie-talkie from beneath his costume and called for help, at the same time making his way through the crowd and pounding up the stairs. Reaching the bathroom, he handed the device to Lucy and immediately began CPR.

"Tell 'em it's a drug overdose," he said, panting a bit as he compressed Heather's bird-like chest. "We need 'em fast."

Lucy obliged, learning from the dispatcher that the ambulance was already on its way. Moments later, she heard the siren, growing louder as the ambulance grew closer; then it abruptly ceased when it arrived at the haunted house. The party was still in full swing but fell silent as the rescuers entered; Lucy went to the top of the stairs and yelled for them to come on up.

Then she and Barney stepped aside as Heather was quickly examined. An oxygen mask was fixed to her face, and she was then lifted from the tub and laid on a stretcher. One of the EMTs quickly established an IV line, and then they were off, carrying her downstairs. Lucy watched from the upstairs hall, which gave her a bird's-eye view of the scene below. She saw them pause at the bottom of the stairs, where they popped open the legs to raise the gurney, which they wheeled through the watching crowd to the door. There they were suddenly confronted by Ty, still dressed in his scarecrow costume. "What's going on?" he demanded. Recognizing Heather beneath the oxygen mask, he reeled a step or two backward, then gathered himself together and followed them out to the waiting ambulance.

Lucy turned back, expecting to see Barney, but he was already searching the bathroom for evidence, along with several other officers, including police chief Jim Kirwan, who was dressed as a magician in top hat and tails. Seeing her, Kirwan joined her in the hall. "So tell me what happened," he coaxed, recording her on his cell phone.

"I was at the party," began Lucy, speaking rapidly, "and realized I hadn't seen Heather, so I came upstairs to check on her. I found her in the tub, unconscious, so I grabbed Barney—he was the first person I saw—and he called for help and started CPR."

"Why did you think you should check on her?"

"Well, these tableaux are all kind of patched together, there's wiring and lights and scenery, and when I didn't see her at the party, I thought she might have tripped on a cable or got tangled up and fell climbing out of the tub. She was supposed to be the model for a famous painting of Ophelia. Kevin Kenneally was the artist. He might know something . . ."

"Kevin was here?"

"Yeah. He was there at the easel," said Lucy, pointing at the easel, now folded and propped against the wall. His palette was there, too, on the floor.

"And she was unconscious when you found her?"

"Yeah. Still in the tub." Lucy pictured the scene in her mind. "I was afraid she was dead. One arm was out, hanging over the side, and I felt it for a pulse. I thought I felt something, so I ran downstairs for help . . ."

"You did the right thing," said the chief, patting her shoulder. "You've probably saved her life."

Barney came to the bathroom door, and Kirwan turned to him. "You oughta see this, Chief," he said.

"Thanks for your help, Lucy," said the chief, with a nod, dismissing her. Lucy was dying to know what the investigators had found, but the chief had closed the bathroom door behind him, shutting her out.

Sighing, she went back downstairs, slowly. The Lobster Claws had toned down the volume and were playing a James Taylor tune; a few people were slow-dancing, but most were gathered in small groups, talking quietly. After searching through the living room area, Lucy found Sue and her husband, Sid, standing with Bill in the dining room, just outside the kitchen door.

Bill quickly wrapped her in his arms. "How are you?"

"I'm okay."

"That was real quick action," said Sid. "The minute I saw you, I knew something was up."

"Barney said it was a drug overdose," she said, speaking slowly and sounding doubtful. She turned to Sue. "Do you think that's likely? Do you think Heather was a user?"

Sue shrugged. "Who knows what people do in their spare time? It's possible, I guess, but I have to say I never thought that Ophelia gig was a good idea. Too many things could go wrong."

"Well, something did," said Sid, taking his wife's hand. "I guess we'll call it a night."

"Us, too," said Bill, wrapping his arm around Lucy's waist and leading her through the nearly empty rooms, where the Lobster Claws had begun packing up their instruments. The once-festive rooms were now nearly deserted, the floor strewn with fallen paper streamers and crushed cups.

"Hell of a party," said Bill, opening the door.

Lucy didn't respond. In her mind, she was back in that bathroom, replaying the awful moment when she'd found Heather.

Next morning, she went to the IGA to do her weekly grocery shopping and ran into Barney's wife, Marge, at the deli counter. Marge was tall and carried a few extra pounds, but they didn't slow her down. She was a brisk, no-nonsense woman who kept her curly gray hair clipped in a short cut and wore comfortable plus-size knits. After requesting two pounds of ham, two pounds of American cheese, and one pound of roast beef, she greeted Lucy.

"Terrible news about that poor Heather Moon." She clucked her tongue and shook her head. "Drugs."

"I guess she's got a long road ahead. I hope she goes straight into rehab and gets herself straightened out."

Marge pressed her lips together. "Haven't you heard?"

Lucy had a horrible sinking feeling in her stomach. "Heard what?"

Marge wasn't one to beat about the bush. "She died. She was DOA. Fentanyl, they say."

Lucy reached for the glass-fronted deli case to steady herself. "She didn't make it to the hospital?"

Marge reached up and took the packs of cold cuts off the counter. "Thanks," she told the clerk, with a little smile, then turned to Lucy. "They gave her Narcan, did everything they could, but . . ." She shrugged and put the packs of meat and cheese in her cart. "I'm sorry, Lucy. I thought you'd heard. It was on the radio."

"No, I hadn't heard," said Lucy, who could almost feel Heather's fluttery pulse beneath her fingers, and could still see the way her long hair fell across her pale face, her colorless lips.

"It's a terrible thing; she was so young," said Marge. "What a waste." She sighed heavily and put her hands on the cart's handle. "Imagine going through all that chemo and beating cancer and then," she lifted one hand in a little wave, "pffft."

"Can I get you something?" asked the clerk.

Lucy couldn't remember what she'd intended to buy. "Uh, no, thanks," she said, turning back to Marge. "Her poor husband. They had such plans. They were going to fix up the house and start a family." She paused, remembering how happy and excited Ty had seemed when they were working together to paint the hallway. "He must be devastated."

"I don't know about that," said Marge. "The police brought him in for questioning, took him straight from the hospital."

"They did?"

"Of course. Those were illegal drugs, and they want to know how she got them." She leaned close to Lucy and lowered her voice. "They suspect he actually supplied them."

Lucy didn't like the way this was going. "But that means . . ."

Marge nodded. "That means he could be tried for manslaughter—even murder, if they can prove a motive."

Lucy wandered through the store, shopping list in hand, but even though she knew the store like the back of her hand, she couldn't seem to find anything. The products all merged together in a blur; she couldn't tell the Raisin Bran from the Froot Loops, the toilet paper from the paper towels, and the wall of yogurt completely baffled her. Her cart was only half full when she went to the checkout.

The cashier, Dot Kirwan, noticed right away. "Light week?" she asked, scanning a loaf of bread, then moving on to some canned goods.

"I'm not myself," admitted Lucy. "I just heard about Heather Moon."

"Jim told me you found her and called for help." Dot was the police chief's mother and related to numerous other Kirwans who worked in the police and fire department. She plopped a bunch of bananas on the scale. "Must have been upsetting."

"I thought they'd be able to save her."

Dot reached for a pound of butter. "These drugs are so risky, I don't know why people do it. They call it 'recreational,' but I don't get it; I don't see how it's worth risking your life to get high." She shook her head, scanning a pack of ground beef. "My Danny, he's an EMT, he tells me half the time you save somebody from an overdose on Friday, and on Saturday you get another call and have to do the same thing all over again. You'd think they'd learn from a close call like that, but they don't; the first thing they do when they get out of the hospital is get more drugs." She hit the TOTAL button rather harder than necessary. "That'll be forty-three nineteen."

On the way home, Lucy detoured down School Street past the Moon house. She drove slowly, noticing that the sign advertising the haunted house fundraiser was still in place, the black-painted plywood cutout of a witch on a broomstick still rode above the roof, and strips of yellow crime-scene tape fluttered from the porch. That yellow tape would have been a nice touch yesterday, a sort of macabre flourish, thought Lucy. Today, however, it had an entirely different meaning. It was for real.

She went through the rest of her weekend chores in a sort of haze: She changed the sheets on the beds and cleaned the bathrooms; she cooked up a big batch of chili and raked leaves off the lawn. She yanked the dying tomato plants out of the garden, but left the leeks and the kale, which benefited from cool weather. She did these things automatically; it was as if her brain had split in two. One half took care of these familiar tasks, while the other half struggled to understand why Heather had indulged in such risky behavior. Why would she take possibly lethal drugs after surviving a grueling battle with cancer? Why?

That question was still on her mind when she went to work at the newspaper on Monday morning.

Phyllis greeted her with a small smile, and Lucy noticed she hadn't dressed with her usual flair. Phyllis enjoyed dressing to suit the holiday, all holidays, and in October went in for sweaters and sweatshirts trimmed with falling leaves, jack-o'-lanterns, and witches on broomsticks, occasionally even going so far as to dye her hair orange. Today, however, she'd opted for a plain, navy-blue turtleneck and jeans; a pair of dangling black cat earrings was her only reference to the coming holiday. "Heck of a thing, a young woman dying like that," she said, adding a big sigh.

"You said it," agreed Lucy, starting to unzip her lightweight parka.

"I wouldn't bother to settle in. Aucoin's announced a press conference at nine at the police station, and Ted wants you to cover it."

Lucy glanced at the antique Regulator clock on the wall, which informed her it was a quarter to. "I guess I might as well go now. Maybe I can get some background." She paused at the door. "Have you heard anything?"

Phyllis shrugged. "I saw Franny at church yesterday,

and she said she hasn't seen hide nor hair of Ty since he went off with Heather in the ambulance."

Lucy knew that Franny Small was the Moons' next-door neighbor. "That doesn't mean anything," said Lucy, unwilling to admit that Ty might have had anything to do with Heather's death. "The house was a mess; he might be staying with friends."

"You'd think he'd come by to check on it."

"He's got a lot to deal with right now," said Lucy. "His wife just died. The house is probably the last thing on his mind."

"You're probably right."

"I'll know soon enough," said Lucy, pushing the door open. The little bell was still jangling as she crossed the sidewalk and made her way to the police station on the other side of the street.

"You can go straight down to the Emergency Control Center," said the dispatcher, buzzing her through. The Emergency Control Center in the basement did double duty as a meeting space in the cramped police station. Lucy knew the way, taking the stairs located just beyond the locked steel door that sealed the lobby off from the rest of the station.

A number of chairs had been set up in the underground bunker, and they were already filled by a handful of other reporters. NECN and the Portland news station had set up cameras, which Lucy took to be a bad sign indicating that the DA was prepared to make a major announcement.

Aucoin and Kenneally entered on the dot of nine, along with Jim Kirwan, and all three took their places, lining up behind a podium containing a couple of waiting micro-phones. Aucoin was first to speak, thanking everyone for coming. He then cleared his throat and began reading from a sheet of paper. "After a thorough investigation, this department is charging Tyler Monteith Moon, age thirty-three, with first-degree murder in the death of his wife, Heather Moon, age twenty-nine, on Friday evening. It is believed that Moon caused his wife's death by substituting a lethal dose of fentanyl for the opioid painkillers she occasionally used."

Lucy had been expecting this, after her conversation with Marge, but it still came as a shock. She sat for a minute, trying to process this development, trying to reconcile the Ty she'd worked alongside painting the haunted house with Ty the accused murderer. She was struggling to imagine how Ty—or anyone, for that matter—could even dream of killing the fragile, ethereal, beautiful creature that was Heather.

"And now, I'm passing the mic to my colleague, Assistant District Attorney Kevin Kenneally," said Aucoin, stepping back so Kenneally could take the podium.

"I would now like to speak to motive," he began. "We believe Ty Moon was motivated by the fact that Heather Moon, who had recently undergone chemotherapy for non-Hodgkin's lymphoma, had recently come into a large inheritance. Ty Moon wanted the good life, he wanted a family, and he didn't want to be tied to a sickly wife." He paused. "Any questions?"

Lucy's hand shot up, and she got a nod from Kenneally. "Has Ty Moon confessed to any of this?"

"No. He denies the charges."

Another reporter jumped in. "When's the arraignment?"

"Later this morning."

"What's the evidence?" demanded another.

Kenneally turned to the chief, who stepped up to the mic. "I'm not free to disclose details, but I can say that our investigation found ample evidence that clearly links Moon to his wife's death."

The questions and answers flew fast and furiously, but Lucy just sat there, scribbling it all down in her notebook. Her ears were hearing, her mind was processing the data, and her hand was writing it all down, but her heart was not accepting the information. She simply couldn't believe that Ty was guilty.

Chapter Five

Lucy was just leaving the police station when she got a text from Ted informing her that Ty had hired Bob Goodman to defend him and assigning her to write a profile of Ty. Bob was already at the courthouse, awaiting the arraignment, so she decided to start by calling Rosie Capshaw.

Rosie wasn't eager to talk. "This is for the paper, right?" she asked.

"Yeah. I'm just looking for some perspective from the people who knew Ty and Heather best." Lucy was at her desk, staring at the photos of her kids, taken when they were still in elementary school, and wondering how well she knew them now that they were adults living out in the world. "Did you know that Heather was into drugs?"

"Pot's legal now, you know, so sure. I've been growing my three plants, and so are a lot of other people. Heather was dealing with a lot, you know, with the chemo and cancer and moving into a new community. She said that grass really helped with the pain and anxiety she was experiencing."

"She didn't die from using grass," said Lucy. "What about heavier drugs?"

"I wouldn't know about that," said Rosie, in a clipped tone.

Lucy decided to change her tactics. "Would you say that Ty and Heather were a happy couple?"

Rosie took her time before answering, and Lucy was beginning to wonder if she was still on the line when she finally spoke. "Who knows what really goes on in a marriage?"

"What do you mean by that?"

"Exactly what I said. They seemed happy, but now Ty's been charged with killing her. The cops must've found some evidence; I don't think they just made up a charge like that. It makes you wonder if what you thought was happening was actually what was going on." She paused. "I'll say this, I always thought Ty was the dominant partner. Heather always seemed to defer to him. She wouldn't do anything unless he approved. Like if I asked her to meet me for lunch or to come by for a glass of wine, she'd always say she had to check with Ty."

"And did Ty ever say no?"

There was another long pause. "Yeah. Sometimes he did."

"Did she give a reason for that? Like she forgot they made plans or something?"

"No. She'd say something like 'Ty doesn't think I should.'" She paused. "Sometimes I wondered if that was just an excuse, something Heather made up because she didn't feel like going out."

"Interesting," said Lucy, remembering her initial suspicion about Ty when she first met him and thought he was extremely controlling and even suspected he was abusing his wife. As she got to know him better, she'd changed her opinion, but now she was wondering if her first impression was possibly correct. "Anything else you'd like to add?"

"Uh, no. I've probably said too much already."

"I don't have to use your name," offered Lucy, hoping to get more information.

"Thanks. That makes me feel better."

"No problem," said Lucy. "Who else should I call?"

"Matt and Luisa, maybe? Brendan? We all hung out together. Kevin, too, but as assistant DA, he's prosecuting . . ."

"Right," said Lucy. "Thanks for your help."

Lucy's next call was to Luisa Rodriguez, but she said she was too upset about Heather's death to talk. Her brother, Matt, claimed he knew nothing about any illegal drugs in Tinker's Cove and declared he believed Ty was one hundred percent innocent. Brendan Coyle said only that he refused to judge people. "My mother used to say that if you want to know someone, you should walk a mile in their shoes."

That caused Lucy to smile. "That's what my mother used to say, too."

"Well, it's good advice."

Figuring that she'd struck out in her conversations with Ty's friends, Lucy decided to tap into a richer source of information and dialed Franny Small.

After exchanging pleasantries, Lucy got down to business. "You were the Moons' next-door neighbor, after all. How did they seem to you?"

"Weird, that's how they seemed. There was all that business with the moans and noises and flashing lights when they moved in, but that was all connected to his work, so I got used to it. But they were never friendly. Not at all, not even a wave if you happened to see them coming or going. And that's the only time I saw them outside the house. They didn't use their backyard at all; they were always either in the house or leaving to go somewhere. They didn't work in the yard or garden, nothing like that. They had landscapers mow the grass, but they never even sat outside of a summer evening, say, to relax and enjoy the fresh air." Pausing a moment for breath, she added her most damning observation. "They didn't even feed the birds!"

"Did they have company? Did people come for dinner or anything?"

"Not until they started working on that haunted house party. That was the first time I saw other folks at the house."

"Did they give you and the other neighbors a heads-up about the haunted house? You know, do the neighborly thing and let you know what was going on, and maybe even ask for your help?"

Franny laughed. "Not a peep. Even after that whole thing with your grandson and the SWAT team, not a word. He just kept on doing what he did, noises and lights and all. I mean, sometimes it was impossible to sleep."

"Did you approach him? Tell him he was disturbing you?"

"No," admitted Franny. "To tell the truth, I was afraid of him. I didn't want to get involved, if you know what I mean."

Lucy thought she did. Some people were approachable, and some weren't, and Ty Moon was one of the latter. There was something about him that was like a big warning sign—danger, falling rocks, something that made you want to keep your distance. She'd thought she'd broken through the barrier and discovered there was nothing to fear, after all, but now she was beginning to wonder if she'd been fooled. Abusers were often master manipulators, and maybe he'd simply told her what she wanted to hear and convinced her of what she already wanted to believe.

At home that night, she asked Bill if he thought Ty was

guilty and got a strong denial. "No way. He adored Heather. Remember, I saw them together when we worked out the plans for the remodel, and he always included her, always asked for her opinion. That's not always the case, you know. A lot of men shut their wives out of the planning or demean their ideas. But not Ty. He sincerely wanted to give Heather everything she wanted."

Lucy had done numerous stories about domestic abuse and was familiar with the abuser's cycle of violence, which often included a period of contrition and even apology. She found herself wondering if Ty had a guilty conscience and was trying to make amends with Heather for something he had done.

"Do you think he was afraid of losing her?" she asked.

"What kind of question is that?" demanded Bill, who was seated at the kitchen table. "A guy treats his wife nicely, and you start suspecting his motives?"

"Well, it's not an unreasonable reaction," said Lucy, putting a pot away in the cabinet. "He has been charged with killing her."

"Sorry, but I just don't see the guy as a wife killer."

"Maybe that's what he was counting on," said Lucy, standing behind her husband and stroking his hair. "Maybe he was just playing the part of a loving husband."

First thing on Tuesday morning, Lucy got a call from Bob Goodman. "I just want to let you know that I'm planning to mount a strong defense for Ty Moon, who is definitely not guilty of murdering his wife. And I'm happy to say the judge was not impressed by the prosecution's argument that Ty was a flight risk and a danger to the public. He pointed to Ty's absolutely clean record, not even a parking ticket, and decided to grant bail. I'm happy to report that Ty has been released from custody and is now ea-

gerly awaiting trial and the opportunity to prove his innocence of these outrageous charges."

"Thanks for the update," said Lucy, wondering how the
community would take this news. She had a feeling that
many people would not be happy with the judge's decision. "So is he going back to the house on School Street?"

"Not just yet," said Bob. "We decided it would be best
for him to lay low for a while, until things die down."

"So where's he going?"

"I'm not free to give you that information. But I will remain in constant touch with him, and he will appear for
trial. The date has not been set yet, but I will let you know
when it is."

"Well, thanks, Bob. Anything you want to add about
your client?"

"Only that he is devastated by the loss of his wife; he's
grieving, and he won't rest until the truth about her death
is known."

"Okay," said Lucy, who had been clicking away on her
keyboard, getting every word.

"And, oh, before I go, Rachel wanted me to remind you
about the Hat and Mitten Fund party on Friday. Make
sure there's a notice in the paper, okay?"

"I haven't forgotten; it's on page one," said Lucy, smiling.

When Friday rolled around, Lucy was ready for some
welcome distraction from the Moon story. She understood
why readers were fascinated by the sensational tale involv-
ing drugs and murder that was unfolding in their own
town, but for the most part, they had the advantage of a
certain distance. Ty and Heather were like actors on a
stage to them, but she actually knew them and found the
whole story terribly depressing. As she drove through
town to the Community Church, where the annual Hat

and Mitten Fund Halloween party took place, she resolutely tucked all thoughts of the Moons into the back of her mind and focused instead on all the various holiday decorations people had put out. It seemed that staid, reserved Mainers who limited Christmas décor to a simple swag on the front door tended to go overboard for Halloween. Maybe it was the riot of fall color in the forest that inspired them, or maybe it was the hint of the macabre that impelled them to set out scarecrows and harvest figures on their lawns. Not to mention huge, inflatable jack-o'-lanterns, enormous purple spiders perched on porch roofs, and fluttering ghosts hanging from trees. And there was always the classic witch that had unfortunately crashed into a tree or even a chimney.

The party was just getting started when she arrived, and a line of costumed kids and their caregivers were entering the basement room. She could hear the DJ playing "Monster Mash," and the cries of the kids as they discovered the games and treats inside. She slipped past the line with an apologetic smile and popped into the kitchen to change into her witch costume. Sue was not impressed.

"You're not going to be a witch again?" she said, watching as Lucy wiggled into the long black dress.

"Why not? It's a classic." Lucy noticed that Sue was dressed entirely in gray and had added a necklace of paint chips, also all gray. "What in the world are you supposed to be? A foggy day?"

"Think, Lucy, think."

"Gray Gables?"

Sue exhaled and rolled her eyes. "Come on, Lucy. You've certainly heard of *Fifty Shades of Gray*, haven't you?"

Lucy plopped her pointy witch's hat on her head and grinned broadly. "That is clever! I wish I could think of something like that."

"Once more into the fray," said Sue, as they left the quiet of the kitchen and entered the madhouse beyond the swinging door.

The music was pounding, kids were dancing and dashing from game to game, dropping candy and spilling drinks in their haste to see and do everything. There were all sorts of games: bean bag tosses, bobbing for apples, a marshmallow shooting gallery, a ball toss, and, of course, Rachel's Madame Zenda. Lucy took her place behind at the refreshment table, which was covered with a colorful assortment of ghoulish treats: zombie fingers, meringue ghosts, eyeball cupcakes, mummy pretzel rods, jack-o'-lantern cookies, and devil's food Draculas. Lucy was particularly impressed by the Franken-munchies, Rice Krispies treats that had been dyed purple and trimmed with fruit leather and marshmallows to resemble Frankenstein's monster.

Stella Rose Levitt, however, was not impressed. "There's no such thing as purple Rice Krispies," she declared, stamping her foot and making her curly hair bounce. She was dressed as a fairy, in a gauzy dress complete with wings and a little sparkly wand.

"Wouldn't you like to try one?" asked Lucy, smiling down at the little four-year-old. "Give them a taste test?"

"No! I know everything, and I know there's no such thing as purple Rice Krispies! Yuck!"

"Perhaps you'd like a smiling skeleton cookie?" offered Lydia Volpe, taking her place beside Lucy at the table. "They're just plain cookies with some sugar icing."

"Sugar's not good for you, you know."

"It's all right to have a treat once in a while," said Lucy.

"No. My mom says sugar makes me crazy."

"Your mother may have a point," said Lydia, who was a retired kindergarten teacher. "Why don't you try bobbing for apples?"

"I don't wanna get wet!"

"Do you see that little tent over there?" asked Lucy, pointing. "There's a very wise fortune-teller in there, who can see the future and tell you all about it."

"My mom says nobody can see the future."

"Well, you might try dancing to the music, or what about the bean bag toss," suggested Lydia.

"This party is dumb," said Stella Rose, turning on her heel and running off.

"Wow," said Lucy, turning to Lydia. "She's a tough little cookie."

"They all are; kids are a lot smarter than they used to be. I retired just in time, before the screen generation arrived."

"I was so shocked one day when I saw a tiny toddler in a stroller swiping away on her mother's cell phone," said Lucy.

"It was probably the tyke's own cell phone," said Lydia, offering a tray of cupcakes to a little boy in a superhero costume and watching with dismay as he took two. "Hey, it's one to a person," she informed him in her teacher voice.

"Not if you can't catch me!" he cried, dashing off with a cupcake in each hand.

"Typical," said Pam, joining her two friends. "Kids today."

"The winds of change do seem to be blowing, even here in Tinker's Cove," said Lucy.

"And not in a good way," offered Lydia. "I've seen young people wearing pajamas in the supermarket!"

"And the cars, have you noticed the cars?" said Lucy. "I was happy to have a second-hand Subaru when I was a young mom, but now they're all driving Audis and Volvos and Range Rovers."

"Not everybody," said Lydia. "A lot of kids qualify for reduced lunch, you know."

"And I bet a lot of others are bringing fancy whole-grain goodies in their reusable, organic lunch bags," said Pam.

"Face it," said Lucy, "house prices around here are out of reach unless you're a professional with a big income. That means we've got yuppie newcomers with plenty of money and the poor folks who are living with Mom and Dad in the old family farmhouse, or maybe they've plunked down a trailer in the front yard."

"Ted says it's not sustainable," offered Pam. "He worries about the future of towns like Tinker's Cove. He says we're losing the sense of community and shared values that made us special."

"I think he's right," said Lydia, with a sigh. "It's getting harder and harder for folks to raise a family here."

Looking out across the room at all the children in their Halloween costumes, Lucy hoped Lydia and Pam were wrong. Times changed, but kids were kids, weren't they?

Chapter Six

Lucy was out campaigning for Bob at the IGA again on Saturday morning, distributing handouts and chatting up potential voters. She found it quite a pleasant experience, as she discovered she knew more people than she thought and was enjoying catching up with folks she hadn't seen in a while, like her Prudence Path neighbor Frankie LaChance, whose daughter, Renee, was pursuing graduate studies at the University of St. Andrews in Scotland. She was enjoying a vicarious glow of pride over Renee's accomplishments when she spotted Rosie Capshaw, dressed in her usual uniform of paint-stained farmer's overalls, pushing an empty cart across the parking lot.

"Hi, Rosie," she called, adding a little wave. "Have you got a minute?"

Rosie didn't seem inclined to linger. "Actually, I'm in a bit of a rush . . ."

Lucy suspected Rosie might be trying to avoid further questions about Ty and Heather and was quick to inform her that she was campaigning for Bob Goodman. "Can I give you one of these flyers? It's full of good information about Bob."

"Sure, thanks," said Rosie, giving the cart a push and then stopping in mid-stride, as if she suddenly remembered something. "Hey, you know, I've got the money from the haunted house party, and I don't know what to do with it."

"Oh, golly," exclaimed Lucy, horrified that the money had been overlooked in the excitement about Heather. "I never gave it a thought. I figured whoever was supposed to have it actually had it."

"No. The kitty was sitting there by the door after everybody left, so I grabbed it to keep it safe. What should I do with it?"

"I don't really have a clue," said Lucy, who knew the Hat and Mitten Fund hadn't been involved in the financial arrangements. "I suppose there were expenses and donations and all. Who was keeping track of all that?"

"It was actually Heather. Well, she was supposed to do it, but she found it was too much, so I was helping her."

"So you've got all the figures?" asked Lucy. "Why don't you just tote it up, pay any outstanding bills, and give whatever's left over in a check to the Hat and Mitten fund?"

"I'm really not comfortable doing it all by myself." Rosie glanced down at her black-and-white-checked Vans. "I'm no bookkeeper; I can't actually balance my checkbook," she confessed. "And considering everything that's happened, I'd really appreciate some oversight, in case there are any questions." She glanced around. "I don't want anybody to think that the finances weren't, well, you know, aboveboard."

"I don't think you need to worry about that! After all, you're the one who saved the cash," said Lucy, giving her a reassuring smile. "But I do see your point. Why don't Pam and I meet with you and go over it all? Out of an abundance of caution? Pam's the fund treasurer."

"That would be a big relief. That cash box just weighs

on me every time I see it," said Rosie, letting out a huge sigh. "When do you want to meet?"

"I'll check with Pam and get back to you."

The three women met a few days later, choosing the morgue in the newspaper office as the most practical spot. There they had plenty of room to spread out all the various invoices and checks on the big conference table, and the locked door made it a secure place to count up the cash. Lucy was amused to see that Rosie and Pam hit it off immediately; it turned out that they both had been high school cheerleaders. When they were finally done, Pam gave a quick rah-rah cheer and announced that they'd made a tidy profit, thanks to some unexpected donations from Hollywood movie people, including a few celebrities.

"Well, at least something good came out of that nightmare," said Rosie, grabbing the museum tote bag she used as a purse and standing up, ready to leave.

"Before you go, I want to ask about something," said Pam. "This is quite a bit of money. I've been thinking that perhaps we should set it aside in a separate fund; we could name it after Heather and use it for a special scholarship."

Rosie sat back down, dropping the bag on her lap. "That's such a nice idea," she said. "Could you do that?"

"The committee would have to vote, but I think they'd support it," said Pam. "What do you think, Lucy?"

"I think it's a great idea, and I don't think there'd be any problem getting it approved. It would be nice to have some recognition of Heather's contribution. After all, the party was her idea, wasn't it?"

"Absolutely," declared Rosie, excited about Pam's proposal. "Ty wasn't for it at first, you know. She had to convince him it would be good for his career, which had actually kind of fizzled out. He wasn't getting work, and she thought it would be a way to get his name out there.

It's the new thing, you know. Get yourself associated with a good cause, like Prince Harry and Meghan Markle."

"I don't think they donated," said Pam, with a naughty grin.

"I don't think they were asked," said Rosie. "Heather stuck to people she and Ty had worked with, or friends of friends, that sort of thing."

Lucy was trying to process this new information; she remembered Bill saying that Ty had landed a big contract that enabled him to renovate their house. "But you say Ty wasn't getting work? How were they going to pay for the renovations?"

"This is completely off the record, Lucy," began Rosie, giving Lucy a stern warning, "but the haunted house was a last-ditch effort by Heather to save her marriage. Ty was jealous of all the attention she received because she was sick, and then she got that inheritance, and he somehow got the idea that she didn't need him anymore, that she thought he wasn't pulling his weight."

"So she came up with the haunted house to show her support for his career?" asked Pam.

"More than that. It was all to prove to him that she loved him," said Rosie.

"I guess that didn't work," observed Pam, "since he killed her."

"You said it," said Rosie, lowering her voice and leaning forward, making eye contact with Pam and Lucy. "I heard, from one of his best friends, that he suspected she was having an affair."

"Was she?" asked Lucy, finding this hard to believe. First it was drugs, now infidelity.

Rosie shrugged. "Not that I knew about. If she was fooling around, she was being very discreet."

"But Ty was suspicious?" asked Lucy.

"More than that, he was determined to find out. And word is, from this friend, that Ty said he could forgive her if she ended the affair, but he'd never let her leave him. He said he'd rather see her dead."

Lucy wasn't convinced that Rosie was telling the truth; she suspected that this so-called friend had concocted the story, but she also couldn't imagine why. She also wondered why Rosie believed it and would pass along such damaging gossip about her friends. On the other hand, Ty's alleged sense of failure and his suspicions about his wife were typical behaviors of abusers. "Do you think that's what happened? Do you really think Ty killed her?"

Rosie nodded and stood up, pausing at the door to put on her jacket. Then she twisted the button that unlocked the door. "That's what it looks like, and if he's guilty, I never want to see Ty again. I hope he goes to jail forever," she said, opening the door and marching through the newsroom.

The little bell on the outer door was still jangling when Lucy turned to Pam and asked, "Do you think she's telling the truth?"

Pam's eyes were large with amazement. "I dunno. That was, well, pretty weird."

"Quite a performance, I'd say," said Lucy, remembering that Rosie was a puppeteer, skilled at manipulating an audience's emotions. "I worked side by side with Ty, and I got no bad vibes at all. He was a hard worker, and I really got to like him."

"I don't know, Lucy." Pam spoke slowly. "I've done some volunteer work on the domestic abuse hotline, and I know that it's often the people you least suspect who are actually abusers."

"I know," said Lucy, who'd covered terrible stories of abuse, one of which involved a very popular local pediatrician. She gave a wry smile. "Actually, I don't know. I'm really confused."

"Well, the one thing I believe is the need to really listen to victims of abuse, especially women. For too long, their stories have been disbelieved, or mocked, or turned against them. We've all heard 'she asked for it,' right? Or accusations that she was lying because of some ulterior motive, like getting a decent, hardworking fellow into trouble." She paused to stuff the money into a blue leatherette bank wallet for deposit, then zipped it shut. "I'm not saying we have to believe every word, but I do think we have to listen and take these stories seriously."

Lucy nodded in agreement, but she was determined to keep an open mind about Rosie's accusations. The more she thought about it, the more she thought Rosie, or more probably the mysterious "friend," was simply trying to muddy the waters. On one hand, Heather was portrayed as a loving wife trying to save her marriage, while on the other, she was the unfaithful wife of an abuser. Was it possible that Heather was both?

After Pam left the office, Lucy settled herself at her desk, preparing to write up a story about new recycling regulations at the town's disposal area. It wasn't exactly riveting material, and her mind kept returning to the moment she'd discovered Heather lying unconscious in the tub. In the end, she decided, all she knew for certain was that Heather's death seemed monstrously unfair. She was young, she'd successfully battled cancer to regain her health, and she should have been looking forward to a nice, long life.

She had finally finished up summarizing the new regulations, including the fact that pizza boxes would absolutely not be accepted henceforward, when her phone rang. It was Bob, inviting her to interview Ty Moon, who was now eager to share his side of the story. "He's at your disposal, Lucy, any time you want."

"The sooner, the better," replied Lucy, who was ready to drop everything in order to talk to Ty. Maybe now she'd finally get the answers she was looking for.

As arranged, Lucy went to Bob's law office that evening to interview Ty, bringing with her a list of questions. Bob himself greeted her at the doorway, explaining that since his secretary had left at five, they'd have plenty of privacy. "It's not that I don't trust her, but Ty is understandably nervous these days. There have been threats and nasty phone calls, and he feels as if he has a target on his back."

Lucy wasn't sure how to take this bit of information. Was Bob expecting her to write a flattering puff piece? If so, she decided, he'd chosen the wrong girl for the job. "I've been a reporter for a long time, but people never cease to amaze me," she said. "Just when you think they couldn't go any lower, down they go."

"So true," agreed Bob, helping her take off her jacket and hanging it in the closet. "Come on into my office."

Ty was sitting in one of the two captain's chairs arranged in front of Bob's desk, and he stood up when Lucy came in. "Thanks for coming," he said, looking very serious. It seemed to Lucy that he had shrunken a bit in the last few days, and there were dark circles under his eyes.

"Always interested in a good story," said Lucy, taking the other chair.

Bob settled himself in his usual spot behind the desk, but tilted his chair back and propped his feet on an open drawer, signaling that he was merely an onlooker. Lucy wasn't fooled; she knew it was a pose and that he wouldn't hesitate to jump in and intervene if he felt they were getting into dangerous territory.

"Well, I'm very grateful for the opportunity to clear things up," said Ty. "Thanks for coming, Lucy."

"Let's get started then," began Lucy. "How have you been?"

Ty seemed a bit surprised by the question. "What do you mean? My wife's dead, and I'm accused of killing her. How do you think I am?"

"I don't know; you have to tell me," prompted Lucy.

He let out a huge sigh and slumped forward. "I'm sad; I miss Heather terribly. And I'm angry. I'm angry that somebody took her from me, and I'm angry that I've actually been accused of killing her, and mostly I just want things to go back the way they were, but I know that can never happen." He stared at Bob's framed diplomas from Colby College and the University of Maine School of Law that hung on the wall behind his desk. "Nothing can bring Heather back."

"Did you know she was using drugs?" asked Lucy.

"Yeah. Because of the chemo. She said marijuana really helped her; she had a prescription for medical marijuana."

"But that didn't kill her," said Lucy. "What else was she using?"

"Recreational stuff, nothing serious. A little cocaine now and then. To perk her up, she said."

"Where did she get it?" asked Lucy.

Ty shrugged. "Friends. There's plenty of stuff around."

"You didn't know about any other drugs? Like opioids?"

"Looking back, I should've been more suspicious, I guess. She was tired and depressed a lot, and I figured it was from the chemo and everything. I should've paid closer attention, but I was busy, working. You know how it is."

"I heard you weren't getting much work," said Lucy. "Is that true? Was the haunted house fundraiser designed to promote your career?"

"I don't know where you got that idea," said Ty. "I've been busier than ever, actually turning away work." He looked down at his hands. "Well, until this happened. I've been open with my clients, letting them know that I'm finishing up my current projects, but I'm not taking on anything new, pending the trial."

"And how are they reacting?"

Ty sat up a bit straighter. "I've been surprised. Really quite supportive. They all say they don't believe a word of it, and they're sure I'm innocent." He gave her a half grin and shrugged. "That's what they say; I don't know if it's what they really believe. It's Hollywood, after all."

"There's also a rumor that your marriage was in trouble," said Lucy, uncomfortably aware that she was venturing onto thin ice.

Bob took his feet off the open drawer and sat up, ready to protest, but Ty waved his hand.

"It's okay. There are always rumors, and the DA thinks I was trying to get my hands on Heather's inheritance. It's stupid; we were married. My stuff was hers, and hers was mine; it was always like that with us. We were going to use part of that money to renovate the house. We were happy; we had plans." His voice broke. "We were going to start a family."

Bob gave Lucy an *I hope you're happy now* look, and she felt a bit ashamed of herself, but only a bit. Ty had requested the interview, and if he wasn't ready to answer the tough questions, well, that was just too bad.

"I think we should wrap this up," said Bob, standing up.

"Before I go, is there anything you'd like to add?"

Ty glanced at Bob, then began. "I just want to say that I'm innocent; they've got the wrong guy. I would never do anything to harm Heather, never. And the thing that really bothers me is the fact that while I'm waiting for trial, a dangerous killer is at large and may be ready to strike again."

Bob cleared his throat. "I'd like to add something. I want to make it very clear that Ty is looking forward to the trial, and we are planning a strong defense that will prove beyond any question that he is entirely innocent." He paused. "Did you get that, Lucy?"

"Every word," said Lucy, turning off the cell phone she'd been using to record the interview. There were smiles and thanks all around, but when she left the office and walked to her car, she had mixed feelings. Who should she believe? Was Ty telling the truth? Or was Rosie?

Chapter Seven

L ucy checked her phone for messages when she left Bob's office and noticed a text announcing that Andi Nardone, one of Bob's opponents in the state rep race, was holding a press conference the next morning. Andi hadn't been getting much traction in the campaign so far; her platform was similar to Bob's, but she wasn't as well known, so Lucy was intrigued. Did Andi have some sort of trick up her sleeve?

She was sitting front and center next morning at the Gilead Senior Center, where Andi was scheduled to speak at ten o'clock, but there was no sign of Andi. "Par for the course," said Luke Halloran from the *Portland Press Herald*. He was a veteran reporter who'd pretty much seen it all and wasn't shy about sharing it. "All these candidates run late because they want to look as if they're in great demand and campaigning hard, when what they're mostly doing is deciding what to wear and checking that nothing is stuck in their freshly whitened teeth."

Lucy couldn't help laughing, and he continued. "Andi, for instance, has got to do something about that frizzy hair of hers, and she's got that New York accent, which doesn't fly in Maine. Of course, her biggest handicap is that she's got two X chromosomes; don't ask me why, but voters don't seem to like women much."

Lucy knew there was some truth in Luke's observations but, as a feminist, felt she had to stick up for her gender. "We're making progress, especially in state and local races. There are quite a few women governors these days and growing numbers of women reps in Washington, along with a handful of senators."

"True enough," he admitted, "but, by and large, politics is a man's game."

Lucy was about to challenge that assertion when Andi arrived, accompanied by her campaign manager and sister, Haley Glass. They were both smiling broadly, greeting in-dividual reporters by name as they made their way to the mics in the front of the room. Haley did a quick sound check and then handed the mic over to Andi.

She hadn't straightened her hair, observed Lucy, but she had adopted a blue blazer and red-and-white-striped shirt as her campaign outfit, along with a tight blue skirt and red high heels. It was quite a change from the jeans and duck boots Andi usually wore for her work as owner of Green Thumb Landscaping.

"Thank you all for coming," she began. "As you know, I'm a candidate for state rep, eager to bring some fresh air into that stale old state house."

A good beginning, thought Lucy, and it earned some chuckles from the assembled reporters.

"It's definitely time to weed out some of those non-producers," she continued, getting a few more chuckles. "I think many voters will agree that the incumbent, George Armistead, began to wilt a long time ago."

By now, the media audience was definitely with her, ap-preciating the quotable material she was serving up for them, and Andi was ready to dish. "While George is stuck back in the nineteen-fifties, I have to say my other opponent isn't much better. Bob Goodman claims to be a progressive, but the fact that he has chosen to defend Ty Moon, an alleged domestic abuser accused of murdering his wife, reveals that his so-called progressive agenda is nothing of the sort. Bob Goodman is a walking, talking example of male privilege, and I challenge him to prove otherwise."

That accusation didn't go over very well, and when Andi paused for breath, hands shot up all over the room. Andi chose Lucy to ask the first question.

"Aren't you forgetting that defendants have the right to a lawyer, and that they are considered innocent until proven guilty?" she asked.

"I have no quarrel with the American system of justice, when it's applied equally and fairly, which we all know it is not. Just ask any African-American or Hispanic citizen who's been forced into a plea deal," declared Andi. "But every attorney also has the right to decide who he or she is going to defend. I submit that by choosing to defend Ty Moon, Bob Goodman has revealed himself to be a misogynist committed to perpetuating male dominance."

"Don't you think you're oversimplifying the situation?" asked Bob Mayes, who was a stringer for the *Boston Globe*. "We don't know what really happened to Heather Moon."

Andi bristled at this challenge. "Don't know! Heather Moon is dead! What more do we need to know? This young woman was victimized by a society that encourages and permits men to abuse and mistreat women. A society that refuses to take women seriously when they find the courage to speak up and accuse a man of sexual misconduct. Even today, if a woman accuses a man of abusing her, she often finds the tables are turned, and she becomes the defendant."

Catching a warning glance from her sister, Andi realized her voice had risen and she was beginning to sound shrill. She took a moment to catch her breath, then pivoted to a safer topic.

"It's simply true," she continued, in a lower-pitched conversational tone, "that this society discriminates against women across the board, whether it's career advancement, health care, or education. Do you know that women pay double what men do for a haircut? Check out the prices at the dry cleaner for women's and men's clothing; you'll find that women are charged more. And what about drugs? If a menopausal woman needs a little hormone lift, she has to pay ten times more than a man pays for his Viagra! All this at the same time that women earn only eighty cents compared to the dollar that men take home."

As she listened to Andi's back and forth with the reporters, Lucy had to admit that Andi had earned her grudging respect. She'd certainly managed to revive her lackluster campaign with new energy by accusing Bob Goodman of being a male chauvinist, but Lucy wondered if the accusation would stick or if the issue would actually matter to voters. George Armistead had held his seat for decades, and he could hardly be described as a feminist. Eventually, the questions died down, and Andi closed the press conference by declaring that she was ready, willing, and able to take on both George Armistead and Bob Goodman at the upcoming debate.

As Lucy gathered up her things and made her way to the door, she was met by Haley Glass. "Lucy, I'm so glad you could come," she said, blocking the exit.

"Just part of the job," said Lucy.

"I know you and Bob Goodman are friends," said Haley, "and your publisher, too, I think."

Lucy didn't like the sound of this. "I don't know what you're insinuating."

"Nothing at all. I'm sure you and Ted strive to maintain the highest journalistic standards." She paused. "But it would sure look funny if Ted endorsed his friend as the best candidate, wouldn't it?"

Lucy found herself laughing. "Readers know and trust Ted; they know he's fair and honest, and his endorsements are thoughtful and well-reasoned. He will endorse the candidate he feels will best serve the community." She paused. "Satisfied?"

"Of course, that's all I'm asking for."

"Well," said Lucy, climbing on her high horse, "you didn't need to ask. It's a given." And with that, she brushed past Haley and marched out the door.

When she got back to the office, however, her sense of satisfaction at putting down Haley quickly evaporated. "A new poll from Winchester College is just out," said Ted, looking glum. "Bob's lead has dropped five percent."

"But he's still ahead?" asked Lucy. It occurred to her that even though professional ethics required impartial reporting, it was impossible for journalists to remain personally impartial, especially when they were covering friends. Or, she realized with a sense of dismay, enemies.

"Barely," said Ted. "Believe it or not, George Armistead is gaining. His 'old-fashioned morals' issue is working for him. Never mind income disparity, climate change, institutional racism, and voter suppression; according to George, the most pressing issue facing the nation is moral decay."

That was a bit of a surprise to Lucy. "What about Andi?"

"Her numbers are flat."

"I have a feeling they're going to start climbing; she's accusing Bob of perpetuating male dominance by defending Ty Moon."

"Smart move," said Phyllis, playing with the orange bead necklace resting on her ample bosom. "Combines the moral issue and a play to women voters."

"Time will tell," said Ted, philosophically. "Write it up, Lucy, okay? Run the poll as a sidebar with the Andi Nardone press conference."

"Okay, boss." Lucy got to work, resolutely shelving her fondness for Bob and striving to present Andi's accusations in a completely straightforward manner, even though they angered her. Her instinct was to defend Bob, a man she knew well and highly esteemed, but that wasn't her job. Besides, she had every confidence that Bob was more than capable of defending himself at the debate and would score an easy win over both his opponents.

Her confidence was shaken, however, when a press release arrived from the DA announcing he was dropping all charges against Ty; Lucy feared Andi would claim that as further proof of the old boys' network in action. "We simply don't have enough evidence to go forward," said Phil Aucoin, when Lucy called to follow up on the announcement. "A supply of drugs, including various opioids, cocaine, and heroin, was found in the bathroom vanity, but there were no prints and no evidence at all linking them to Ty Moon. That house was like a sieve, people were in and out for weeks preparing for the fundraiser. Anybody could have stashed them there."

"Why would they do that?"

"Maybe somebody was dealing; all those volunteers coming and going would have been great cover for a dealer. Remember, this was an artsy crowd, probably not averse to a little recreational drug use. Or maybe the drugs were going to be distributed at the party." He sighed. "All I know is, the forensics simply weren't there. And as for motive, that didn't pan out either."

Her next call was to Bob, who shared her fears that voters would take Aucoin's action as proof that Andi Nardone's accusations rang true. "Now people will think there's some sort of underhanded dealing between me and the DA's office. All us guys sticking together . . ."

"That's outrageous," said Lucy, who knew that Bob and Phil Aucoin had their differences, which sometimes erupted in contentious conflicts in and out of court.

"Honestly, I'm happy for Ty, but this couldn't have come at a worse time for me, what with Andi Nardone's claims of sexism and the debate only days away."

It was after one o'clock when Lucy hit the SEND button and decided to treat herself to a couple of cider donuts from MacDonald's farm stand. Not the most nutritious lunch, she reminded herself, but she hadn't had even one cider donut this fall, and she knew they would soon be gone, along with the brightly colored foliage on the maple trees.

It was only a short drive to the farm stand, which offered a corn maze, pick-your-own pumpkins, and dozens of varieties of apples. Apple cider was also featured, along with the delicious donuts. Lucy found herself browsing among the bins of apples, eventually deciding on a peck of winesaps, and it was there that she spotted Juliette Duff.

Lucy had helped Juliette during a family tragedy a few years ago, so she didn't hesitate to greet the famous supermodel. While some models looked marvelous in photographs but tended to be gaunt and emaciated in real life, Juliette looked terrific all the time, whether she was posing for *Vogue* in a designer ball gown or shopping for apples in jeans and a sweatshirt. She had perfect proportions, and each feature was exactly where it should be; her gorgeous blond hair looked natural, even though it wasn't, and she had an easy-going, friendly attitude that seemed to say, "I'm just a regular girl."

"Hi, there," said Lucy, greeting her with a big smile. "Are you here for long?" She knew that Juliette's career kept her away from her home in Tinker's Cove for much of the time.

"I've got a week off, and this is my favorite season. I love the apples and"—she sighed and rolled her eyes—"the cider donuts."

"Me, too," said Lucy. "I'm having a late lunch. Want to join me?"

"Sure." The two women supplied themselves with a half-dozen donuts to share, along with a jug of apple cider, and seated themselves on a convenient bale of straw.

"I'm sorry about Heather," began Lucy, "I know you were friends."

"It's terrible, and they accused Ty! I felt so bad for him."

"They've dropped all charges," said Lucy, biting into her donut.

"That's a relief." Juliette was studying her donut, as if considering where to begin eating it. "He adored Heather; he would never hurt her."

"That was my impression, too," said Lucy, polishing off her first donut. "I got to know him a little bit when we were working to set up the haunted house. I really liked him. He was fun and so creative. And a hard worker."

"That's Ty." Juliette took a tiny bite of her donut and chewed thoughtfully. "I'll give him a call."

"I know he'd love to hear from you. He really needs his

friends now." Lucy was considering eating a second donut but didn't want to seem piggy in front of Juliette, who still had only taken a few tiny bites of hers.

"I suppose people are being terrible," said Juliette, who'd experienced the hate mail that was the downside of a high-profile career.

"He's been lying low," said Lucy, deciding that the donuts really were rather small and reaching into the bag for another. "I gotta say, I never suspected Heather of using drugs, especially after all she'd been through with chemo. Did you?"

"I think a lot of people use medical marijuana during chemo," said Juliette, speaking slowly and thoughtfully.

"She was doing more than that," said Lucy, realizing that she'd almost finished that very small donut. "The cops found cocaine, oxy, all sorts of bad stuff, including heroin, in the bathroom."

Juliette sighed. "There's a lot of drugs in the modeling world, I'm afraid. Mostly diet pills, amphetamines, stuff like that, but I've always stayed clear of them. I don't even take aspirin."

Juliette was wrapping up the remaining half of her donut in a paper napkin, and Lucy wondered if she was actually saving it for later. "If I have a headache, I go for a walk, get some fresh air. Or do some yoga, something like that. I know myself pretty well, and if I have aches and pains, I know just what to do. Or if I'm anxious, I go for the deep breathing. I concentrate on the in and out and clear my mind."

"What if you're hungry?" asked Lucy, thinking about a third donut.

Juliette laughed. "I'm always hungry. That's just the way it is."

"Wow," said Lucy, unscrewing the cap on the cider and filling the paper cup decorated with the MacDonald Farm logo that was offered with cider purchases. "I wish I could be like that."

"Believe me, when I retire, I'm going to eat everything, and I mean everything! Every darn thing that I've been denying myself, starting with pizza!"

Lucy laughed. "Good for you." She drank some cider, savoring its delicious tangy taste and the slight fizz that tickled her tongue. "I don't suppose you know where Heather got her drugs, do you?"

Juliette filled her cup halfway with cider and took a sip, then stared into the cup, running her finger around the rim. "No idea," she said. "If I did, I'd be tempted to commit murder myself."

"I know how you feel," said Lucy, biting into that third donut.

Chapter Eight

Okay, thought Lucy, starting her car. So Juliette pleaded complete ignorance about illegal drugs—good for her. She drove carefully through the busy parking lot and paused at the road, wondering which way to go. Left would take her back to town and the office, but right would take her to Shore Road and Rosie Capshaw's studio at the Van Vorst estate. She drummed her fingers on the steering wheel, uncertain about what to do, and then, impulsively, turned left. She'd only interviewed Matt and Luisa Rodriguez briefly, on the phone, and hadn't really pressed them for information. Now, she decided, she could put it off no longer and headed for their restaurant, Cali Kitchen, where she knew the lunch rush would be ending and the staff would be preparing for the dinner crowd.

Reaching the restaurant, which was located on the harbor, Lucy parked in the town parking lot, which was now filling up with white-shrink-wrapped yachts stored high and dry for the winter. Making her way to the restaurant, Lucy remembered when it had been an Irish pub that had fallen on hard times and had attracted a rough crowd. That had all changed when Rey Rodriguez, Matt and Luisa's father, bought the place and transformed it into a trendy eatery offering an international fusion menu. Gone were the gingham curtains, sticky tables, and dusty fake geraniums, replaced with blond wood, gleaming chrome, and uncluttered windows offering harbor views. Also gone were the four-dollar beers; now a craft brew would cost eight or nine bucks, and a glass of white wine would set you back a cool twelve dollars.

Stepping inside, Lucy saw a handful of diners were lingering over their lunches and enjoying the view of the cove and the lighthouse perched out at Quissett Point; a couple of servers were clearing away the ketchup bottles and lunch menus and setting the empty tables with white cloths and candles. Matt was behind the bar, staring at a computer screen, and he greeted her with a big smile. "Kitchen's closed, Lucy, but I could make you a sandwich," he offered.

"I'm not here to eat, Matt. I'm working on a story, and I've got a few questions I'm hoping you can help me with."

"Sounds like trouble," he said, biting his lip and giving a half-smile.

"Just background stuff, completely off the record."

"Now I am worried," he said, closing the laptop. "Shall we sit in a booth?"

"Good idea," replied Lucy, following him to the far corner of the dining room.

Sliding onto the salmon-colored leather banquette, Lucy thought she and Bill really ought to eat out more. It would be lovely to come here of an evening and relax, have a delicious dinner without the bother of deciding what to make and gathering the ingredients, cooking it all, and cleaning up afterward. Of course, it would cost a lot more than one of her homemade meatloaf dinners, so she pushed that thought aside and smiled at Matt, who was seated opposite her.

"I'm sure you know about Heather's overdose," she began.

"That was awful," said Matt. "Luisa and I were at the party . . ."

"I don't remember seeing you there . . ."

"She was Wonder Woman, and I was a bumble bee . . ."

Lucy could easily picture Luisa as Wonder Woman but couldn't quite see tall, dark, and handsome Matt as a bumble bee. "I wish I'd seen you buzzing around," she said, shaking her head.

"I was mostly in the kitchen, keeping the platters filled." His expression was serious. "And then, well, you know what happened. All of a sudden, the party was over. We cleaned up and left."

Lucy remembered the sense of desolation and shock that had befallen the revelers after Heather was taken away in the ambulance. "The DA has dropped all charges against Ty."

Matt's dark eyebrows rose in surprise. "I hadn't heard."

"Yeah," admitted Lucy, "but it opens the question of who gave Heather the drugs? And did that person know it was fentanyl?"

"And why do you think I know the answers to those questions?" As Lucy had feared, Matt's tone was challenging, defensive.

She knew she was venturing into sensitive territory and had to be as diplomatic as possible. "Well, it's no secret that restaurant work is demanding, and sometimes people, um, well, self-medicate . . ."

Matt laughed. "So you think I've got a drug dealer on my list of contacts?"

Lucy was quick to backtrack. "Listen, I'm not making any judgments. I just thought you might have heard something from an employee, or maybe had to let somebody go . . ."

"Luisa and I have worked very hard to keep this a drug-free establishment. We're very clear about our policies when we hire somebody, and if there's the least sign that somebody is using, we give them a warning and offer help with treatment. If the problem persists, we regretfully let them go."

Lucy glanced around the restaurant, now empty of diners, where there was a sense of quiet purpose as the workers went about setting the tables. Soothing jazz played on the sound system, and one server was at the bar, filling small glass vases with fresh clusters of chrysanthemums. "I know how seriously you take this issue," said Lucy, making eye contact. "I'm asking because of Bob, Bob Goodman. Andi Nardone is accusing him of sexism because he was defending Ty. If I can prove somebody else supplied the drugs to Heather, her accusation will be groundless; Bob was simply defending an innocent man."

"But you said the charges against Ty have been dropped."

"Right. But suspicions linger, especially when it's the husband. The spouse is almost always the prime suspect. And the charges were dropped because there wasn't enough evidence to prove the case, not because the DA decided Ty is innocent."

Matt nodded. "You and Bob are friends, right?"

"For a long time," said Lucy, smiling at Luisa, who had come out of the kitchen and was distributing the flower arrangements. "Bob's a good man. I'd really like to see him win this election."

"Andi Nardone's a good woman," countered Luisa, setting one of the vases of bronze chrysanthemums on their table. "And electing her will help even the balance of power in the male-dominated legislature."

"She's not as qualified as Bob . . ."

"She'll bring a fresh point of view and represent women's interests . . ."

"So will Bob."

"Be realistic, Lucy," said Luisa, with a nod toward her brother. "A man can claim to support women's rights; he can even actually do it, but it's not the same. How can a man know what's really important to women? I bet Bob's wife takes care of all the nitty-gritty details of life so that Bob can concentrate on his work, right? Does Bob go the dry cleaner? Does he remember to pick up bread and milk? Prescriptions? I bet his wife makes sure his underwear drawer is full and dinner's on time every night, right? How would he manage without her?"

Lucy found herself smiling at this description of Rachel, which was spot-on. "I see your point," she admitted. "But it does seem a bit unfair to accuse a lawyer of chauvinism simply because he defended a person accused of a crime who happened to be a man. Wasn't Ty entitled to have a strong defense, and his rights protected? If you ask me, Andi is implying he's guilty when everybody is presumed innocent until proven otherwise."

Luisa rolled her eyes. "It's never quite like that, now, is it? And one big reason is people like you, the media, who seize on sensational crimes and dig up every nasty little salacious detail."

"Only because we're trying to discover the truth!"

"Wouldn't that be better left to the courts?"

Lucy felt deflated; she didn't like to argue, especially when she wasn't scoring many points. She didn't want to give up, though, and desperately reached for something, anything that would convince Luisa and Matt to help her. "Well, it looks as if the courts aren't interested in finding out the truth about Heather's death, so it's up to people like you and me." She paused. "Do you really think Ty gave Heather the lethal drugs?"

Matt shook his head. "No, but I'm pretty sure he knew where she was getting them, and he certainly wasn't trying to get her to stop. There's a term for what he was doing; he was an *enabler*, right?"

Lucy didn't like the idea but had to admit the possibility that Ty had enabled Heather's drug use. Husbands and wives often had shared secrets that they kept to protect each other. Ty had admitted knowing that Heather used marijuana and occasionally cocaine, but had denied knowing that she was into heavier drugs. Now Lucy was rethinking the truth of that claim, which seemed increasingly unlikely. She pressed on, pleading with them: "C'mon, you must have some suspicions, some idea who she was getting them from?"

"I don't know for sure," began Luisa, letting out a big sigh, as if she was finally getting a weight off her chest, "but I got the feeling it wasn't some random dealer, some stranger. I think it was somebody she knew, somebody she trusted."

"Why do you think that?"

"Just because of Heather's personality. She really wasn't very adventurous. She had a small circle of friends; she wasn't spontaneous. She wasn't comfortable leaving home; she refused to use public transportation or stay in motels. She didn't even like the hospital; she wasn't convinced it was really clean." She paused. "It's just a hunch, but I don't think she would have taken any drugs unless whoever gave them to her looked her in the eye and told her they were perfectly safe."

"So you think she got the drugs from someone in that small circle of friends?" asked Lucy, turning to Matt.

He picked up a salt shaker and ran his fingers down the smooth ceramic cylinder. "Look, I don't know for sure. My drug of choice is a nice, cold IPA, but it's no secret that illegal drug use is practically an epidemic around here. People die of overdoses all the time; just check the obits. And like the social workers say, it involves people in every class, including college-educated professionals with high incomes. So do I think somebody I know is dealing? I think it's more than likely, but I don't know who."

"Not even a suspicion?" prompted Lucy.

Luisa turned to her brother and shrugged. "I've got enough to think about. I just don't let my mind go there. I try to take people at face value. What you see is what you get." She picked up the vase and adjusted the flowers. "Now that's better, isn't it?" she asked, stepping back and cocking her head to one side.

"Thanks for the chat," said Lucy, who knew when it was time to quit. "See you at the debate."

Luisa smiled mischievously. "May the best woman win."

Leaving the restaurant, Lucy was struck with the fact that in Tinker's Cove, as in many coastal Maine towns, the town fathers had seen fit to locate the parking lot in a piece of prime, waterfront real estate. A strip of grass with a few benches was a recent addition, and she paused to snap a photo of an old gentleman who was enjoying the fine day and watching a flock of geese heading south. After getting his permission to use the photo and jotting down his name, she continued on her way back to the office, trying to decide if Matt and Luisa had been telling her the truth. Now that she thought about it, it seemed that Luisa had rather smoothly managed to change the subject when she joined the conversation. They had given her one bit of interesting information, however, and that was their belief that Heather had gotten the fatal drugs from someone she trusted, someone in her close circle of friends.

Driving the short distance to the *Courier* office, Lucy's thoughts turned to Brendan Coyle, another member of the group, who ran the local food pantry. He provided healthy food for an ever-increasing number of families who struggled to make ends meet by juggling several part-time jobs in the new "lean" economy. She'd interviewed Brendan often, learning that the great majority of pantry clients were working at low-paying jobs that didn't offer guaranteed hours, which meant that shifts were only allocated as needed. A cashier or stock clerk who was expected to work overtime in the busy tourist season would only get fifteen or twenty hours a week, at minimum wage, come winter.

She'd always enjoyed talking to Brendan, who was passionate about his work and seemed to her to have a generous, kind spirit. He was a big man, with a full beard and a huge smile, who laughed a lot. Now, as she drove along, she wondered if she'd missed something.

Was the pantry a convenient cover for the distribution of illegal drugs? Was Brendan himself a user?

Pulling up at a stop sign, she decided she was being ridiculous. Brendan was a salt-of-the-earth kind of guy; it was absurd to think otherwise. Perhaps she ought to take Luisa's advice and start accepting people at face value, instead of suspecting them of all sorts of devious behavior.

Turning on to Main Street, and parking in front of the police station, she found herself wondering about Kevin Kenneally. He was a member of the group, and he'd portrayed the artist Millais in Heather's tableau. She knew he must have been present at the haunted house, but now that she thought about it, she didn't remember seeing him at the party afterward. That didn't mean he wasn't there; the party had been crowded and spread throughout several rooms. Or he might have left early, moving on after doing his duty in the tableau. He'd certainly had the opportunity to give Heather the fentanyl, but motive and means? He was an assistant district attorney, clearly a man with an eye on the future. He was active in community organizations like the Hibernian Knights and other clubs; he was always available for a quote or interview, and was clearly laying the foundation for either a run for public office or a successful private practice. More importantly, she thought, he had the trust of DA Phil Aucoin, who often said he had complete confidence in Kevin. That was something Aucoin didn't give easily; he certainly didn't take people at face value. He thought the worst of everyone, and Lucy admitted ruefully that everyone included her!

Gathering up her bag and getting out of the car, she stopped at the police department to pick up the weekly log. The log was a popular feature of the weekly paper, and whenever Ted tried to discontinue printing it, considering it a waste of space, he got complaints from readers. They apparently enjoyed reading the carefully worded notations that suspicious activity was reported on Parallel Street or that a traffic violation had occurred on Route 1. Details such as the name of the offender or the exact description of suspicious activity were never included, offering readers plenty of opportunity to speculate about who among their neighbors was involved.

The log was always waiting for her at the dispatcher's desk, and it was there in the lobby that she bumped into Kevin Kenneally, who was on his way out. He greeted her warmly and seemed in no rush to leave, so Lucy took advantage of the situation to ask him about the steps his department was taking to stop drug trafficking in the county.

"Well, you know DA Aucoin created the Drug Task Force to tackle that very problem, and they've had terrific success seizing more than a ton of illegal drugs and hundreds of thousands of dollars," he said.

Lucy knew all about the task force, which in her opinion worked at an exceedingly slow pace. Investigations were inevitably drawn out and took years, which was difficult to understand since she herself had witnessed drug deals in broad daylight, often in public parking areas. That was her next question.

"Well, the task force has to operate very carefully and must abide by strict legal guidelines or their cases get thrown out of court," said Kenneally. "Any sort of undercover activity or phone tapping, anything like that must be closely and carefully supervised. And, of course, it takes time to build the trust of suspected offenders."

"But I've seen drug deals take place in the parking lot at Blueberry Pond," protested Lucy, mentioning a popular swimming spot.

"Those folks are low-level bottom feeders," said Kenneally. "The task force is after much bigger fish."

"I understand that, but isn't there a community policing theory about broken windows, that if police stop petty crimes, it changes the environment in which more serious crimes can take place?"

"I think that's been discredited," said Kenneally, giving her a rather patronizing smile. "That sort of thing involves racial profiling, stop and frisk, and we certainly don't want to perpetuate that sort of discrimination. Besides, here in Tinker's Cove, I don't think you'll find many broken windows."

"We have some pretty run-down areas," said Lucy.

"Well, poverty is always with us, but just because a family doesn't have much money doesn't mean it's involved in criminal activity."

Lucy could think of several exceptions to this rule that everybody in town knew about, but decided not to press the issue.

Kenneally had taken a step toward the door and seemed ready to end the interview. "I guess I'll see you at the debate," he said. "Should be interesting."

"I'll be there," said Lucy, giving him a little wave. "Thanks for the interview."

"Always happy to chat with you, Lucy." He pushed the door open, holding it for Lucy, and the two walked down the steps together. He strode down the sidewalk to his car, and Lucy paused at the curb, preparing to cross the street to the newspaper office on the other side. She was waiting for a pickup truck to pass when she heard a female voice calling her name. Turning around, she saw Officer Sally Kirwan waving at her from the station steps. She waved back and waited for Sally, who was in a hurry to talk to her.

"What's up?" she asked, as Sally met her.

"Let's move along a bit," said Sally, casting an eye at the police station. "This is a bit sensitive."

Lucy knew that Sally handled a lot of confidential matters, especially domestic disputes and crimes against women. She expected to hear about something along those lines as she accompanied Sally for a little stroll down the street. Reaching the alley between the hardware store and the fudge shop, she stepped inside and Lucy followed, eager to hear whatever tip Sally was so eager to share.

"This is on the QT, and you can't say it came from me, but I really think people ought to know what's going on," began Sally.

"No problem," said Lucy. "I'm always grateful for background information."

"It's about the evidence room in the station. It seems that some illegal drugs that were seized and stored there have gone missing." Sally paused, giving Lucy a meaningful look. "That's why Kenneally was at the station today. He met with the chief to discuss the problem."

"If these drugs are missing, they must have been taken by somebody in the department," said Lucy. "They're the only ones with access, right?"

Sally gave a knowing nod. "That's right."

"But won't they be missed? I imagine they're evidence needed for a trial, right?"

"A lot of defendants end up plea bargaining. The court's backed up, and instead of waiting months for a trial, they want to get on with their lives, so they plead to a lesser charge and take a couple of months in the county jail, sometimes just probation."

"What happens to the evidence then?"

"It sits there, piling up, and when they run out of space, they destroy it."

"How much is missing?" asked Lucy.

"Heroin, hundreds of tabs of oxy, some fentanyl, a lot of pot."

"Any suspects?"

Sally pressed her lips together, thinking. Finally, she spoke. "A couple of officers have had issues with drugs in the past—went to rehab and recovered—and I imagine they'll start with them." She paused. "I'm not going to name names; I'm sure you understand."

"Of course not," said Lucy, who would have given anything to get those names. "You've been a great help. Thanks."

Sally looked a bit uneasy, already regretting what she'd done. "Don't tell anybody where you got this, right?"

Lucy took her hand. "Don't worry. I never reveal my sources." She smiled. "Besides, I'm not exactly sure how to use this. I'll have to talk it over with Ted."

"Do whatever you think is best," said Sally, straightening her heavy utility belt. "Just keep me out of it."

"Right," said Lucy, watching as Sally marched down the road in her blue uniform. Not many women could carry it off, thought Lucy, but Sally had a trim little figure and looked rather smart as she marched along.

Chapter Nine

On the night of the debate, the high school auditorium was packed; it was standing-room only. The Hat and Mitten Fund always held a bake sale at these civic events, and Lucy was pleased to see they were doing a brisk business, selling homemade treats and hot coffee. She stopped and bought some shortbread and coffee, which she figured would provide the energy she needed to cover the event and write it up before heading home to bed.

Walking down the aisle to the front of the auditorium, where she had been assured there would be a reserved seat for her, she paused here and there to greet friends and neighbors. Finding the promised seat, she didn't have long to wait for the debate to begin. Roger Wilcox, a veteran local politician who had chaired the town's board of selectmen for eons, was moderating the event and was a stickler for promptness. When the hands on the clock over the stage clicked into place at 7:00 p.m., he tapped the microphone, calling for silence.

"Welcome, all," he began. "It's great to see so much interest in the upcoming election for state rep. We have three highly qualified candidates: incumbent George Armistead, and two challengers: businesswoman Andi Nardone and attorney Bob Goodman." Roger was a tall man, well into his sixties, with gray hair and wire-rimmed spectacles, and Lucy knew from experience that he always held the door for a lady. So she wasn't at all surprised when he gave Andi a gentlemanly bow of the head and invited her to be the first speaker. "Ladies first," he said, adding a brief introduction summarizing her qualifications for office, which included a college education, community involvement, and a successful business career.

Andi didn't seem pleased with his choice of words, however. "I don't know that I'd call myself a lady. Ladies stay home and drink tea like this," she said, miming taking a sip from a tea cup with her pinky raised.

The audience laughed, enjoying her little joke at Roger's expense.

"I don't spend my days drinking tea," she continued, "I bet you've seen my Green Thumb Landscaping trucks around town. I started that business from scratch, and I now employ dozens of workers and have hundreds of satisfied customers.

"But why am I running to be your state rep, you may wonder, when I have so many other responsibilities?" She paused and looked at the audience. "Well, it's because my experience starting a business opened my eyes to the many hurdles women face in our society. When I applied for my first small-business loan, I had to ask my father to co-sign for me. The bank wasn't willing to grant me a loan based on my business plan; I had to be sponsored by a man.

"Nowadays, they're practically begging me to borrow money," she continued, with a naughty smile that got a laugh from the audience. "So I have to admit that women are making progress, but it's slow. We're a long way from being treated equally with men, and that's especially true when it comes to state government. Women are fifty-one percent of the population, they say, but we do not have fifty-one percent representation in the legislature.

"In closing, I don't want you to think I am a one-issue candidate. It's true that I'm a feminist and will work to establish equal rights for women, but I am a citizen of Tinker's Cove, and I will work hard for all of you, for this very special, unique community. So I humbly ask for your votes come Election Day. Thank you."

Andi got a healthy round of applause, and not just from the women. A lot of men, she noticed, were nodding along in agreement and clapping. Lucy was relieved that Andi hadn't attacked Bob directly, but that sense of relief faded when Andi took the first question, which Lucy suspected had been planned all along.

The questioner was Lori Johnson, a mom who coached youth soccer and was a strong advocate of equal funding for girls' athletics. "You've spoken about your strong feminist convictions, but can't men also be feminists? Do you think you will do more for women than the other candidates?"

"I'm so glad you asked that question, Lori," said Andi, moving into an obviously carefully prepared answer. "I have to say I have seen no evidence at all that George Armistead supports women's rights; in fact, he has consistently voted to reduce funding for women's health programs. He has also voted against legislation designed to extend the time period in which victims of sexual abuse of both sexes can take legal action against their abusers."

Lucy glanced at George, who she suspected wasn't the least bit bothered by these accusations but instead regarded Andi as little more than an annoying upstart.

Moving right along, Andi turned her attack on her primary target, Bob. "As for Attorney Bob Goodman, I was very surprised when he chose to defend a man charged with murdering his wife. Bob claims to support women's rights, he calls himself a feminist, but when push comes to shove, I fear he's just as much a member of the old boys club as George Armistead."

This caused quite a buzz in the audience, and Bob raised his hand, demanding an opportunity to rebut Andi's charges. Roger Wilcox demurred, saying he would have a chance to explain his views shortly, and allowed Andi to take a few more questions.

When Bob took the podium, he abandoned his prepared speech and instead defended his decision to represent Ty Moon, reminding the audience that the DA had dropped all charges against him. He argued forcefully for the right of the accused to a strong legal defense, regardless of sex, religion, or race. "Everyone is presumed innocent until proven otherwise," he declared, "and I am innocent of these aspersions on my character. If you vote for me, you will find I will do everything in my power to represent the interests of all citizens in this district, whether boy or girl, man or woman, cat or dog!"

That got quite a laugh from the assembled crowd, but Bob soon found himself answering some tough, even hostile questions. "Why haven't you spoken out before in support of increased funding for girls' athletics at the high school?" "How do you intend to make sure women in Maine don't lose access to abortion clinics?" "Can we really trust you to defend a woman's right to choose?" "You're on the board of directors of Seamen's Bank, which has a dismal record of promoting women to executive positions and has been challenged in court by female employees claiming they are paid less than male employees. What have you done to change these policies?"

Bob did his best to explain his positions and to defend his actions, but his questioners were not satisfied with his responses and persisted in peppering him with questions that were thinly veiled accusations of male chauvinism. Lucy suspected he was in trouble when Andi's campaign manager, Haley, stepped up to the microphone provided for audience questions. "As a white, heterosexual male, wouldn't you say you've been blind to the many advantages and privileges you've had throughout your life?"

Bob sighed, seemingly defeated. "All I can say is that I find it hard to imagine myself as anybody except myself. Perhaps I have been blind," he admitted, then rallied a bit. "But I would like to say that I've always followed the advice my mother gave me . . . to treat everyone as I'd like to be treated myself."

"And with that," said Roger Wilcox, "let's hear from our incumbent state representative, George Armistead."

George was the very picture of a prosperous member of the establishment, with a head of snowy white hair; he was dressed in the regulation navy-blue suit, white shirt, and red tie. He made no bones about his old-fashioned views, calling for a return to traditional Yankee values like thrift and hard work, and lamented dwindling memberships at local churches. He called for stricter drug laws and tougher sentencing of convicted criminals, and reminded everyone that he was a strong supporter of Second Amendment gun rights. "Moral turpitude is this country's biggest problem," he insisted, "and I, for one, am not afraid to stand up, as I always have, for the American family and this great country, one nation under God. Thank you."

George got a warm round of applause, mostly from older members of the audience, but Lucy wasn't entirely convinced that the support would translate into enough votes to return him to the state house. On the other hand, it seemed that Andi's attack on Bob had lost him some votes, and she now doubted he was the shoo-in she'd believed him to be before the debate. Andi had managed to change the direction of the campaign, and it seemed that any one of the three might win the election.

She lingered afterward to offer some words of support to Bob and Rachel, then joined the crowd heading out to the parking lot and home. She found herself next to Officer Sally in the crush, and when they were outside, Sally drew her aside into a shadowy spot. "Golly, I feel like I'm in a spy movie," said Lucy, laughing.

"I know; I'm paranoid," admitted Sally. "Working in the department will do that to you. As a woman, I'm an outsider. I'm not in the club, and there are some who'd love to see me fall on my face."

"But you're related to most of the guys in the department," said Lucy. As a Kirwan, Sally was a member of a large family that included many workers in the town's police and fire departments, as well as the Department of Public Works.

"That's the problem," said Sally, with a rueful sigh. "I was supposed to be a dispatcher, or an admin, but silly Sally went all out and got a degree in criminal justice. Just who did I think I was, hunh?"

"Well, I think you do a hell of a job; I think you're the best cop on the force."

"I try," said Sally. "So listen, I got a peek at the ME's report on Heather, and it seems she was no amateur when it came to drugs. She had needle tracks up and down her arms."

Lucy remembered that Heather always wore long sleeves, mostly fluttery chiffon, and sometimes even added lacy gloves. She'd thought it was a fashion statement, a preference, but now it seemed she was hiding her addiction.

"Couldn't it have been from the chemo?" asked Lucy. "Those IVs can be brutal."

"No. According to the ME, they were quite recent."

"That's a bit of a surprise," said Lucy. "I never would have guessed."

"That's how it goes," said Sally. "I've been in a state of constant surprise since I started this job. You wouldn't believe some of the stuff I've seen."

Lucy saw an opportunity for a story. "Well, maybe, one of these days, you can tell me all about it," she coaxed, with a naughty smile.

"No way," said Sally, chuckling. "That would certainly get me chucked out of the department, and the family!"

Chapter Ten

Next morning, when Bill barged into the bathroom, looking for a toenail clipper when she was brushing her teeth, Lucy came to a conclusion. The more she thought about Heather's addiction, the more she thought that Ty must have known. It would have been impossible for Heather to keep it a secret, especially since she was mainlining. It was one thing to sniff up some powder, quite another to manage an injection that required a syringe and other equipment. Unless a married woman had a room and bath of her own, it was very difficult to keep secrets from a husband; she'd discovered with some dismay that even her much-desired en suite master bath didn't give her all the privacy she craved because she had to share it with Bill. But even if Ty hadn't discovered Heather's drug paraphernalia, he must have noticed mood swings and changes in behavior that would have led him to suspect that she was using. That meant there was a good chance he knew who was supplying the drugs. The trick was to convince him to tell her.

She waited until mid-morning to call him, figuring that, like her, he might be taking a break. You could only sit at a computer for so long before you had to get up and stretch, give your eyes a rest by looking out the window, and recharge with some caffeine. So she took her coffee and her phone over to the big plate-glass window in the *Courier* newsroom that overlooked Main Street and dialed his number.

"I was just thinking about you," she began, when he answered. "You've been through so much. How are you doing?"

"Okay," he replied, in a noncommittal voice.

"I'm just calling as a friend," she continued. "I really enjoyed working with you on the haunted house. It was all so shocking. I'm having a hard time processing it all, and I know it must be much harder for you."

"It's no picnic," he confessed. "I've got my work. It's a good distraction, but I find my mind wanders. I can't say I'm being very productive."

"It's important to keep up the routine, even if you're pretending. It will get easier with time. Trust me." Lucy took a deep breath, remembering some scary moments. "I've been through some things that I'd rather forget—I was even captured by a religious cult once. It takes time; you need to be patient with yourself. Maybe talk to a therapist, even. But eventually you find you're more in control of your emotions and you begin to feel better."

"If you say so," said Ty, unconvinced.

"I do." Lucy paused. "Say, can I take you out to lunch? I bet you haven't been eating much or seeing other people."

"You would be right. But believe me, I'm not good company. I don't know anybody here in Portland, I've become a bit of a loner."

"I have some errands in Portland anyway," said Lucy, fibbing in an attempt to persuade him to meet with her.

Much to her surprise, he accepted her invitation, saying, "Thanks, Lucy. To tell the truth, I've got to start seeing people again. I've heard there's a great little small-batch brewery near here. It's called Blackbeards. Want to meet me there?"

"Great. I'll meet you there around one."

Ending the call, Lucy wondered how on earth she was going to get Ty to confide in her, but figured it was worth a try. She didn't like the way Andi Nardone was using him to smear Bob in the campaign, and the best way to end it was to prove his innocence by finding the real killer.

That's what she planned to tell Ty, when she found him in the brewery, sitting at a small table against an exposed brick wall, with a half-drunk glass of beer. The actual brewing machinery, including huge stainless-steel vats, was enclosed behind a glass partition.

Spotting her, he stood up and gave her a little wave. Lucy hurried to meet him, smiling broadly. As she made her way to the table, she noticed that he was much thinner, his face had acquired some lines, and he needed a haircut. His smile, however, was welcoming.

"Thanks for coming; it's good to see a friendly face," he said, indicating a chair.

When she'd taken it, he added, "This seasonal pumpkin ale is quite good."

When the waiter arrived, he ordered one for Lucy and another for himself, along with a fried-fish sandwich. Lucy chose her usual BLT. The drinks came first, and they chatted about a range of topics: his work, the scene in Portland, news from Tinker's Cove. They were both hungry, and conversation halted while they tackled their sandwiches and fries. Once their plates were bare, the waiter returned to remove them and asked if they'd like another drink. Lucy chose tea, but Ty went for a third beer.

"I hope you don't have to drive home," said Lucy, somewhat concerned.

"Nope. I walked. My place is just round the corner."

"You know, when we moved to Tinker's Cove, I thought I'd be able to walk everywhere because it's a small town, but I soon discovered that our house was too far out, and I had to drive. I walked a lot more when I lived in New York City."

"The walking is one of the things I like about Portland." He looked up as the waiter set down his beer and Lucy's tea, along with the folder containing the bill. "That and the anonymity."

"Yeah, I can appreciate that," said Lucy, spooning out the tea bag and setting it on the saucer. "Especially since Andi Nardone won't let it rest."

He took a slurp and set down his glass. "What do you mean?"

Lucy took a cautious sip of her tea and discovered it was actually barely warm. "Oh, you know, in the campaign. She's calling out Bob as anti-feminist because he defended you. The implication is that you're really guilty but got off because of some technicality."

Ty looked shocked. "That's terrible. It's unfair to Bob, and it's slanderous to me. Why does she think she can do that?"

"It's pretty clever, in a nasty way. She knows how suspicious people can be in a small town, and she's exploiting that and manipulating them. It's very hard for Bob to defend himself since the police haven't charged anybody else."

"He's such a great guy; I'm really grateful for everything he did for me. I wish there was some way I could help."

This was her chance, thought Lucy. "Well, actually, there is a way."

Ty sat up a bit straighter. "How? How can I help? I've already said I didn't do it; I wouldn't hurt Heather. I've said it over and over, but nobody believes me."

Lucy caught his gaze and held it. "Come on, Ty. You must've known Heather was using. How come you didn't tell Bob who she was getting the drugs from?"

He turned away, looking out the window at the loading dock, where a truck was being filled with metal kegs of beer. "It was Pretendsville," he said. "Heather pretended she wasn't using; I pretended I didn't know."

"I guess I can see that," admitted Lucy, thinking of the things she knew about Bill but never mentioned, like the money he spent on lottery tickets and the occasional winnings he kept for himself. As for herself, she had a few secrets, too, like the exorbitant amount she spent getting her hair professionally colored at the salon, following Sue's advice. "But you really knew, and you must have some idea who was supplying the drugs, don't you?"

Ty hesitated for a few minutes, then the dam seemed to break, and he blurted out Kevin Kenneally's name. "He stole them from the police evidence locker, said nobody'd ever suspect, and I guess he was right."

"Why didn't you tell Bob?"

"Because of Heather. I didn't want anyone to know. She'd been through such a bad time with the cancer, and she was so fragile." He paused, his eyes brimming, then let out a big sigh. "She was so beautiful . . ." He sniffed and wiped his eyes with the back of his hands. "I loved her so much." He screwed up his mouth. "I still do."

Lucy sipped her awful tea, then decided it wasn't worth the bother and shoved the cup and saucer away from her. "I understand that you wanted to protect Heather, but the secret is out. She OD'd. And Kenneally is sending people to jail for doing the exact thing he's been doing. He even fingered you for murder."

If she'd expected outrage and indignation from Ty, she was about to be disappointed. "So what's new?" he asked, rhetorically. "There's always people like him who think they're better and smarter than everybody else and they don't have to play by the rules. It's always been that way, and it always will be." He flipped open the leatherette folder, glanced at it, and stood up, pulling a fifty from his wallet.

"Oh, let me," said Lucy, protesting. "I invited you."

"We're all set," he said, snapping the folder shut and tossing it on the table. "It was great catching up, Lucy."

"No chance you'll name Kenneally?" she asked, in a last-ditch effort.

He shook his head. "Nah. I'm just trying to get through one day at a time."

Lucy remained at the table, watching as he made his way to the door. Then she gathered up her things and headed for the ladies room; it was a long drive home.

On the ride back to the office, Lucy struggled with her emotions. On one hand, she sympathized with Ty's reluctance to tarnish his wife's reputation by admitting she was an addict. As things stood now, her death was the result of an accidental one-time overdose. People might speculate that she was a user, but the ME's findings were only known to law enforcement and hadn't been released to the public. Her addiction would remain a private matter unless there were further legal proceedings, such as a demand for the release of public records by a media organization or a wrongful death lawsuit, or if criminal charges were pressed against another individual. All of which were unlikely at the moment. Ted certainly didn't want to jeopardize his relationship with local police authorities by taking them to court, and Ty, who would be the logical person to pursue a wrongful death lawsuit, certainly wasn't interested in exposing Heather's life to further examination. Most frustrating of all to Lucy was his reluctance to identify Kenneally as the person responsible for giving her the tainted drugs, but she understood that any decent defense attorney would do everything possible to implicate Heather in her own murder. The victim would be put on trial, too.

She had almost reached Tinker's Cove when she got a text from Ted informing her that something was going on over at the county courthouse complex and instructing her to find out what it was all about. Lucy loved covering breaking news, so she flipped down the visor with her PRESS card on it and stepped on the gas.

As she negotiated the back roads leading to Gilead, she speculated about what was going on. A fire? Auto accident? Those were certainly possibilities, but the fact that whatever was occurring was taking place at the county complex, which included the county jail as well as the district and superior courthouses, implied some sort of criminal activity. Sometimes prisoners attempted to escape, sometimes defendants attacked their accusers, and sometimes the losing parties expressed their disappointment in the justice system in carefully orchestrated statements. There was also the possibility of some sort of disorder in the county jail itself, like prisoners attacking a guard or holding a hunger strike. Anything could happen, really, and Lucy was eager to find out what was going on.

Gilead seemed peaceful enough when Lucy crossed the town line and cruised down Main Street, past the usual shops and restaurants. She had the road to herself when she turned into the access road for the county complex, and she was beginning to think Ted had gotten bad information, but when she arrived at the parking lot, she found several police cruisers were parked, blue lights flashing, outside the DA's office building. Closer examination revealed that two of the cruisers were state police vehicles and another was from Tinker's Cove, which she suspected might mean that the jig was up for Kevin Kenneally.

Whatever was taking place was happening inside, she decided as she noted the absence of any police presence in the parking lot apart from the cruisers. No snipers were posted on the rooftops; there was no SWAT team lurking in the shadows, waiting to strike. Concluding that she was not likely to be caught in any crossfire, she got out of her car and started walking to the DA's office, which was a small brick building tucked alongside the stately granite county courthouse that was listed on the National Register of Historic Places.

She was just stepping out from the first row of parked cars when the courthouse door burst open and Kenneally dashed out, looking rather frantic. Lucy stared at him, wondering why he hadn't bothered to put on his coat. It took a few seconds for her to figure out that he must be making a run and trying to escape, and that's when he saw her. Lucy looked around for help, thinking she could use that SWAT team about now, and that's when Kenneally grabbed her arm and shoved something that sure seemed like a gun into her side.

"Let's go," he growled, shoving her between two parked cars toward the empty row of spaces where her car with its PRESS card proudly displayed was parked. "Get in your car."

Behind them, Lucy heard the sound of a door banging open and thudding feet. Then somebody yelled, "Stop where you are! Put your hands up, Kenneally!"

Kenneally looked back over his shoulder, and his grip on her arm weakened. Lucy seized the opportunity to pull away from him and ran as fast as she could. Terrified they would begin shooting at Kenneally, she wanted to get as far away from him as she could, and she sheltered behind a large green metal dumpster.

Kenneally ducked down and scooted behind the parked cars, hunched over. This maneuver was observed by several cops who had their guns out but were holding fire. This enabled Kenneally to reach his sporty Corvette and climb in; he backed out right into a parked Volvo and, shifting gears with an audible grind, zoomed straight toward Lucy. She was boxed in; the dumpster was enclosed by fencing, and Kenneally's car was blocking the opening. "Get in!" he ordered, waving the gun at her. Lucy knew that would be a fatal mistake and leaped behind the dumpster just as Kenneally fired a shot; then he hit the gas and zoomed up the hill toward the county jail and the access road.

Now sirens could be heard as more cruisers started pouring into the parking lot, blocking all the exits. Kenneally circled around the perimeter, desperately looking for an escape that didn't exist; finally, returning back to the little brick DA's office building, he stopped his car. He got out, raised his hands over his head, and was arrested by Tinker's Cove police chief, Jim Kirwan, who read him his rights.

The election took a back seat to Kenneally's arrest at Cali Kitchen, where Bob's friends and supporters had gathered to await the results of the vote. The mood was generally upbeat, albeit with a tingle of nervous anticipation. But even the possibility of victory couldn't top the scandalous revelation that one of the county's assistant district attorneys had been stealing drugs from various local police department evidence rooms and selling them, which was followed by the even more disturbing news that the DA was preparing to charge Kenneally with Heather Moon's murder, presumably because he feared she would expose him.

"Those kids get paid peanuts," observed Sid Finch, helping himself to a handful from one of the bowls on the bar. "They've got tons of student loan debt from law school; they're trying to get started in life, you know, buying cars, paying rent, getting married." He paused to enjoy a big swallow of beer. "Of course, that doesn't excuse what he did. And now they're saying he killed Heather Moon, who thought he was her friend. I just don't get it."

"Stealing was bad enough, but actually selling the drugs and taking advantage of desperate people, that really stinks," observed Zoe.

"Zoe's right," said Rachel. "Addiction is a disease, an effort to treat psychic pain, which is every bit as serious as actual physical pain."

"You can't dismiss actual physical pain as a causal factor," volunteered Eddie Culpepper, who, as an EMT on the town's rescue squad, had responded to countless overdoses. "That's how a lot of users get started."

"It's the hypocrisy that gets me," said Pam. "You wouldn't have thought butter melted in Kenneally's mouth."

"You said it," chimed in high school teacher Charlie Zeigler, his voice trembling with outrage. "He actually did an entire assembly presentation on the dangers of addiction and illegal drugs. I guess we were lucky he didn't give the kids his phone number in case they wanted to try some oxy or pot."

"And he actually tried to convict Ty of killing Heather, when he was the murderer. It's unbelievable." Sue shook her head. "Wow."

"I think we do deserve a certain level of integrity in public officials like district attorneys," observed Franny Small, neat and prim as ever in a crisp white blouse with a gold bar pin clipped to both sides of her Peter Pan collar. "Don't forget he was prosecuting Ty Moon for the very crime he committed." She took a very small sip of white wine. "I find that unforgivable."

"I'm pretty sure the bar association agrees," said Bob.

"Have you heard from Ty?" asked Lucy. "What was his reaction?"

"Mostly relief, I guess," replied Bob. "He did say he never really took to Kenneally."

"I do hope he continues renovating the house," said Franny, who lived next door. "I miss him. He wasn't actually such a terrible neighbor. Not like the woman on my other side, who lets her cats out to kill the birds at my feeder and use my hydrangea bed as a potty."

"I think he wants to finish the reno and sell the house," said Bob, giving Bill a nod. "He's thinking of going back to LA."

"I don't blame him," said Sue. "Why would he stay here where there must be so many bad memories?"

"I do hope he finds a good therapist," observed Rachel, picking up her phone. "We have some early results . . ."

Lucy clanked her spoon against a glass, and conversation paused. Everyone remained silent as Rachel stood, finger in the air, listening intently to her cell phone; more than a few people were holding their breath. Then she smiled broadly and announced, "Bob took Tinker's Cove, getting seventy-two percent of the vote!"

Cheers and clapping erupted; there was back slapping, and someone called for a speech.

"Too early for a victory speech," said Bob, blushing with pleasure. "We've got to hear from the other precincts, but we're off to a good start!"

Unfortunately, the numbers soon turned as other districts were counted. Andi Nardone had a surprisingly strong showing in Gilead and got the college vote, too. But it was the more conservative inland areas that finally dominated and returned George Armistead to the assembly.

"I guess that male privilege issue was a non-starter," grumbled Zoe, who Lucy suspected had voted for Andi Nardone.

"Oh, well, you can't win 'em all," proclaimed Sue. "Let's have a toast for our Bob, anyway."

Glasses were raised, somebody started singing "For He's a Jolly Good Fellow," and there were hugs all around. "There's always next time!" proclaimed Bob, raising his glass.

His significant other and major supporter wasn't quite as enthusiastic, however. Rachel, gathered with Sue, Pam, and Lucy in a corner, rolled her eyes. "Over my dead body," she muttered. "One campaign was enough. Over my dead body."

DEATH OF A
HALLOWEEN PARTY
MONSTER

Lee Hollis

Chapter One

"Wait, don't tell me!" Reverend Ted exclaimed, stopping Hayley as she passed by with a plate of hors d'oeuvres. "Prom Night Carrie!"

"Bingo," Hayley said with a wink. Although pretty much everyone at the party had nailed her costume on the first guess. There were only so many movie-monster characters who would wear a cheap metal tiara and a satin, white prom gown splattered with fake pig's blood. She had set down the flower bouquet that completed her look earlier so she could serve more food to her guests.

Hayley was excited to be hosting her first-ever private function at her new restaurant.

Hayley's Kitchen.

She still could not believe it, even with the beautifully stenciled signage outside.

Hayley Powell officially owned her own business.

After she'd opened the doors to her new eatery, just two months ago, in the small coastal tourist town of Bar Harbor, Maine, Hayley's Kitchen had quickly become the new local hot spot. Although most of the island summer visitors had departed immediately after Labor Day, Hayley had remained open, hoping to serve the town until at least Thanksgiving. And given the unexpected support from the community, she was now considering possibly even staying open until Christmas, almost unheard of in a tiny New England tourist town. But Bar Harbor desperately needed a year-round place for friends and families to enjoy a nice dinner out during the cold, unforgiving winter months, and Hayley was itching to fill that void.

She had decided to celebrate her newfound success by throwing a party. Halloween was her favorite holiday of the year, and so, with the help of her BFFs Liddy and Mona, she'd e-mailed invitations for what she hoped would be her first annual Halloween party at Hayley's Kitchen, with many more in the years to come.

Once word got out that Hayley was having a soirée at her new restaurant, half the town had clamored for invites. But Hayley had insisted on keeping the guest list down to a manageable thirty attendees, at least for her first time out. But, of course, to no one's surprise, about a third of those invited asked if they could bring a guest, and Hayley just couldn't say no, so at last tally, thirty-nine people in a wide variety of colorful Halloween costumes were packed into her restaurant's main dining room.

"What about me? Can you guess who I am?" Reverend Ted asked eagerly as he struck a pose, arms out.

Hayley smirked.

This was hardly a huge mental challenge.

Reverend Ted was in a tunic and sandals, wearing a gray wig and fake beard, holding a tablet made of Styrofoam with the Ten Commandments printed on the front of it.

"Um, wild guess, Moses?" Hayley shrugged.

The invitation had specifically requested, in the spirit of Halloween, that everyone come dressed as their favorite *movie monster*. Reverend Ted had obviously missed the memo. Moses was a far cry from the Creature from the Black Lagoon.

Reverend Ted relaxed. "I know, it's a little on the nose. Local pastor comes as religious figure, but I didn't have time to go buy a new costume, so I recycled this one from last year. I'm still new to town, so no one has ever seen me wear it before. By the way," he said, snatching one of the hors d'oeuvres off her silver tray, "these little cheese pumpkins are delicious."

"Thank you, Ted," Hayley said, not wanting to be rude, but quickly moving on. She had so much to do. The party had only started a half hour ago, and she was already running low on food. She had spent the past week cooking and baking in the few hours she was not busy running the restaurant. She was closed on Mondays, so that finally gave her a full day to finish preparing. Although she was not about to admit it to anyone, Hayley was using her guests as guinea pigs. She had made a wide array of recipes from her card file for the party, and she was hoping to see what was popular and what was not before she decided whether or not to add them to her permanent menu or nightly specials.

Suddenly, there was a loud crash.

Hayley spun around to see Freddy Krueger, with the iconic molded face mask, hat, striped shirt, and glove with fake steel claws. He had dropped his cocktail glass, and it had shattered all over the floor. His eyes were bulging out at the sight of a giant shark standing next to him.

"Sorry, Cappy," the shark said.

Hayley instantly recognized the voice inside the big bulky foam shark costume.

It was Mona.

As if reading her thoughts, Liddy was suddenly at Hayley's side. "Why on earth would she choose such a cumbersome costume, knowing the room would be so packed with people? I tried to warn her, but since when does she listen to me? That's the fourth person she has bumped into in fifteen minutes. If this keeps up, you'll have no glassware left by the end of the party!"

Freddy Krueger bent down to pick up the shards of glass off the floor. Feeling guilty, Mona bent down to help, but she was weighted down by her unmanageable costume and pitched forward, landing flat on the floor, facedown.

"Shark down! Shark down!" Mona cried, her voice muffled. She rolled over onto her back, arms and legs sticking out of the costume, flailing.

Liddy couldn't help but giggle, and Hayley nudged her, flashing an admonishing look. Mona's greatest fear was anyone laughing at her. She dreaded embarrassment of any kind.

Freddy Krueger tried to lift her up but couldn't do it on his own, so he signaled a couple of buddies, a sexy vampire and a furry thing—maybe the Wolfman, was Hayley's best guess—who bounded over to help with the heavy lift. Together, they managed to haul Mona back up to her feet; they could see her red, puffy face inside the shark's mouth, a border of shark teeth surrounding it, almost as if she was inside a big, round picture frame.

"Thanks, guys," Mona barked as she marched over to Hayley and Liddy. "He should have watched where he was going!"

"Oh, it's *his* fault?" Liddy gasped, incredulous.

They could see Mona glaring at them from inside the shark's mouth. "At least I came as a famous movie monster! Liddy, you didn't even bother dressing up! You just came as yourself!"

"What are you talking about?" Liddy scoffed. "I did not come as *myself*!"

"You're wearing your own wedding dress, the one you had custom-made for your big wedding day that blew up in your face! Who else could you possibly be?" Mona argued.

Poor Liddy's ill-fated wedding day had involved the groom not showing up, but that was another story that neither Hayley nor Liddy were anxious to revisit anytime soon.

Liddy put her hands on her hips. "And I suppose the green makeup, black lipstick, and giant fright wig don't give you *any* clues as to who I'm supposed to be?"

Mona casually shook her head. "The green complexion did give me pause, but I figured you just ate too many of those gravestone-shaped sugar cookies and were feeling nauseous . . ."

"*Bride of Frankenstein*!" Liddy wailed. "I'm supposed to be the Bride of Frankenstein!"

Mona studied her from inside the shark's mouth. "Oh . . . I see it now . . . I guess . . ."

Liddy was coming to a slow boil.

Hayley put her hand on Liddy's shoulder to help calm her down. "She's just messing with you, Liddy."

"I know. I guess I just don't get Mona's peculiar sense of humor. Maybe it works on some other level, some different frequency, like one that only dogs can understand."

Liddy brushed some cookie crumbs off her white wedding dress. She had lent the same dress to Hayley's daughter, Gemma, the year before when she wanted to go to a Halloween party as Glinda the Good Witch from *The Wizard of Oz*. At least they were getting some good use out of the dress after Liddy was forced to box it up and store it in her attic, since it had been custom-made and she was unable to return it to the dress shop.

"Food's getting pretty low; people are scarfing it down faster than I can put it out. Would you two mind helping me restock?" Hayley asked.

"Lead the way, Carrie," Liddy said before turning back to Mona. "Come on, Jaws."

"I'm not Jaws, I'm Meg," Mona protested.

"Who's Meg?" Liddy asked, puzzled.

"Meg! The megalodon from that Jason Statham movie!" Mona sighed.

"The mega-what?" Liddy laughed, shaking her head.

"A megalodon, which means big tooth, a giant extinct shark! My kids *loved* that movie!"

"Whatever happened to a simple great white like Jaws? I wouldn't even get in a swimming pool for two years after seeing that movie!" Liddy said.

"Jaws is old news, so twentieth century," Hayley joked.

As the three women made their way to the kitchen, they passed a woman with flat brown hair, wearing a flannel shirt underneath a denim coverall dress, filming the party with her phone while lugging around a large sledgehammer.

Liddy cranked her head around to get a good look. "Hayley, who is that woman? I don't recognize her."

"That's Randy," Hayley answered, chuckling.

"*What?*" Liddy gasped, surprised. "Who is he supposed to be, the mother from *Psycho?*"

"Oh, come on, Liddy, it's so obvious. He's Annie Wilkes," Mona howled.

"Who?"

"From *Misery*, the Stephen King book. Kathy Bates won the Oscar for playing her?" Hayley said.

"Oh, right," Liddy said. "What's the sledgehammer for?"

"You really are not a movie person, are you?" Hayley remarked as they headed through the swinging doors into the kitchen.

Hayley stopped suddenly.

From the moment she'd stepped foot into the kitchen, she'd sensed something was amiss.

Liddy instantly noticed her tensing. "Hayley, what is it?"

"Some food's missing," Hayley said ominously.

"What do you mean? I see plenty of it on the table over there," Mona shouted from inside the shark's mouth.

Hayley nodded. "Yes, but I also had several pans of my Mummy Meat Sliders and Pepperoni Pizza Pockets shaped like jack-o'-lanterns that I took out of the freezer to thaw so I could pop them in the oven. But now they're gone."

They heard rummaging coming from behind the pantry door.

"Who's in there?" Hayley shouted.

The rummaging suddenly stopped.

"There is nowhere to go!" Hayley warned. "You better just come out here right now!"

There was a little stalling, but finally, the evil Chucky doll emerged from the pantry.

Or at least it was someone dressed like the evil Chucky doll.

It was actually Mona's sixteen-year-old son, Chet.

"Chet, what the hell are you doing? You know you're not supposed to be back here!" Mona yelled.

"I know," Chet mumbled. "But Hayley's out of those little Thai-Spiced Deviled Pumpkin Eggs, which were awesome, so I came to see if there were any left."

"I'm sorry, Chet, we're totally out. I should have made more," Hayley said with an apologetic smile.

"Did you move the pans that were sitting right over there?" Mona demanded to know.

Chet quickly shook his head. "I didn't touch anything!" He paused for a moment, then reached into the pocket of his Chucky-inspired overalls. He withdrew his hand, which held some cookies—one bat, one ghost, one black cat. "Except these. But I only took three for later. Okay, five. I already ate two . . ."

Suddenly, they heard a bloodcurdling scream.

It echoed throughout the kitchen but had come from the dining room. Hayley, Mona, Liddy, and Chet all dashed out of the kitchen to investigate.

The main dining room had quieted down, everyone shocked by the ear-splitting outburst.

Hayley stepped forward to address her shocked guests. "What happened? Who screamed?"

There was silence as everyone waited for the guilty party to confess, but no one stepped forward.

Finally, Annie Wilkes, or Randy, stepped forward and pointed a finger. "It was the Mummy."

All eyes fell upon someone dressed as the Mummy, who stared down at the floor, embarrassed.

Hayley gasped. "Sergio?"

The Mummy nodded slightly.

"But it sounded like a *woman* screaming," Liddy said.

The Mummy sighed again, now utterly humiliated. "No, Liddy, it wasn't a woman; it was me. I apologize for startling everybody. I got scared, and I lost it for a second and yelled."

"That was no yell," Mona said. "That was a full-on, damsel-in-distress scream if I ever heard one!"

All the party guests erupted in laughter.

Sergio was normally the brave, macho chief of police of Bar Harbor, and so it was quite disconcerting that such a high-pitched cry had come flying out of his mouth.

Although wrapped up like a mummy, Sergio Alvares's handsome face was still exposed, and he looked as if he wished he was anywhere else in the world at this moment.

"What scared you so badly, Sergio?" Hayley asked.

Sergio again did not want to admit anything. He just stared at the floor, lips pursed.

"Pennywise," Randy, his husband, answered for him.

Suddenly, Pennywise the Clown, from the *It* movies and another popular Stephen King novel, proudly stepped forward, white-gloved hand raised. He certainly looked exactly like the creepy killer with the white painted face, large forehead, gray crinkle clown suit with ruffled pant legs and puffed sleeves. In one hand, he held a red balloon. Pennywise moved slowly, eerily toward Sergio, holding out his balloon.

Sergio shrieked again and jumped back.

The partygoers erupted in laughter, even louder and more raucous this time.

"So I hate clowns! Sue me!" Sergio bellowed.

In an effort to alleviate her brother-in-law's supreme embarrassment, Hayley recruited everyone nearby to help set out whatever food was left and not missing. Pretty soon her guests forgot all about the Pennywise incident and were focused on the appetizers fresh out of the oven, while Hayley, Liddy, Mona, and Randy gathered around Sergio, who was shaking slightly, more than a little discombobulated.

Hayley gently patted his back.

"He just snuck up behind me and scared me half to death. I'm fine now, please don't everyone make a fuss," Sergio said, waving them off.

Liddy turned to Pennywise. "Who are you anyway?"

He gave her an awful, shiver-inducing, I'm-going-to-kill-you-in-your-sleep wide grin. "I'm Pennywise."

Liddy was hardly spooked. "Okay, cut the crap, clown. I mean, who are you *really*?"

"You don't recognize me? It's Boris. Boris Candy."

The high school music teacher.

At first, Hayley forgot she had even invited him. But then she remembered that it had been Mona who had strong-armed her into e-mailing him a last-minute invitation. Mona wanted to stay on his good side because she was afraid Mr. Candy might flunk her son, Chet. Apparently Chet, who played the trombone in Mr. Candy's jazz band, had had a few truancy issues and was also having trouble in his music appreciation class. Hayley barely knew the music teacher since both her kids had long graduated before Mr. Candy started at the school, but she had decided to grant Mona's request. Hayley had to admit, Boris Candy's Pennywise costume was well thought out and highly effective. It had made Bar Harbor's chief of police scream like a frightened little baby.

And, frankly, Boris was quite proud of that fact.

"I should get some kind of prize for scariest costume, right? Let's face it! If the big, strong, strapping Chief Alvares was so spooked by me as Pennywise that he screamed at the top of his lungs and nearly ran to the bathroom and locked himself inside, that deserves something!" Boris excitedly turned to Hayley. "What do I win? Might I suggest a free dinner at Hayley's Kitchen?"

"I'll figure something out," Hayley said, politely brushing him off.

Sergio had finally managed to calm his nerves. "This all started when I was a boy . . ."

"Back in Brazil?" Liddy asked.

"Yes. There was this crazy old man in our village who sat on his porch every day drinking cachaça and yelling at all the kids who passed by. Then, when he was drunk, he would dress up as a clown and take a perverse pleasure in hiding until we were close enough, and he would pop up and terrorize us," Sergio solemnly explained. "I was so scared every time it happened. Finally, one day, I could not take it anymore, and so I went to the local municipal guards and complained, and he was given a warning to stop. Well, that just chickened him on even more . . ."

Hayley, Mona, and Liddy exchanged confused looks.

"*Egged* him on, Sergio. Not chickened. The warning just *egged* him on even more . . ." Randy said softly, correcting his husband.

English was not Sergio's first language.

Sergio sighed. "Chicken, egg, who cares? Anyway, because I had dared to stand up to him, he decided to exact his revenge. One night while I was asleep in my bed, I heard tapping on the window, and when I turned over to see what it was . . ." He stopped, quivering at the horrible memory. "There was that evil clown staring at me. I screamed bloody murder until my parents came running in to see what was happening. I pointed at the window, but the clown was gone, and my parents thought I had just had a bad dream. But I never forgot the terror I felt, and I have been afraid of clowns ever since."

"Well, I can certainly see why," Liddy said. "That's terrible. Whatever happened to the old man?"

"As far as I know, he's still alive in the village; he's just a *really* old man now, probably still yelling at the kids and dressing up as a clown at night to scare them."

Somebody tapped Sergio on the shoulder.

He turned around and was face-to-face with Pennywise again.

"Boo," Pennywise blurted out, wearing that grotesque evil grin.

Sergio yelped, but thankfully this time didn't scream.

It looked as if he wanted to punch Boris in the clown face, but as a law-enforcement officer, he refrained and just stalked off, trying to get away from him.

"Who knew this costume would be such a big hit and so much fun?" Boris gushed, chasing after Sergio.

"Randy, he's not going to stop needling Sergio. You should do something," Hayley suggested.

"You're right," Randy said. "I missed recording Sergio screaming earlier on my phone; maybe Boris will be able to get him to do it again, so I get it on video!"

"You are not being a good husband right now, Randy," Hayley scolded.

Randy nodded. "I know, but Sergio says we can't afford to go to Provincetown next summer on vacation. He's being pretty stubborn about it actually, but if I have him screaming like Janet Leigh in the *Psycho* shower scene on a phone video that I can post on YouTube at any time, well, then maybe I'll have more leverage to convince him!"

Randy excitedly trotted off.

Hayley felt the burning need to remind him one more time, "Not a good husband!"

Chapter Two

"You're late," Hayley said, clutching her phone to her ear as she supervised Liddy and Mona setting out the last few remaining trays of food for the guests.

"I know, sorry, babe," Hayley's husband, Bruce, said on the other end of the call. "I was leaving the office when a report came over the police scanner about a residential break-in on Hancock Street."

"*Another* break-in?"

There had been an unsettling rash of home burglaries over the past several months. Well, "rash," in a town as small as Bar Harbor, actually meant *four* break-ins. But that was still a lot and was a developing pattern, especially since the summer tourist season, which ordinarily caused a spike in local crimes, was long over.

"There was no one else around to go cover it; all the reporters are probably at your party, so it was left to me. You know only a late-breaking story would keep me away," Bruce said apologetically.

"Is it the same M.O. as the others?" Hayley asked.

"No," Bruce said solemnly.

Hayley immediately tensed up. "How is this one different?"

"All of the previous break-ins occurred at empty houses;

the residents were either not home at the time or out of town," Bruce quietly explained.

"Oh, dear . . ." Hayley heard herself saying.

"Apparently the thief broke in thinking no one was inside the house, but the elderly widow who lives there was upstairs taking a nap. She heard some kind of commotion, and when she came out her bedroom to investigate, she came face-to-face with the burglar."

Elderly widow.

Hancock Street.

"Was it Clara Beaumont?" Hayley gasped.

"Yes," Bruce said quietly.

Clara Beaumont was about eighty-six years old, widowed fifteen years ago when her husband Irving died at seventy-six following complications from a stroke. Clara had lived in Bar Harbor her entire life, married Irving straight out of high school, and had one daughter, who went on to give her three grandchildren, all of whom lived in California but visited once a year for the holidays. Hayley had had the pleasure of interacting with Clara at the Congregational Church services, a number of library bake sales, and at the village green during the summer band concerts, since Clara was an avid music lover. She was a sprightly, happy woman, and still remarkably sharp for her age.

Hayley held her breath. "Is she all right?"

There was a long pause on the other end of the phone.

"Bruce?"

"I'm afraid not, babe."

Hayley's heart sank. "Oh, no . . ."

"From what the cops can gather, Clara suddenly appearing out of nowhere spooked the guy. One of the neighbors walking his dog past the house at the time heard Clara screaming and called 911. What happened next is a little fuzzy. Either Clara slipped and fell down the stairs, trying to get away, or there was a struggle and the guy pushed her," Bruce said. "The police found her lying at the foot of the staircase when they arrived. At that point, she was still conscious."

"Did she know the man who broke into her house?"

"Hard to say. All she managed to get out was that the thief took off with her diamond wedding ring. I guess she saw it in his hand when she came out of her bedroom. But she passed out before she had a chance to identify him. She's at the hospital in intensive care right now. The cops are still combing the house for clues."

"Poor Clara . . ." Hayley moaned.

"I'm still waiting to talk to one of the officers at the scene, but I will get to the party just as soon as I can," Bruce promised.

Bruce continued talking, but Hayley could not hear what he was saying due to an argument happening right behind her just a few feet away.

"What was that, Bruce?" Hayley asked, holding the phone closer while pressing a finger into her other ear.

"I said I've got my King Kong costume in the trunk of my car so I can change in the parking lot and make a grand entrance."

"I can hardly wait," Hayley laughed. "See you when you get here." She ended the call, then spun around to discover Annie Wilkes and the Mummy, or Randy and Sergio, snapping at each other in a heated exchange.

"You're completely overreacting," Randy insisted.

"No, I am not," Sergio griped, his hand held out. "Now give me the phone."

Hayley quickly interceded. "Please, you guys, I really want this party to go off without a hitch, so I'm begging you, don't fight. Not tonight."

Her emotional appeal seemed to do the trick and brought the temperature down a bit between the bickering couple.

"He wants me to erase the video I've been recording of the party because he can't stand the thought of anybody seeing him scream like a little girl," Randy sighed.

"I am the chief of police in this town, and so I have a certain image to maintain. I do not want that video getting passed around and making me look like a fool!"

"I'm not going to post it on social media, Sergio, I promise; it's just for family and friends," Randy said with a Cheshire-cat-like grin.

Sergio glared at him, skeptical.

"Don't you think he's making too much of this, Hayley?" Randy asked, turning to his sister to back him up.

"I think it's none of my business, and so I plead the fifth."

Sergio's phone buzzed. He glanced at the screen. "It's Donnie. I better take this."

Randy turned to Hayley. "He's been calling all night. There was another break-in on Hancock Street . . ."

"I just heard. Bruce is covering the story for the paper. I pray Clara Beaumont recovers," Hayley said.

"What's the status, Donnie?" Sergio asked, listening intently.

Officer Donnie, after eight years with the Bar Harbor Police Department, had finally been promoted to lieutenant. It had been a long time coming. Sergio had been grooming him, putting him in charge when he was out of town on vacation. Donnie had grown quite a bit from his early days as a wet-behind-the-ears rookie and was now ready to do the chief proud. Hayley was not surprised that Sergio had not immediately rushed out of the party to the crime scene the moment he heard about the 911 call, because Donnie was anxious to prove his mettle and run an honest-to-goodness police investigation all on his own without the chief there to look over his shoulder. This was Donnie's big chance, but Hayley could tell just from Sergio's agitated tone and gestures that staying out of it was killing him.

"Are you sure you don't need me there, Donnie? Not in any supervisory capacity, just as an observer? No, I promise, you are point man on this, but I can just be there if you have any questions," Sergio said, pausing to allow Donnie to argue his point. Sergio nodded. "Okay, if you are sure. But you will call me the minute you are done sweeping the house for evidence, or if Mrs. Beaumont's condition changes? I can be over at the house or at the hospital in less than five minutes!"

Hayley smiled to herself. Sergio was obviously desperate for any excuse to ditch this party and the embarrassing moment he had endured earlier.

"No, Donnie, I trust you. Just keep me updated, that's all I ask," Sergio said before ending the call. With a half-smile, he cracked, "I just promoted him to lieutenant last month, and I think he's already gunning for *my* job."

"Donnie's loyal to you, Sergio, and he's developed into a good cop over the years. Give him a chance to spread his wings a little," Randy said.

Sergio nodded. "You're right."

"Now relax, and enjoy the party," Randy said, aiming his phone at a nearby gaggle of guests in a wide variety of colorful Halloween-movie-monster costumes. "Everyone looks so great. Although if there was a costume contest, I would be a shoo-in to win. You have to admit, I make an awesome Annie Wilkes."

"It's like you're channeling Kathy Bates. Hey, what happened to your sledgehammer?" Hayley noticed.

"It was too heavy to carry around, so I left it in the

kitchen," Randy said, swiveling his phone around to capture all the revelers in his video.

"Just keep the camera away from me, or the Mummy here will mummify you," Sergio warned.

"Promises, promises," Randy joked.

Hayley busted up laughing.

Chapter Three

What sounded like a woman's bloodcurdling scream pierced the air, startling Hayley, who was in the kitchen, lining a garbage bin with a big plastic bag in order to begin the clean-up effort. She raced back out into the dining room to see what was happening, stopping short at the sight of Sergio confronting Pennywise, who had snuck up behind him yet again.

"I warned you, Candy! If you don't stop following me around, I will arrest you for stalking!" Sergio yelled.

Mona, who was sweeping the floor with an industrial broom, and Liddy, who was folding up a linen tablecloth, both suppressed smiles. Mona's son, Chet, was slumped down in a chair in the corner, eyes glued to his phone but with a smirk on his face. Randy gulped down the last of the spiked punch, red-faced, trying not to laugh too hard. There were no other guests left at the party.

Pennywise, who had been stacking leftover cookies and brownies on a paper plate, just stared at Sergio without saying a word.

"Don't look at me like that!" Sergio warned.

Pennywise didn't budge.

It was almost as if he wasn't sure what to do.

Sergio pointed a finger at his clownish, exaggerated, scary red lips. "Did you hear me? This is *not* funny!"

"It's a little funny . . ." Randy interjected.

Sergio threw him a fierce glare, and Randy mimed zipping his lips. He was not going to say another word and upset his husband any more than he already was. Randy also held up his phone to show Sergio he was not still recording.

Sergio returned his attention to Pennywise. "Would you at least take off that mask?"

Again, Pennywise stood frozen, not moving a muscle.

Sergio took a deep breath, collected himself, and then said calmly, "Look, Boris, the party's over. Unless you're going to help us clean up, maybe you should consider just going home."

Pennywise continued to stand motionless a few more seconds, ratcheting up the tension.

Hayley stepped forward. "Boris, is everything all right?"

He then nodded his head slightly, grabbed the last few remaining cookies off the table, piled them onto his paper plate of leftover desserts, and lumbered away. But he did not head for the front door. Instead, he wandered toward the kitchen, passing by Chet, who reached out and snatched a praline square off the plate and stuffed it in his mouth.

"Chet, stealing sweets from your music teacher is not going to help get you a better grade! Now get off your duff and help us clean up!" Mona ordered.

Chet stood up and sighed, annoyed, then reluctantly took the garbage bin from Hayley and began half-heartedly dumping empty cups and paper plates into it.

Pennywise disappeared out the back of the restaurant.

"What was that all about?" Hayley wondered. "And why isn't he leaving out the front door?"

"Front door, back door, who cares? As long as he's gone. What an odd seagull," Sergio said, shaking his head.

"Duck," Randy corrected him. "Odd duck."

"Fine. Whatever," Sergio snorted. "We are on an island off the coast of Maine. I do not understand why the saying just cannot be a seagull!"

Liddy chuckled. "You know, Sergio does make sense in his own strange way."

Randy crossed to Sergio and gently patted his back. "I'm sorry for laughing at you earlier. I'm sure it wasn't easy to talk about your fear of clowns. Forgive me?"

Sergio glanced at Randy, appearing to soften, but then spit out an emphatic, "No!"

Hayley wasn't too worried. Her brother and his husband rarely stayed mad at each other for too long. Sergio would probably forget why he was even upset by morning. Still, she was confused by Boris Candy's bizarre behavior. She was about to follow him out the back to see if she might find out what, if anything, was wrong with him when suddenly the front door burst open and Cruella de Vil blew in, looking wild-eyed and discombobulated. She wore an oversized fake fur coat, a black dress, long, red gloves that stretched out to her elbows, and a half-black, half-white wig. Her face was caked with white makeup, and her lips were painted a ruby red. The costume was spot-on.

"I can't find Pia!" Cruella roared.

"Is Pia one of your dalmatian puppies?" Randy cracked.

"No! My daughter!"

Cruella was actually Dr. Mira Reddy, a physician at the Jackson Lab, a biomedical research facility founded in Bar Harbor, Maine, way back in 1929. Although she was smart as a whip and at the forefront of her field—mammalian genetics and human genomics research—the common opinion around town was that Dr. Reddy's personality was no match for her brains. Many in town found her snobbish and dismissive. In fact, Hayley would never have even thought about inviting the doctor to her Halloween party, especially since she had culled the guest list to only include a small number of close family and friends, but Mona had begged Hayley to include her, just like she had with Boris Candy.

Dr. Reddy's daughter, Pia, was Mona's youngest child Jodie's best friend, and Jodie was desperate to have her BFF at the party so she had someone to play with. Unfortunately, Pia had told Jodie that her mother refused to allow her to come on her own, that she would have to accompany her as a chaperone, so Hayley was left with no choice but to include Dr. Reddy on the final guest list. The irony of her showing up dressed as Cruella de Vil was not lost on anybody.

"Well, has anyone seen her?" Cruella huffed. "It's late, and it's a school night! I want to go home!"

Everyone exchanged blank looks.

Except for Chet, who stopped picking up paper plates off the table and asked quietly, "Was Pia dressed as a witch?"

"Yes," Dr. Reddy said. "She and Jodie came as characters from that old movie *Hocus Pocus*, which they saw recently. Did you see them? Where are they?"

"In the back, near the storeroom," Chet said. "But that was a while ago."

Everyone fanned out to find the girls, no one having a clue what was about to turn up.

Chapter Four

After bumping into tables and knocking over a few chairs, Mona mercifully shed her bulky foam shark costume to lead the search for her daughter, Jodie, and her friend, Pia. Sergio slipped out of his Mummy getup as well, and Liddy continued with the cleanup. But the rest of the remaining group were already spread out in the restaurant, checking everywhere for the missing girls.

Not two minutes passed before they heard Randy call out, "Found them!"

They all raced in the direction of Randy's voice, which, as Chet had already told them, was coming from the storeroom in the back. Hayley, with Dr. Reddy breathing heavily down her neck, was the first to enter after Randy. The two girls sat in the middle of the floor, opposite each other, in their *Hocus Pocus* costumes. Jodie had a red wig on and was wearing a green dress, like the Bette Midler character Winifred in the movie, and Pia, who was smaller, wore a blond wig and pink dress, presumably the Sarah Jessica Parker character, aptly named Sarah. Between them was a large hardcover tome embossed with the title *Witchcraft: A Book of Spells*, along with lit candles and various potion bottles.

"Girls, what are you doing in here?" Hayley asked.

They stared up nervously at her.

Finally, Jodie squeaked out, "Nothing."

Dr. Reddy pushed her way past Hayley and gasped. She reached down, picked up the book, and began thumbing through it. "What exactly is going on here? Where did you get this book?"

Another long pause.

This time Pia spoke. "Amazon."

By now, Mona and Sergio had joined Hayley, Dr. Reddy, and Randy in the storeroom with the girls.

Dr. Reddy slammed the book shut, her mouth open in shock. When she finally managed to collect herself, she kneeled down, took her daughter by the arm, and said firmly, "Were you two practicing *witchcraft*?"

The girls glanced at each other, not wanting to get themselves into any trouble, but after some tortured hesitation, Pia ultimately nodded slightly and broke down, her eyes pooling with tears. "Yes. I'm sorry, Mommy."

Dr. Reddy released her grip on her daughter and shot back up to her feet. "This is outrageous! What kind of party is this, allowing little girls to engage in this kind of behavior?"

"Oh, come on, they're just having a little harmless fun," Mona snapped, rolling her eyes.

This did nothing to tamp down the mounting tension.

Dr. Reddy whipped around to Mona and marched up to her until their noses were almost touching. "I can't say I'm surprised to hear you say that, Mona Barnes. You've unleashed an army of misbehaved troublemakers onto the streets of this town over the years, so why should I expect some decent parenting with the last runt in the litter?"

Absolute silence.

Except perhaps the sound of Mona's blood boiling.

Mona rolled up the sleeves of her sweatshirt in a threatening manner and took a step toward Dr. Reddy. "I think I have put up with enough of you, you sanctimonious, snobby—"

"Let's just *all* calm down," Hayley pleaded.

Sergio instinctively reached out and grabbed Mona, pulling her back by his side, gripping her tightly by the arm and preventing a potential all-out brawl.

Mona struggled a bit to free herself from his iron grip, but thankfully she slowly cooled down and stopped fighting him.

Still, Sergio wasn't taking any chances. He casually threw an arm around Mona's shoulders, so he was in a good position to take her down in case she unexpectedly tried to lunge at Dr. Reddy and attack her, which, given Mona's legendary quick temper, was not a difficult scenario to imagine.

"I find it reprehensible that anyone would think something like this is acceptable behavior. Come on, Pia, we're going home right now," Dr. Reddy spit out.

Pia grabbed the book and scrambled to her feet.

"No, you give that back to Jodie. I will not have my daughter reading that blasphemous filth!"

"B-but . . ." Pia sputtered.

"But *what*?" Dr. Reddy snapped.

"It's my book," Pia muttered, eyes downcast.

Mona snorted through her nose, trying to suppress a laugh.

Dr. Reddy's nostrils flared. She snatched the book out of her daughter's hand and tossed it in a nearby garbage bin. "We'll talk about you ordering items off the internet without my permission when we get home. Now come on, Pia!"

Liddy suddenly popped her head in the storeroom, carrying a casserole dish wrapped in tinfoil. "Hayley, there was half a Chicken Cordon Boo casserole left over. No sense letting it go to waste. Should I put in the fridge for later?"

"No, take it to the freezer; thanks, Liddy," Hayley said, returning her attention to a rattled Dr. Reddy and a remorseful, teary-eyed Pia.

"Where's your coat?" Dr. Reddy asked her daughter.

Pia shrugged. "I don't know."

Dr. Reddy sighed. "Well, go find it, so we can get out of here."

Pia dashed off.

Hayley knelt down to Mona's daughter, Jodie, who had remained tight-lipped since they had first been caught. "Jodie, do the candles and bottles belong to you?"

Jodie shook her head, eyes glued to the floor, and said quietly, "No, Pia brought them, too. It was her idea to be real witches and cast spells."

Mona relished this moment by throwing a self-satisfied smile in Dr. Reddy's direction, which the doctor willfully ignored.

Randy surreptitiously leaned in and whispered in Hayley's ear, "I only see one real witch here," as he nodded toward Dr. Reddy, stifling a chuckle.

Hayley was about to ask Dr. Reddy if she would like them to put the candles and bottles in a paper bag so she could take them home with her, too, when suddenly they heard another woman's high-pitched, bloodcurdling scream.

All eyes turned to Sergio.

"It was *not* me!" Sergio protested.

"Liddy . . ." Hayley said under her breath as she shoved her way out of the storeroom and ran toward the walk-in freezer located in the opposite far corner of the kitchen.

The large, stainless-steel freezer door was open when Hayley arrived on the scene, with Sergio, Randy, Mona, and Dr. Reddy bringing up the rear.

Hayley suddenly came to an abrupt stop.

The casserole dish had slipped out of Liddy's hands, shattering the glass and sending Hayley's Chicken Cordon Boo Halloween recipe flying everywhere. Just past Liddy, on the floor in the freezer, was a man's body, sprawled out on his back, limbs akimbo.

Hayley's eyes zeroed in on the man's pale ghostly face, his glassy, lifeless eyes staring up at her, his crooked mouth wrenched open as if frozen in a silent scream.

"Oh, no . . ." she moaned.

There was no mistaking who it was.

The dead man was Boris Candy.

Chapter Five

Liddy couldn't stop screaming.

The shock of stumbling over a corpse had been too much for her.

Hayley whipped around and grabbed her by the arms. "Liddy, please, get a hold of yourself!"

Liddy managed to catch her breath, heaving gulps of air and fanning herself in an attempt to calm down, but then her eyes would drop back down to Boris Candy's corpse, and she would start screaming all over again.

Hayley shook her by the arms. "Liddy, I don't want to slap you!"

That seemed to do the trick.

Liddy finally managed to get herself under control, grabbed Hayley's hand, poised to strike, and growled, "Don't you dare . . ."

Sergio was already circling the body, inspecting the scene. He knelt down to examine the back of Candy's head.

Hayley pushed Liddy toward the door. "Go and make sure Jodie and Pia stay far away from here. I don't want them to see anything!"

But it was too late.

Hearing Liddy's terrified scream, Jodie had already

rushed to the freezer and pushed her way through the group to see what was causing such a commotion. The little girl's eyes popped open wide, and she emitted a frightened gasp.

Mona instantly covered her daughter's eyes with her hands and hustled her out. "Come on, Jodie, there is nothing to see here!"

"I'm going to go check on Pia," Dr. Reddy said, mostly to herself, before taking one last glance at the dead body and shaking her head in distress before rushing out.

Sergio sprang back up when he was done investigating. "There is a bloody wound on the back of Candy's head."

Hayley gasped, even louder than Jodie. "*What?*"

"It appears as if someone bludgeoned him to death with some kind of blunt object. Near as I can tell, Mr. Candy must have decided to change out of his clown costume back here before going home, and while he was distracted, someone came up behind him, whacked him good in the back of the head, then dragged the body into the freezer, hoping to hide it long enough for him . . . or her . . . to escape out the back door."

Randy bolted from the freezer, only to return a few moments later. "There is one problem with your theory, Sergio. The back door is locked from the inside. The killer could not have gone out the back, unless someone locked it *after* he left."

"No," Liddy whispered. "It was already locked when I came back here to clean up after the party. I know because I checked. Boris Candy was still in the main dining room."

"Then the killer had to have left out the front door, but most of the party guests had already left by the time we all last saw Mr. Candy alive," Hayley noted. "Which means . . ."

Sergio nodded, a solemn look on his face. "It would

have to be one of us still at the party . . . me, you, Randy, Mona, Liddy, Dr. Reddy, Mona's boy, Chet . . ."

"No, that's preposterous!" Hayley protested. "Why would any one of us want to harm poor Mr. Candy?"

Sergio shrugged. "I don't know. But it's all we've got at this point."

Mona appeared at the freezer door, her face ashen and her whole body trembling. "You all better come out to the dining room, right now!"

"Why? What's happened now?" Hayley groaned, almost dreading to find out.

Mona didn't answer her. She just whipped around and led them all out of the freezer, leaving behind the body and taking them back out front to the dining room.

There they saw Dr. Reddy pacing back and forth in full Cruella de Vil mode, sucking on a cigarette and rubbing her tired eyes with her black-gloved fingertips. Chet sat in a corner, legs stretched out, arms folded, obviously wishing he was anywhere else. Jodie and Pia were sitting crosslegged on the floor, close together, shoulders touching, sticking together, both with long, solemn faces.

Mona marched over to the two little girls, bent down, and said gently, "Okay, Jodie, repeat to Sergio exactly what you just told me."

Sergio eagerly stepped forward. "Did you girls see something? Do you know who killed Mr. Candy?"

Jodie and Pia exchanged petrified looks.

Then Jodie turned back to the Chief and nodded slightly.

Sergio rested a hand on Mona's shoulder, signaling for her to get up. Mona rose and took a step back, allowing Sergio to kneel down and take her place. He smiled at the girls and said in a warm, reassuring voice, "It's okay, girls.

You're not in any trouble. Everything is going to be okay. Just tell me who it was. Who killed Mr. Candy?"

Another nervous glance between the girls.

Pia was now on the verge of tears. "Tell him, Jodie!"

Finally, Jodie, after a lot of wriggling and hemming and hawing, stared down at the floor and whispered under her breath, "We did. We killed Mr. Candy."

Island Food & Cocktails
by
Hayley Powell

It's never been a secret that Halloween has always been my kids' favorite holiday, probably because every year their father made such a big deal out of it when they were growing up. Every October, my husband, Danny, would try to top himself by going bigger with his scary costumes and elaborate pranks. The kids loved it. I just found myself exhausted. Mostly because, nine times out of ten, I was the target of his pranks. One year involved dressing up in a giant raccoon costume and hiding in the laundry room, so when I came to get the towels out of the dryer, he could jump out at me. The kids, of course, were in on it and fell to the floor holding their sides and laughing hysterically as I came screaming out of the laundry room, frantically waving my hands in the air. But I never complained too much because I had long accepted the fact that it had become a family tradition.

That is, until the year Danny and I separated and he moved out of state a couple of months before Halloween. The kids were heartbroken, and as Halloween drew closer, I could tell they just didn't have the same spirit without their dad around to get them excited. I didn't want them sulking at home, so I convinced the kids to dress up in their favorite costumes and march in the middle-school Halloween parade. I also rallied them to go trick-or-treating with me, Mona, and her kids in the early evening. I was certainly no substitute for their father, but I did my best to whip up a little enthusiasm.

It seemed to work. Dustin dusted off his go-to Batman costume, and Gemma transformed herself into Hermione Granger from the *Harry Potter* books for the next day's parade. The kids had set off for school, and that's when things took a decidedly dark turn.

As I was leaving for work, I noticed that the pumpkins I had placed on the railing of the deck were gone. I cursed to myself, assuming some kids must have smashed them on the road. So I went down the street to investigate, but I didn't see any pumpkin guts anywhere. When I returned, both pumpkins had mysteriously returned. They were sitting on the front steps unscathed, except they were now each wearing a clown's hat, which I found somewhat disconcerting.

Later, when I arrived home for lunch to let my dog, Leroy, outside to take care of his midday business, I opened the refrigerator to get some turkey and cheese for a sandwich, and screeched at the sight of a sandwich already made, sitting on a plate, with a knife plunged into the middle of it, sticking straight up. It *had* to be the kids. Who else could have done it? They had learned from the best, and as the saying goes, the apples don't fall far from the tree, and let's face it, my ex, Danny, was that mighty big tree!

Then, after work, when I went to grab the mail out of the box in front of the house, waving to my neighbor Jim across the street, who was already raking the fall leaves in his yard, I reached inside the box and felt something thick and fuzzy brush across my hand. I instantly yanked my hand out, peeked inside, and let out a shriek loud enough to wake the dead! Poor Jim dropped his rake and came running across the street to help me. A few curious neighbors peered out their windows. My kids raced out the front door as I stood there blubbering about a giant spider in the mail box. Jim peeked inside, then reached in and pulled out a big, black, fake fuzzy spider with a note attached that said, "Boo!"

Jim couldn't stop himself from busting up laughing; Dustin thought the spider looked cool and wanted to keep it; Gemma just rolled her eyes and moaned that I was embarrassing her in front of the neighbors. I knew right then by their reactions that the kids had had nothing to do with this bizarre series of pranks.

I marched inside and called Danny, who swore he was still in Iowa and had not snuck back to town to engage in his typical Halloween revelry.

So who was behind this unexpected reign of terror?

That's when I opened the kitchen cabinet for a box of pasta to make for dinner and was met with a giant ghoul face bobbing up and down and laughing maniacally. More screaming. More running around. Both hands in the air. Not my most calm and composed moment.

That was the last straw. After taking a few deep breaths, I dragged the kids out to the car and drove straight over to my brother Randy's house, hoping to coerce an invitation to stay for dinner because I was not about to spend another moment in my own home, dreading what might happen next.

Randy and his husband, Sergio, were more than happy to host us, and we all gorged on one of Randy's specialty dishes, Chicken Cordon Bleu—or Boo, as he liked to call it around Halloween—a name I adopted for my own Chicken Cordon Boo Bites appetizer, but more on that later. I spent most of the meal breathlessly recounting the day's heart-stopping pranks, and how I was clueless as to who could be behind them! Sergio promised to have a squad car patrol the neighborhood to be on the lookout for anything out of the ordinary. I thanked him profusely. I was determined to get to the bottom of this.

The next day was Halloween. I made plans with Mona, who offered to pick up my kids and her own brood and take them back to her house for a quick dinner before we would all meet up to go trick-or-treating. After a long day at work, including a mid-morning break to step outside on the sidewalk of the *Island Times* office to watch the parade pass by and wave at all the children in their costumes, I rushed home to feed Leroy and grab a quick bite to eat before Mona arrived with the car full of kids, ready to load up on trick-or-treat sweets.

I tossed my purse on the kitchen table and glanced around for Leroy, who, oddly, was nowhere to be seen. I started to get an eerie feeling. The house was so quiet, almost too quiet, as I stood in the middle of the kitchen, just listening for a moment.

I slowly walked out of the kitchen toward the living room when I thought I heard soft music playing. I strained to hear what it was as I silently crept down the hallway. As it seemed to slowly grow in volume, I recognized the tune. It was the theme from that creepy 1960s super-natural soap *Dark Shadows*! My stomach was in knots as I rounded the corner and suddenly saw a man sitting in a chair facing away from me. I covered my mouth to muffle my gasp. I quietly backed away, keeping my eye on the man in the chair, and then spun around to make a run for it. That's when I found myself face-to-face with a lumbering, black-eyed, de-caying zombie with pieces of skin hanging off his face. I screamed and turned to see the man in the chair stand up and turn around. It was *an-other* zombie! Perhaps I had woken the dead with all my screaming outside at my mailbox the day before!

I was just about to faint dead away when the zombies began chuckling and snorting, softly at first, then building to all-out guffawing. That was the moment I knew I had been had. The zombie masks came off. It was Randy and Sergio!

Suddenly, the basement door flew open and Dustin and Gemma, who apparently had not gone to Mona's, came running out, with Leroy yipping at their heels, laughing and yelling, "We got you! We got you!"

When Randy and Sergio finally managed to stop howling, they explained that the kids were very sad about their dad not being here to play a Halloween trick on Mom like they did every year. Danny had decided that if he couldn't be there to supervise the prank personally, he would enlist a little help from their two uncles, who were more than happy to lend a helping hand to scare the living daylights out of their poor mother. Why I am always the target, I will never know. But I have to admit, they got me good!

Later that night, after trick-or-treating, Gemma and Dustin called their dad to fill him in on how well the plan had worked and how terrified I was, and then they handed me the phone. Danny rather sheepishly asked me if I was mad, but I told him no. I couldn't be upset when I saw how excited the kids were to be doing something with their dad, even if he was 1,500 miles away. But as I hung up the phone, I thought to myself, *You better watch out next year, Danny Powell. What goes around comes around.*

Then I went to make myself a Hot White Russian, hoping that might do the trick in getting my heart rate to come down.

Hot White Russian

Ingredients
4 ounces hot coffee
2 ounces Kahlua
2 ounces milk
1 ounce vodka
Whipped cream (optional)

Pour all the ingredients into a coffee mug and stir, topping with whipped cream, if you like. Sit back and enjoy!

Chicken Cordon Boo Bites

Ingredients
2 boneless chicken breasts
1/3 to 3/4 cup vegetable oil
1 cup flour
2 tablespoons Cajun seasoning
1 teaspoon granulated garlic
1 cup milk
1½ cup seasoned Panko bread crumbs
4 slices of ham cut into 1-inch squares
4 slices of Swiss cheese cut into 1-inch squares

Dipping sauce
2/3 cup mayonnaise
1 tablespoon mustard

Instructions
Mix the two ingredients for the dipping sauce in a small bowl, and set aside.

Pound the chicken breasts with a kitchen mallet to equal thickness.

Heat the oil to medium heat.

Add the flour, Cajun seasoning, and garlic to a 1-quart ziplock bag.

Cut the chicken into bite-size pieces. One by one, dip the chicken bites into the milk, then into the flour mixture. Shake off excess flour and dip back into the milk, then roll the bite around in the panko bread crumbs, making sure it is fully coated. Add the coated chicken to the heated oil, and cook until golden brown and cooked through (7–10 minutes), turning as needed. Remove from oil and place on a cooling rack placed on a baking pan.

To each bite, add a piece of cheese, a piece of ham, and another piece of cheese, and secure with a toothpick. When ready to serve, you can warm for a bit in the oven or even for a few seconds in the microwave, just long enough to melt the cheese. Put out the bowl with the dipping sauce, and you are in business!

Chapter Six

"This is preposterous! The girl is obviously making up stories to get attention!" Dr. Reddy cried.

"Please, let the girl speak," Sergio demanded, before swiveling back around and kneeling down so he was eye-to-eye with Jodie. "Now, Jodie, are you saying you hit Mr. Candy in the back of the head with something?"

Jodie shook her head, blinking back tears.

Sergio nodded. "Okay, then why do you think you killed him?"

Jodie turned to glance at Pia, who was sucking her thumb nervously, eyes wide with fright. Jodie then returned her gaze to Sergio and whispered, barely loud enough for the others to hear, "We cast an evil spell on him."

"I have heard enough!" Dr. Reddy sighed, marching forward and grabbing her daughter by the hand, dragging her toward the door. "Come on, Pia, we're leaving."

Sergio sprang back to his feet, chasing after her until he managed to insert himself in front of her and her daughter and block their exit. "I'm sorry, Dr. Reddy, but I cannot allow you to leave until we figure all this out."

"You can't force me to stay! I will not be held prisoner!"

"Then I will consider your refusal to cooperate as an

obstruction of justice, and I will call Judge Crowley to issue an arrest warrant."

Dr. Reddy gasped. "You wouldn't dare!"

"Try me," Sergio threatened.

Hayley suspected Sergio was bluffing, but Dr. Reddy appeared convinced enough that he would make good on his threat that she plopped down at a table near the door, still squeezing Pia's hand, keeping her firmly by her side. She sat there pouting, refusing to make eye contact with anyone.

Sergio walked back and knelt down next to Jodie again. "Okay, dear, I want you to tell me exactly what happened. Start from the beginning."

Jodie looked toward her mother, not sure what to do.

"Go on, tell him, Jodie. Sergio wants to help you," Mona said as gently as the irascible Mona was capable of.

"Mr. Candy came to the storeroom, where we were playing with the spell book, and he accidentally stepped on one of our candles, and his costume nearly caught on fire before he stamped it out. He got really mad at us and called us 'silly, stupid little girls,' and then he grabbed a bottle of wine and stormed out. He was so mean, and he made us so mad . . . that's when we . . ."

"Cast your spell?" Sergio asked.

Jodie nodded.

Sergio put a comforting hand on Jodie's shoulder. "What kind of spell did you cast?"

Jodie stared at the floor, ashamed. "A death spell . . . We didn't think it would actually work, we were just playing around . . . But then . . . then he died."

Tears streamed down Jodie's face.

Dr. Reddy piped up. "Well, I certainly hope you are proud, Mona Barnes! You've managed to spawn your very own *bad seed*!"

"I swear, if she doesn't button it, I am going to knock her head to kingdom come!" Mona seethed under her breath.

"Violence is never the answer," Liddy warned.

"Since when?" Mona groused.

Pia tugged on her mother's Cruella de Vil fake fur coat. She also had tears pooling in her eyes. "It was me, Mama . . ."

"What do you mean?" Dr. Reddy snapped.

"I was the one who went to the chapter on black magic in the book and found the death spell. Jodie just went along with it."

"Why on earth would you ever do something like that, Pia?" Dr. Reddy cried.

"Because Mr. Candy called us names and hurt our feelings, and we just wanted to get back at him. But it was just a game! We didn't really want him to *die*!" Pia wailed.

Dr. Reddy hugged her daughter, trying to comfort her as the girl sobbed uncontrollably, while still glaring at Mona, refusing to believe her poor daughter was at fault in the slightest despite the girl's full confession. In the doctor's mind, no matter what Pia was willing to admit, she had to be under the bad influence of the juvenile delinquent Barnes girl.

Hayley walked over to Jodie and gingerly put a hand underneath her chin, raising it up so she could offer the distraught child a reassuring smile. "It was wrong to cast a nasty spell on anyone, even someone who mistreated you, but, Jodie, believe me when I tell you, your spell did *not* kill Mr. Candy—"

"That's right! He died from a blow to the back of the head!" Dr. Reddy yelled. "Obviously, neither girl is big enough, or tall enough, or strong enough to do that kind of damage, so that puts Pia in the clear. Are we free to go now?" Dr. Reddy said as she stood back up.

"Sit!" Sergio barked, pointing a finger at her as if she was a misbehaving Great Dane.

Dr. Reddy dropped back down in her chair again, still gripping Pia tightly by the hand.

"It was just a coincidence," Hayley promised Jodie, who used the back of her hand to wipe away the tears streaking her apple cheeks.

"But the spell could have made him trip and fall and crack his head open!" Jodie sniffed.

Sergio pulled Hayley aside and said in a low tone, "That's not possible. The wound is not consistent with him tripping and falling. This is definitely a homicide. Someone whacked him pretty hard in the back of the head."

"I know," Hayley whispered back to Sergio. "I just don't want to scare the girls. They're upset enough as it is without having to worry about an actual murderer being among us."

"So what do we do now, call the police?" Liddy asked.

"I am the police, Liddy, in case that little fact slipped your mind," Sergio sighed. "All of my officers have their hands full with the break-in at Clara Beaumont's house at the moment, so I want you all to just sit tight until I have had a chance to question everyone."

"Uh oh . . ." a man squeaked.

All eyes turned to Randy, still in his Annie Wilkes overall denim dress and flat, brown stringy-haired wig.

"What is it?" Sergio asked.

"Has anyone seen my sledgehammer?"

They all looked around the dining room, but there was no sign of it.

"I remember putting it down in the kitchen earlier because it got too cumbersome to lug around, but then I lost track of it, and now I can't find it," Randy said quietly.

"What were you doing carrying around a sledgehammer?" Dr. Reddy howled.

"It was part of my costume! Annie Wilkes from the Stephen King novel *Misery*! Didn't you read the book or see the movie?"

Dr. Reddy shook her head. "No, I am not a fan of Stephen King. Too much unbelievable supernatural nonsense. I'd rather live in the real world."

"What about Hayley's awesome costume? You didn't know she was prom-night Carrie in a blood-soaked dress from King's very first novel?" Randy gasped.

Dr. Reddy shrugged and snorted, "I just thought she had a lousy dry cleaner."

Sergio was losing patience. "Okay, let's table the Halloween costume contest for later. We need to locate that sledgehammer. Hayley, why don't you and Liddy fan out and see if you can find it. The rest of us will stay here and try to remember if one of us saw anything unusual during the time leading up to Candy's mur—"—he stopped himself, eyeing the two visibly distraught moppets—"Candy's death."

Randy suddenly gasped. "We don't have to try to remember. I have it all right here." He held up his phone. "I was recording a video of the party for most of the night."

Sergio charged across the room to his husband and snatched the phone out of his grasp. They both began to intently watch the playback of the evening.

As Hayley and Liddy headed toward the back of the restaurant again, in search of the sledgehammer, Dr. Reddy and Mona remained behind, glaring at each other.

Dr. Reddy opened her mouth to say something, but Mona quickly cut her off with a stark warning. "If you say one more disparaging word about my daughter, it will be the end for you."

"I wasn't going to say anything," Dr. Reddy sniffed, pausing, waiting; then, unable to resist, she added, "Except that I'm surprised you know such a big word as *disparaging*."

Hayley winced, glancing back, half-expecting to see Mona flying across the room at Dr. Reddy, but Mona surprisingly didn't go on the attack. She held back, hugging her shaken daughter, whispering some soothing, comforting words in her ear.

Hayley and Liddy decided to split up in the back of the restaurant, in their frantic hunt to track down the possible murder weapon. But after a thorough search, the sledgehammer failed to turn up.

It was as if it had just vanished into thin air.

Or someone had taken great pains to hide it.

But where?

Chapter Seven

Sergio sat at a table in the dining room with Jodie and Pia, going over their story one more time as Dr. Reddy and Mona hovered nearby and Randy watched the video he had recorded on his phone for any obvious clues.

"After you cast this spell on Mr. Candy, did you see anyone else wandering around near the storeroom?"

"No," Jodie said quietly.

"Were you in the storeroom the whole time until we came to find you?" Sergio asked gently.

"Yes," Jodie said, nodding.

Pia tugged on the sleeve of Jodie's witch costume. "No, Jodie, remember, after Mr. Candy yelled at us, we went to get some cookies because we were hungry."

Jodie nodded, then turned back to Sergio. "Oh, yeah. That's right. We went back out front to the party for a little while."

"So you never saw Mr. Candy come back, and you never saw him talking to anyone else?"

Both girls shook their heads.

"They didn't see anything!" Dr. Reddy sighed. "Stop badgering them!"

"Please, Dr. Reddy, I am just trying to do my job, which

would be a whole lot easier if you would stop interrupting me!" Sergio snapped.

Dr. Reddy threw her hands up in the air in surrender.

Liddy had now joined Randy, whose eyes were focused on his phone, and started watching the video of the party over his left shoulder.

Hayley decided to do one more sweep of the whole restaurant just in case she and Liddy had failed to spot the missing sledgehammer, which must be hidden somewhere, during their initial search. She looked in all of the cupboards, under the sink, in every corner—still with no luck.

That's when she realized there was one place where she had not looked.

The walk-in freezer.

Where Boris Candy's body was still lying on the floor.

Hayley took a deep breath, steeled herself, and pulled the freezer door all the way open. Fortunately, Mr. Candy's body was exactly where they had left it. Nothing supernatural had spirited it away. Hayley took a tentative step inside, shivering from the cold, and scanned every nook and cranny.

There was no sign of the sledgehammer.

Just poor Mr. Candy, who would probably die of frostbite if he had not already been dead.

That's when it dawned on her.

Where was his Pennywise costume?

The current theory was that he had changed out of his costume right before he was attacked. If so, then what had happened to the costume? Hayley poked around, but she could not locate it.

Maybe he had already stored the costume in his car but, for some reason, had come back inside before driving home, perhaps having forgotten something.

Hayley then unlocked the back door and walked outside, circling around the building to the parking lot, where only a few cars remained. She knew Mr. Candy drove a red Prius and spotted it instantly, parked next to Liddy's black Mercedes.

Hayley turned on the flashlight on her phone as she approached Mr. Candy's car. She first tried the door handle. It was unlocked. She opened it and scanned the seats and floor with the light. No sign of the costume. Then she popped open the trunk and searched there. Still no costume. What had he done with it?

She walked back inside, bolted the door shut again from the inside, and returned to the dining room.

Liddy quickly noticed the troubled look on her face. "What's wrong? What did you find?"

Hayley shrugged. "That's just it. I didn't find anything. Mr. Candy's Pennywise costume is missing. The mask, the clown costume, the big red shoes, everything."

"Sit tight, girls, I will be right back," Sergio told Jodie and Pia before standing up and crossing over to Hayley. "Are you sure he didn't put it in his car after he changed?"

"No, I just checked; it wasn't there. And he was wearing it right up until the end of the party, after most of the guests had gone, so it should be around here somewhere," Hayley said.

"The sledgehammer, the costume, what else has disappeared without a trace?" Liddy pondered.

Randy marched over to them, clutching his phone.

Sergio turned to his husband. "See anything on your video that was out of the ordinary?"

"No, and I watched it three times," Randy said, holding up the phone so Hayley and Sergio could see the video for themselves. "I started recording pretty early on during the party, and you can plainly see Mr. Candy walking around, mingling with the other guests, generally having a good time."

They watched the video, following Candy, sometimes in the background, sometimes just for a flash as Randy moved the camera around, before stopping on Candy as Pennywise, towering behind Sergio, who casually turns around and screams.

Hayley glanced at the Chief, who grimaced.

"Can you fast-forward through this part, please?" Sergio groaned.

Randy snickered but did as he requested, before slowing the video back down to normal speed. "Now wait, here comes the interesting part. He's having a perfectly good time, and then something changes. Wait, here it comes . . ."

They watched as Mr. Candy suddenly reacts to something, stopping in the middle of the room and spinning his head around frantically, before dashing out toward the kitchen.

Randy pressed pause on the video. "Something just spooked him real bad!"

"Why does he suddenly run to the kitchen?" Hayley asked.

Randy shrugged. "I have no idea." He pressed the fast-forward button up to the point when Pennywise returned to the party. "But he comes back about ten minutes later as if nothing had happened."

"That's strange," Hayley observed, watching as Pennywise threaded his way through all the costumed guests, as if on the hunt again to scare a few unsuspecting people. "Right about here, the party begins to wind down." He paused the video again. "There you can see Jodie and Pia by the dessert table. They did come out to the dining room to get cookies, just like they said. And Mr. Candy is still alive and well. He's right there, loading up on food as the other guests begin to file out."

"When do you lose track of him?" Sergio asked.

Randy continued playing the video. "Right up to this moment, with only a small handful of people left at the party, you can see him heading out again by himself toward the kitchen and storeroom . . ."

The video froze.

"And that's when I stopped recording because the party was pretty much over at that point," Randy said.

Sergio paced back and forth, trying hard to put the pieces of the puzzle together. "So the murder had to have occurred after the point when Mr. Candy changed out of his costume. The back door was locked from the inside, so no one could have entered from there. And the only people left in the restaurant are the ones who are still here now . . ."

Cruella de Vil.

The Mummy.

Annie Wilkes.

Carrie.

Bride of Frankenstein.

A giant land shark.

Chucky the killer doll.

And two pint-sized witches from *Hocus Pocus*.

One of those movie monsters was definitely a killer.

But which one?

And how did the murderer manage to get rid of the clown costume and the sledgehammer, the presumed murder weapon?

"Well, I, for one, find it difficult to believe that any of us here could be some kind of maniacal butcher!" Dr. Reddy sniffed, adjusting her half-white, half-black Cruella wig. "It's just too ridiculous to even consider!"

"Then who else could it be?" Randy wanted to know.

There was a long silence.

"A ghost . . ." a tiny voice squeaked.

It came from Pia, who hid behind her mother's massive fur coat. Dr. Reddy turned, taking a step away from her. "Pia, there are no such things as ghosts!"

"Jodie and I conjured up an evil spirit that murdered Mr. Candy, and then it must have just floated away . . ."

Dr. Reddy opened her mouth to protest but stopped short of speaking, because as they all pondered the little girl's outlandish theory, the more they realized that, at this point, it was the only theory that made sense.

If everyone in the dining room was as innocent as they claimed, then the only other possible explanation had to be rooted in the supernatural.

And with no clues pointing in a more grounded direction, no one present in Hayley's restaurant at this moment was prepared to rule out a ghost with an ax to grind.

Chapter Eight

"If you are finished tormenting my daughter with your barrage of questions, Chief Alvares, I would like to take her home now, because it is well past her bedtime," Dr. Reddy said, grabbing Pia by the hand, anxious to bolt out the front door.

"I am done with Pia, Dr. Reddy, but not with you, so I would appreciate it if you would just take a seat and be patient," Sergio sighed, at his wit's end. "I do not want to have to ask you again."

Dr. Reddy huffed and muttered to herself, but did as she was told, sitting back down at one of the dining tables, Fendi bag in her lap, while gesturing to Pia to take a seat as well.

Hayley held her hand out to Randy. "Mind if I take a look at the video?"

Randy gave her the phone. "Be my guest."

Hayley pressed PLAY and reviewed the video footage of the party again while half-listening to Sergio.

"Liddy, you're up," the Chief said.

"*Me?* Why me? You certainly don't consider me a suspect, do you?"

"I consider everyone here a suspect," he said pointedly.

"Including *yourself?*" Dr. Reddy cracked, annoyed, as

Pia stared at the floor, embarrassed by her mother's obstinance.

Sergio chose not to respond. He just flashed her an annoyed look before turning his attention back to Liddy. "Liddy, it's late; we're all tired. Just try to be cooperative, will you?"

Liddy dramatically sighed. "Fine. You can ask me anything you want. I have nothing to hide. I scarcely knew Boris Candy. I hardly had any interaction with him whatsoever."

"Ha!" Mona piped in.

Liddy turned to Mona, right eyebrow raised. "You have something to say, Mona?"

"Yes! What about the blind date you had with Boris when he first moved to town? Did you conveniently forget about *that*?"

There was a long dramatic silence.

"No, I did not forget about that, Mona," Liddy spit out with a furious look. "I have just tried to bury that awful memory and put it behind me."

Everyone in the room seemed to lean forward, curious.

"It happened a couple years ago, right before Boris started as the new music teacher at the high school. Mona, for some inexplicable reason, decided to play matchmaker. He had only been in town for about a week or so when he came into Mona's lobster shop—"

"He had never tasted a Maine lobster before in his life; can you believe that?" Mona interrupted. "So I set him up good with a three-pack and gave him tips on the best way to steam them. He told me later that it was the best meal he'd ever tasted. He was hooked. He came back every week after that. He seemed like such a nice, decent guy; I don't know what I was thinking, fixing him up with Liddy!"

"Mona, Sergio is questioning me, not you. I do not need your needless and unsolicited color commentary," Liddy seethed.

"Whatever," Mona shrugged. "The floor's yours."

"Thank you," Liddy said evenly, before turning back to Sergio. "In Mona's cluttered, confused mind, she somehow thought the two of you would actually hit it off."

"I'm assuming the two of you didn't?" Sergio asked.

"No!" Liddy scoffed. "From the moment we sat down at the restaurant, there was this underlying tension between us. I knew right away the date was going to be a disaster!"

"What did he say that set you off?" Sergio asked.

"It's not what he said. It was the rude looks he kept giving me as I told him about myself, like he was judging me. I found it very off-putting and uncomfortable."

"Did you ask him about it?"

"Yes, finally I couldn't take it anymore. I asked him why he was being so quiet. And do you know what that obnoxious, rude man said? He had the gall to tell me that he found me self-involved, that I had been talking nonstop about myself for thirty minutes without showing even the tiniest bit of interest in *him*! Can you believe that?"

Mona involuntarily gave a snort, but quickly pretended it hadn't come from her when Liddy shot her a glowering stare.

Sergio tried getting Liddy back on track. "Was Mr. Candy right about that?"

"Of course, he was right! Why should I show interest in a completely nondescript, boring, utterly humorless human being? If I am going to get all gussied up for a date, I want the man I'm meeting to have a little kick to him, like a spicy chili, but Boris Candy was basically a bland bowl of applesauce!"

"So am I safe in assuming there was no second date?" Sergio asked, suppressing a smile.

"No, we didn't even get through the first date. I was so insulted, I threw my glass of merlot at him. He got up from the table to go clean himself off in the bathroom, but then he never came back! Can you believe that?"

There were a few nods about the room that Liddy willfully chose to ignore.

"He ditched me! We had driven to the restaurant in his car! I was stranded!" Liddy wailed. "At least he had the good manners to pay the bill on his way out, but I had to call a taxi to take me home. We were at Jack Russell's, which is outside of town. I couldn't walk all the way home!"

"She called me the next day and demanded that I reimburse her for the cab fare," Mona said, chuckling. "Which I did, because, I admit, it was my fault for thinking those two might get along."

"Oh, I could have killed the man for abandoning me like that . . ." Liddy said, before realizing the implications of her remark and quickly adding, "But I didn't! It was a long time ago, and everyone knows I am never one to hold grudges!"

There was more quiet snickering in the room over Liddy's bogus claim about not holding grudges, enough for her to feel the need to add another caveat, "At least not in this case! Anyway, Mona was right about one thing! It was all *her* fault!"

"I was just trying to cheer you up after you got ditched at the altar!" Mona protested.

"Must we bring *that* up?" Liddy sighed.

"You're the one still wearing the wedding dress!" Mona said.

"How many times must I say this? It's my Halloween costume! I'm the Bride of Frankenstein!"

Randy wandered over to address Mona. "I am a little surprised you called Boris a nice, decent guy, Mona."

"Why is that?" Mona asked.

"Because I remember you two having an altercation at my bar not too long ago," he said.

"That was *nothing*!" Mona snapped.

"What is he talking about, Mona?" Sergio pressed.

"It was just a minor disagreement, that's all! I went in for Chet's parent-teacher conference at the school, and Candy told me that Chet had been acting out in his music-appreciation class lately, and that if he didn't adjust his behavior, he was going to take disciplinary action."

"And you thought he was being unfair to Chet?" Sergio asked.

"What? No," Mona scoffed, glancing over at Chet, who was still slumped down in a chair in the corner, texting. "We all know the kid can be a hellion. I had no problem with making him pay for his bad behavior. But he insinuated that *I* was to blame for failing to keep him in line at home. Well, I stewed about that all day, and then I ran into him at Drinks Like a Fish, and yes, okay, I admit, I had a few beers in me when I approached him. I started yelling at him that maybe if he was a better teacher, he might be able to keep Chet interested in his boring class! It was not one of my prouder moments."

"Imagine an education professional questioning your parenting skills," Dr. Reddy whispered under her breath.

Mona whirled around, eyes blazing. "Lady, you are *this* close to a whole world of hurt!"

Dr. Reddy pointed an accusing finger at Mona. "See, if anyone is capable of causing bodily harm, it's *her*!"

"Dr. Reddy, please stay out of this," Sergio warned.

"The bottom line is, we resolved our differences shortly after that," Mona insisted. "I even brought him free lobsters at the school as a peace offering because I knew how much he loved them. And we haven't had a problem since. I actually like the guy . . . I mean *liked*."

The dining room fell silent again.

And then Hayley let out a gasp as she watched the video on Randy's phone.

"What is it, Hayley?" Sergio asked.

"How did we miss this?" Hayley whispered, running the video back a few seconds and playing it again.

Sergio and Randy rushed over to her, surrounding her on each side to see what had suddenly piqued her interest.

The scene on the phone was Boris Candy walking up behind Sergio and scaring him, causing him to scream.

Sergio sighed, annoyed. "Yes, Hayley, we have already had a good laugh over it. We do not have to watch it yet again."

"No," Hayley insisted. "Look, in the background. We were all laughing at you screaming, and we completely missed what was happening just a few feet away."

Behind Sergio and Candy, they could clearly see Mona's son, Chet, holding a cup of hot chocolate and distinctly dropping some kind of white pill into it. Moments later, he approached Mr. Candy, offering it to him. Mr. Candy happily accepted and chugged the hot chocolate down in a couple of gulps.

"Chet, get over here right now!" Sergio demanded.

Chet looked up from his phone, worried. "What?"

"Now!" Sergio roared.

Chet hauled himself up out of the chair, pocketed his phone, and shuffled slowly over to Sergio with a heavy sigh.

Sergio walked up to Chet so he was inches from him, towering over him in an intimidating manner. "What did you put in the hot chocolate you gave to Mr. Candy?"

There was a flicker of panic on Chet's face.

"Nothing," he said, obviously lying.

Sergio gestured toward Randy's phone. "We have it all recorded. You spiked the hot chocolate with something. Now tell us what it was!"

Mona barreled over to her son, sticking a finger in his face in a threatening manner. "What did you do, Chet? Come clean now, and you may live to see your high school graduation!"

Chet stuffed his hands in his pants pockets and shuffled his feet some more, staring at the floor, and then finally said in a tiny, defeated voice, "Mr. Candy kicked me off my trombone spot in the jazz band . . ."

Mona's eyes widened in surprise. "What? When?"

"A few weeks ago. He said I wasn't taking music seriously. I didn't want to tell you and make you mad," Chet said, hemming and hawing before mumbling, "I wanted to pay him back, so I slipped some Ex-Lax in the hot chocolate, and I sort of gave it to him as a peace offering."

Hayley wanted to laugh, but stopped herself.

"That would explain why he ran out of the party so fast," Randy said, smirking.

"There is a bathroom in the back next to the storeroom. The two out front were probably occupied, and Mr. Candy was in a code-red situation," Hayley surmised. "He must have switched to red wine after that, which would explain why he came into the storeroom to get a bottle and stumbled upon Jodie and Pia practicing witchcraft."

"What else do you want to tell us, Chet?" Sergio asked.

"That's it! It was just a stupid joke! I swear that's all I did!"

Mona shook her head in disgust. "What a rotten, despicable thing to do! I am ashamed of you right now, Chet! Where on God's green earth did you learn such a thing?"

Chet stared at his mother, slack-jawed. "From you, remember? You told all us kids that story from when you were in high school, and you slipped Ex-Lax in your soccer coach's water bottle because he benched you for three games after you deliberately kicked a girl on the opposing team in the shins so you could steal the ball away!"

"I was trying to teach you a lesson about what *not* to do when you're angry!" Mona argued.

"But—" Chet protested before Mona cut him off.

"Do as I say, not as I do! You're grounded until your eighteenth birthday!" Mona roared.

Another deafening silence.

Even Dr. Reddy knew well enough not to comment.

Chapter Nine

Sergio put an arm around Chet's shoulder. "Okay, son. We're done for now. You can go sit back down."

Chet bounded back to his chair in the corner, his phone in hand, to resume texting his friends.

"That's it? He's no longer a suspect?" Dr. Reddy scoffed.

"He came clean about the Ex-Lax," Sergio said.

Dr. Reddy folded her arms, agitated. "Exactly! If he was willing to poison a man, why abandon the credible possibility that the boy took it one step further and bludgeoned him to death?"

Sergio cocked an eyebrow. "Really, Dr. Reddy, I would hardly call a laxative poison."

"What if Mr. Candy was allergic to one of the ingredients. Would you be so dismissive then?"

"No, but he wasn't, and the Ex-Lax was not what killed him," Sergio patiently argued.

"Well, I, for one, think you are letting him off the hook far too easily," Dr. Reddy snorted. "He has already told us his motive. Mr. Candy unceremoniously kicked him out of jazz band, and the kid was thirsty for revenge."

Chet sighed loudly in the corner, dismayed to find all the attention in the room was still on him.

Mona lunged forward, red-faced with fury. "First you

accuse my Jodie of corrupting your innocent daughter. Now you're accusing my son of murder? I've had it with you, lady!"

Hayley reached out and grabbed Mona's sweatshirt, forcefully pulling her back.

Mona whipped around to Hayley. "She's out of line, Hayley! Chet can be a prankster and pig-headed and lazy like his father, but he's a good boy, for the most part!" She then pointed a finger at Chet in the corner. "But you're still grounded!"

"A mother is always blinded by the love for her children," Dr. Reddy said to no one in particular.

Chet had heard enough. He shot back up to his feet and yelled at Dr. Reddy, eyes blazing, "I didn't get anywhere near Mr. Candy after I gave him the hot chocolate! I bet you can't say that, can you?"

It took a moment for Dr. Reddy to realize Chet was addressing her, but when she did, she huffed and threw him a haughty look. "I am quite sure I have no idea what you are talking about!"

"I saw you," Chet growled, eyes narrowing. "I saw you chasing after Mr. Candy. I was sitting right here. You were right in front of me and didn't even notice me, and I heard you threaten him!"

"That is a bald-faced lie! The boy is obviously just making things up to take the heat off himself," Dr. Reddy cried.

"You said you were going to do everything in your power to get him fired, or something like that," Chet said.

"Is that true, Doctor?" Sergio asked.

"No, I . . ." Dr. Reddy glanced around the room, unnerved by all the faces focused on her. "I mean . . . It was *nothing*!"

"I think you'd better explain," Sergio said. "And, please, don't leave anything out."

"There is nothing to explain! We simply had a disagreement, that's all."

She wanted to leave it there, but she instinctively knew that was going to be impossible. After mulling her options, Dr. Reddy was resigned to the fact that she was not going to be able to remain silent or simply brush it off. "Fine. My oldest daughter, Nina, has been struggling in Mr. Candy's music appreciation class, so I requested a meeting at the high school to discuss the situation with him. I told him Nina would do some extra-credit work in order to catch up. I thought we had resolved the situation. Nina worked exceedingly hard to bring her grade up, and I thought she had succeeded, but he still gave her a terribly unfair grade."

"He failed her?" Hayley asked.

"No." Dr. Reddy was so upset that she was near tears. "He gave her . . ." She choked on her words, almost unable to get them out. "He gave her a *B plus.*"

Mona busted up laughing. "B plus? You're talking like that's the end of the world! I would be the proudest mother in the world if just one of my kids came home with a B plus! Hell, I'd throw a party if they came home with a C minus!"

Dr. Reddy bristled. "She deserved an A."

"That must have made you very angry," Sergio suggested.

"Yes, frankly, it did. Nina worked hard to improve her grade. We have very high expectations for her and her future, and a B plus was not going to help get her into Harvard. Mr. Candy's obstinance was going to potentially cost my daughter her future!"

Hayley was flabbergasted. "Do you honestly believe a B

plus in music appreciation is going to hurt Nina's chances of getting into a good school?"

"Yes, I do, as a matter of fact," Dr. Reddy snapped. "I don't want her going to just a good school. I want both my daughters going to the *best* schools. A world-class college education is the first stepping-stone to a life of success."

Hayley glanced over at Pia, who was quietly listening to her mother, taking it all in. Hayley felt sorry for the poor girl, who, much like her older sister, had to be under intense pressure to perform perfectly, even in middle school.

"Look, Doctor, I understand you're a passionate advocate for your daughters. I have read all about you hang-glider parents," Sergio said.

There was another momentary pause before Randy tugged on Sergio's Mummy costume. "Helicopter."

Sergio turned to him, confused, then glanced toward the ceiling. "What? I don't hear anything." He turned to the others. "Do any of you hear a helicopter?"

"No, Sergio. Helicopter parents. That's what they call hard-driving, overprotective parents."

"What did I say?"

"Hang glider."

"My mistake. I grew up hang gliding in Brazil. You get my meaning! Parents who hover around trying to control everything!"

"I am not ashamed of taking a keen interest in the lives of my children," Dr. Reddy said defensively.

"Nor should you be," Sergio said. "I am just curious to know why you did not share this dispute you had with Mr. Candy earlier."

"Why should I? I told you, it meant nothing," Dr. Reddy said, suddenly getting flustered. "Okay, yes, I was mad, but not enough to bash him in the back of the head with a sledgehammer! I didn't say anything, because I knew if I did, I would immediately be a suspect, and I didn't want to have to deal with all that nonsense!"

"Too late!" Liddy interjected.

Dr. Reddy gave her a withering look.

"Now you know how it feels!" Chet blurted out with a self-satisfied smirk, not bothering to look up from his phone.

As Dr. Reddy's meltdown continued to worsen, the front door to the restaurant blew open, and King Kong suddenly came crashing inside, shocking everyone. He roared and pounded his chest as if he was about to grab Fay Wray and climb to the top of the Empire State Building and swat at airplanes.

Dr. Reddy screamed as Jodie and Pia both stared, wide-eyed and entranced. Even Chet glanced up from his phone to take in the sight of a gorilla suddenly in the restaurant, but then casually went back to texting.

The gorilla reached up and removed his head, revealing Bruce, whose face was sweaty and his hair matted. "Man, it's really hot inside this ape mask!"

Liddy turned and whispered into Hayley's ear. "Is it wrong for me to be oddly attracted to Bruce in that gorilla suit?"

"I really don't want to have that discussion with you, Liddy," Hayley said before emphasizing, "*ever.*"

Bruce set the gorilla head down on a table. "Sorry I'm so late for the party. I've been at the hospital, waiting for Clara Beaumont to regain consciousness."

"Is she going to be all right?" Hayley asked.

Bruce nodded. "Doctor said she's in stable condition and should make a full recovery. They were worried she broke a hip from that nasty spill down the stairs, but thankfully that didn't happen. She does have a fractured elbow and a couple of nasty bruises. She finally woke up about ten minutes ago."

"Was she able to identify who broke into her house?" Sergio asked.

Bruce nodded again. "Lenny Bash."

Hayley gasped. "I know Lenny! He used to work here as a busboy. He started when the previous owner, Chef Romeo, ran the place and stayed on a while after I took over before he quit."

"Why did he quit?" Liddy asked.

"I'm not really sure. He never told me why; he just said he wanted to move on," Hayley explained.

"Sounds like he wanted to move on to a life of crime!" Mona added.

"Mona's right," Bruce said. "Lenny has had quite a few run-ins with the cops lately, built up quite a record. He's been shoplifting and writing bad checks all over town."

"So do you think Lenny has been the one breaking into all the houses lately?" Liddy asked.

"It's starting to appear that way," Bruce said. "Like I said, he's been a regular in the *Island Times* 'Police Beat' section for some time now for his petty crimes. But he may have stepped up his game to burglary—and now, unfortunately, assault."

"And he is still on the loose," Dr. Reddy shuddered.

Bruce turned to Sergio. "Donnie has put out an APB. I saw him at the hospital, and he wanted me to assure you that he is on top of this and has everything under control. They're going to find Lenny, so he wanted me to make sure you stay right here and enjoy yourself."

Bruce finally noticed all the glum faces in the room.

"Hey, I thought this was supposed to be a party! You're all acting as if somebody just died!"

Island Food & Cocktails
by
Hayley Powell

I recently ran into a classmate from my childhood, Sabrina Merryweather, at the town's Fourth of July parade. Sabrina now lives in Arizona, but was back on the island for a two-week vacation to visit with her family. What strikes me about Sabrina now is how much she has changed in the ensuing years since high school—or, more specifically, how much her *memory* has changed. You see, Sabrina is always excited to see me and catch up whenever she wings her way back to Maine, and she stubbornly maintains that we were "the bestest of best friends" when we were teenagers.

This could not be further from the truth.

There is a lot of revisionist history going on in Sabrina's brain. Case in point: the week of Halloween when we were juniors at Mount Desert Island High School. I remember it as if it was yesterday.

My two BFFs, Liddy and Mona, and myself had just sat down at a table in the school cafeteria to eat lunch. Everyone had been buzzing all day about a big, blow-out Halloween party that was supposedly happening that weekend. I found myself getting excited until I heard who was hosting the event—Sabrina Merryweather! Her parents were going to be out of town that weekend. My heart sank because I knew there was no way I would be receiving an invitation. Sabrina had made no secret about her intense dislike for me, for reasons I was never clear about. Mona thought she was jealous of me and was always trying to compete with me, but I had no ill will toward her at all. I just thought she didn't like my personality. But whatever.

Sabrina waltzed into the cafeteria carrying a stack of envelopes, followed by her faithful posse of three girls, who tried to dress exactly the same as their beloved queen bee.

We watched Sabrina glide around the cafeteria, magnanimously bestowing her envelopes upon the lucky chosen few, deliberately side-stepping our table to make a point, although it was pretty obvious to everyone she was snubbing us.

When her stack dwindled down to just three envelopes, she circled back toward us, and for a moment, I thought we were dead wrong and were about to receive invites to the party. But then, true to form, Sabrina stopped right in front of us, handed me all three envelopes, and said with a cruel smile slapped on her face, "Could you hand those to Robert, Mike, and Tom behind you. I can't reach them."

I could feel my face reddening, but I was not about to give her the satisfaction of showing any emotion whatsoever. I simply shrugged and said, "Sure."

As I handed the envelopes to Robert, Sabrina cooed, "I really hope you can come, Robert!"

We all knew Sabrina had a wild crush on Robert Shields. She had been chasing him around the whole semester, shamelessly plotting ways to get him to ask her out, but so far failing in her single-minded mission. I would not have been surprised if the whole Halloween party idea had been hatched just as a ploy to get him over to her house, albeit along with about thirty other kids from our class.

Having been shut out of Sabrina's soirée, I suggested to Liddy and Mona that they come over to my house for a sleepover that weekend; we'd watch a bunch of scary movies on DVD and stuff ourselves with a ton of Halloween candy that my mother had bought. Liddy and Mona both thought that was a fabulous idea, but then Mike and Tom stood up behind us and came over and asked Liddy and Mona to be their dates for Sabrina's party. I knew they would decline out of solidarity, so I found myself jumping into the conversation and accepting on their behalf because I knew they would have more fun at a party than watching my little brother, Randy, run crying from the room because he was so scared of *Candyman* on TV.

That's when Robert, out of the blue, asked, "What about you, Hayley. Would you like to go together?"

You could have heard a pin drop.

Liddy had to reach over and gently close my mouth by raising my chin up with her hand. When I could not find my voice to answer Robert's question, Mona finally groaned, "Yes, Robert; yes, she would!"

"Great," he said with a laconic, sexy smile. "See you Saturday."

I could hardly breathe, and I felt faint, but I managed to get through the rest of the lunch period without making an utter fool of myself.

Needless to say, I was overjoyed with excitement. But, to be honest, I was also a little nervous about how Sabrina might react when I showed up unexpectedly at her party, on the arm of the boy she currently was intensely obsessed with.

On the invitation, Sabrina requested that everyone come as their favorite movie dance couple because she detested the typical scary Halloween costumes with all the blood and gore, claiming she got nauseous at the sight of blood. Looking back on that now, I find it rather odd, since she ultimately became a prominent medical examiner and dissected people for a living.

Robert and I decided to go to the party as Patrick Swayze and Jennifer Grey (Johnny and Baby from *Dirty Dancing*).

Of course, when we arrived at Sabrina's house a few days later, I should have known that about seventy-five percent of the party-goers would be dressed as Johnny and Baby, especially since the movie was still so popular, years after its release. Yes, there were a smattering of Dannys and Sandys from *Grease*, a Fred and Ginger from *Top Hat* (movie geeks who knew about those really old flicks on TCM), and a couple of white leisure suits paying tribute to John Travolta from *Saturday Night Fever*, but mostly there were just a whole lot of Johnnys and Babys pretty much everywhere you looked.

I spotted Sabrina as leather-clad bad girl Sandy from *Grease* and was relieved she hadn't noticed me yet, but then Robert suddenly grabbed me by the hand and dragged me toward her. "Let's say hi to Sabrina!"

Well, when our hostess turned around to see us approaching—hand in hand, mind you—let's just say, if looks could kill, I would have been dead on the floor.

It only got worse from there.

Robert appeared oblivious to the simmering tension as Sabrina tried keeping a fake innocuous smile planted on her face, although she was slicing and dicing me with insanely furious eyes.

I had to get away. "You two chat. I'm going to go to the ladies' room. Which way is it?"

Sabrina pointed down the hall and growled, "That way."

I was off.

There was a line of girls waiting, but a girl from my English class who had come up behind me said there was another bathroom farther down, off the laundry room, so I walked to that one with no line and went inside. I was just finishing up, washing my hands, when someone jiggled the doorknob.

"Be right out!" I said.

"No, you won't," someone answered.

I heard a click. I tried turning the door handle, but it wouldn't budge. Someone had locked the door from the outside. I kept jiggling the handle to no avail.

I suddenly heard Sabrina's enraged voice.

"This is for stealing my boyfriend, and having the gall to show up at my house and throw it in my face!"

And then there was silence.

She was gone.

And I was stuck in the bathroom off the laundry room that very few people knew about. I was trapped! My only hope was that Robert would eventually miss me and try to find me.

After about a half hour of pounding and yelling, I realized no one could hear me over all the music and noise. It was a tiny bathroom, and the heat was pumping through the vent. I was starting to sweat, and so I unbuttoned my blouse a couple of buttons, trying to stay cool. I could see in the mirror that my hair was a fright because I kept running my hands through it nervously, trying to come up with some kind of plan to escape.

Finally, like a miracle, I heard a click, and the door flew open. I was hoping it was Robert coming to my rescue, but actually it turned out to be Zach Rivers, one of the hulking high school football players, staring down at me. I tried to explain what had happened, but he didn't seem all that interested, so I gave up and just followed him back down the hall toward the living room.

The party was in full swing as we walked in, and then, quite unexpectedly, Zach put his arm around me and pulled me close to him.

Well, that almost brought the whole room to a sudden standstill.

Hayley and Zach?

I noticed Robert had a disappointed look on his face.

Right next to him Sabrina was beaming, triumphant.

And that's when I knew I had been set up.

I learned later that, after Sabrina locked me in the bathroom, she enlisted Zach's help to execute her evil plan. She found Robert, who had been looking all over for me, and out of the kindness of her cold heart, she told him that she had seen Zach and me leaving together, but that she had no idea where we had gone, heavily suggesting we had snuck away to go somewhere and fool around!

She went on to add that she had heard this was not the first time I had done something as horrendous as ditching one boy for another, but not to worry because she was there to help him through his heartbreak, and thank God he found out in time what kind of person I really was!

My tousled hair, open blouse, and sweaty face only bolstered her ridiculous fake story. But, sadly, Robert bought it. And he didn't speak to me again. In fact, he and Sabrina started dating the following Monday.

Small consolation: Two months later, a hot Swedish foreign exchange student, Helga, arrived at school, and a smitten Robert dumped Sabrina to be with her, and he didn't bother to tell Sabrina. So I believe, in the end, there is such a thing as karma!

I never let that night dampen my enthusiasm for Halloween. Nowadays, I love hosting my own parties, and these next two yummy recipes are popular annual staples! I hope you love them as much as I do!

Boo Boozy Milkshakes

Ingredients

½ pint chocolate ice cream
½ pint vanilla ice cream
8 ounces chocolate milk
5 ounces bourbon

Combine ingredients in a blender, tailoring them to your liking. If you prefer a thinner shake, add a little more milk. If you like thicker, add more ice cream. Divide into 2 large glasses and enjoy.

Monster Meatball Sliders

For this recipe, you'll need 1 12-ounce jar marinara sauce, either one you've made or your favorite from the super-market. You'll also need a package of 12 Hawaiian rolls or slider buns.

Turkey Meatballs Ingredients

(Note: to save time, you can use your favorite frozen
   meatballs)
1 pound ground turkey
1 egg, beaten
2 slices of bread, torn into small pieces
½ cup Italian bread crumbs
½ cup grated Parmesan cheese
½ cup panko crumbs
½ tablespoon Italian seasoning
½ tablespoon garlic powder
½ tablespoon dried basil
½ tablespoon dried parsley
1 teaspoon kosher salt
1 teaspoon ground pepper

Preheat oven to 375 degrees. Line a baking pan with foil and spray with cooking spray.

In a large bowl, add all of the ingredients and, with clean hands, combine them. Shape scoops of the meat mixture into 12 same-size meatballs. Place meatballs in a sprayed baking pan.

Bake in preheated oven for 20–25 minutes or until cooked through. You can cut one to check doneness. Add them to the warmed marinara sauce.

Assembling the Sliders

¼ cup butter
½ teaspoon garlic powder
1 teaspoon Italian seasoning
2 tablespoons Parmesan cheese
12 Hawaiian rolls or slider buns, sliced in half
2 cups shredded Mozzarella cheese
Butter, with Italian seasoning to taste
Parmesan cheese to taste

Use your favorite or homemade marinara sauce. On the stove, warm it in a pan big enough to hold the meatballs.

Preheat oven to 350 degrees.

In a small saucepan, melt the butter with the garlic powder and Italian seasoning, and set aside.

Butter a 9x13 baking pan and place the bottom halves of the Hawaiian rolls in the pan, then top each roll with a meatball, some extra sauce, and sprinkle the shredded Mozzarella evenly over the meatballs. Do this for all the rolls.

Carefully add the top halves of the rolls and gently press. Brush melted, seasoned butter over the tops of the rolls, then sprinkle the Parmesan cheese evenly over the tops.

Cover with tinfoil and bake in a preheated oven for 10 minutes. Remove the foil and put back in oven to bake for 5–7 minutes longer. Remove, slice, and serve warm.

Chapter Ten

As Sergio pulled Bruce aside to bring him up to speed on the dead body in cold storage that was currently lying inside the walk-in freezer, Hayley, Liddy, and Mona huddled together, all of them still rattled by the thought that there could be a cold-blooded killer lurking among them.

Hayley had discounted everyone in her mind, even Dr. Reddy, because she honestly could not conceive that any one of the guests left at her Halloween party was capable of such a malicious, violent act, especially the kids.

Nothing made any sense.

But who else could it have been, especially with the back door locked and all eyes on the front door the entire time?

Jodie tugged on Mona's sweatshirt. "Mommy, I'm tired. When can we go home?"

"Soon, baby, I promise. When Sergio says we can leave," Mona said, rubbing her daughter lightly on the head.

"But Pia got to go home. Why can't we?" Jodie whined.

"No, Jodie, Pia's right over there with her Mom," Mona insisted.

"No, she's not," Jodie said.

They all looked over at the table near the front door, where Dr. Reddy and Pia had sat earlier. It was empty.

Liddy frantically glanced around the dining room. "Where did they go?"

"They couldn't have left out the front door. One of us would have seen them," Hayley said.

"They went out the back," Chet murmured, without taking his eyes off his phone.

"What? When?" Mona barked.

"Just now," Chet said, thumbs furiously tapping on his screen.

"Sergio! She's making a run for it!" Hayley cried, dashing out of the dining room toward the rear exit off the kitchen, next to the storeroom and pantry, where she came upon Dr. Reddy, clutching Pia's hand while sliding the bolt of the back door open to make her escape.

"Stop right there, Doctor!" Hayley exclaimed.

Dr. Reddy froze in place halfway out the door. Guilt was written on her face before she quickly masked it with indignation. "Don't be so dramatic, Hayley. I was just going to take Pia home. She's tired and needs some sleep. Don't panic; I was coming back. I was going to have my older daughter, Nina, babysit."

Hayley stared at her skeptically.

"My daughter has been through enough trauma for one night. I am doing what's best for her. I should think Mona would do the same with her own child."

Sergio and Bruce suddenly appeared behind Hayley.

"I wasn't running away!" Dr. Reddy protested.

Liddy scampered in behind Sergio and Bruce, craning her neck, trying to see past the two much bigger men. "Yes, you were! The guilty always run!"

Dr. Reddy covered Pia's ears with her hands. "There is a dead body not twenty feet away from here. I will stay here all night if I have to, but this is no place for a child!"

"Dr. Reddy, as I have told you multiple times, no one is

going anywhere, not yet. I called the county forensics team, and they're on their way, so we just need to sit tight until they get here. Hopefully, they can help us fill in a few of the blanks. I understand Pia is tired—we all are—but this is a crime scene, and your daughter is a potential witness, and so I insist on everybody's cooperation. Is that clear?"

Dr. Reddy's face flushed; her instinct was to argue some more, and she opened her mouth to protest, before sighing and slamming the door shut and sliding the bolt back into place.

"Can I at least get a cup of coffee to keep myself awake if we're going to spend a few more hours in this god-forsaken place?" Dr. Reddy groused

She then marched back toward the dining room, dragging behind her a yawning Pia, who struggled to keep up with her mother's pace.

Sergio turned to Hayley and gave her an apologetic smile. "Do you mind?"

Hayley waved everyone out. "Go. Just make sure she doesn't try to duck out the front! I'll put a pot on."

Sergio and Liddy returned to the dining room to join the others.

Bruce hung back and gave his wife a comforting hug. "Long night, huh?"

"You could certainly say that," Hayley sighed wearily.

"I sure hope nobody mentions the corpse in the freezer in their Yelp review," Bruce joked.

"You better go help Sergio in case somebody else tries to make a break for it. I'll be right out with the coffee."

Bruce kissed Hayley softly on the lips.

She wrapped her arms around his neck. "Thanks, I needed that."

He winked at her and then bounded out of the kitchen in his gorilla suit.

Hayley took a deep breath, exhaled, then wandered into the pantry to fetch a package of coffee beans. She spotted it on the top shelf, grabbed it, and was turned halfway back around when something on the floor caught her eye.

It looked like a tiny piece of glass at first.

She set the coffee grounds down on a middle shelf and picked up a mini broom and dustpan to sweep it up, fearing someone might cut themselves on the broken glass, but as she bent down, it quickly became obvious the sparkling object wasn't glass.

It was a diamond embedded on a silver wedding band.

Somebody at the party must have accidentally dropped it.

Hayley carefully picked it up and examined it.

Something was inscribed on the back of the band.

Forever Yours, Irving.

Irving.

She only knew one Irving in town. And that was the late Irving Beaumont, who had died long ago. His widow, however, was still very much alive.

Clara Beaumont.

The poor elderly woman who was at this moment in the hospital recovering from a brutal attack during a home robbery.

How on earth did it get here?

It suddenly dawned on Hayley. Bruce had mentioned earlier that Clara Beaumont had told the police before passing out at her home that the robber had made off with her wedding ring.

This was it.

Engraved by her loving late husband, Irving.

And Lenny Bash had stolen it.

Which meant Lenny had been in this pantry at some point.

But how?

And why?

Why would Lenny Bash show up at Hayley's Halloween party with dozens of people present after having just robbed Clara Beaumont's house? There was the possibility that he had arrived in disguise—all the guests were wearing costumes, after all—but again, *why*? What would draw him here? Why would he risk hanging out in public where someone might recognize him, especially since he had no way of knowing whether or not Clara Beaumont had been able to identify him? Any rational burglar would no doubt go into hiding, lie low, and avoid the cops until he could skip town, not crash a party.

It made no sense.

And why was he in the pantry?

That's when Hayley noticed a few empty pans that had been shoved in the corner on the bottom shelf. She pulled one out and noticed small chunks of hamburger meat and crumbs of bread left on the bottom. She examined the other pan and found half of a mini pepperoni and bits of a flaky crust.

Or course!

Her missing food.

She had noticed that two pans of appetizers she had prepared for the party were missing earlier in the evening.

Her Mummy Meat Sliders and Pepperoni Pizza Pockets in the shape of jack-o'-lanterns!

Someone had scarfed them down right here in the pantry.

It had to be Lenny.

But what happened to him?

Where did he go?

On the video Randy had shot on his phone, all the guests had been accounted for as they left the restaurant. And the rear door was locked from the inside, which would have made it impossible for Lenny to flee from the back of the restaurant.

How could he have shown up at the party, chowed down on Hayley's food in the pantry, accidentally dropped Clara Beaumont's wedding ring at some point, and then just vanished into thin air?

This was a real head scratcher.

Hayley closed her hand around the diamond ring and was about to head back out to show Sergio what she had found when her eyes fell upon a deep scratch in the wooden floor of the pantry.

She bent down and ran her finger alongside it. What appeared so odd was the shape of the scrape. It was not your ordinary wear-and-tear scrape from heavy foot traffic or from someone dropping cans of food, causing damage to the floor. No, this scratch formed a large half circle that ran almost the full width of the pantry, almost as if in the shape of a rainbow.

What would cause a scratch like that?

Hayley looked around, failing to find any sharp object someone could have used to dig into the floor.

The shape reminded her of a door sagging from loose hinges scraping across the floor as someone tried to open it.

But the door to the pantry was at an opposite angle.

There was simply no way it would have been able to cause that scratch.

Her eyes settled on the back wall of the pantry.

Then she had a thought. She had seen enough movies set in gothic mansions to suspect that maybe . . . just maybe . . .

The thought made her chuckle.

No, she was being ridiculous.

But what if . . . ?

Hayley stood up and moved slowly to the back wall. She reached up, took hold of the top shelf, and gave it a good yank. Suddenly the wall began moving forward, creaking, as the bottom scuffed across the hardwood floor, following the pattern of the long half-circle scratch.

Hayley couldn't believe it.

The back wall of the pantry was a giant door.

Her new restaurant had a secret room!

Behind the wall, foreboding darkness.

Hayley poked her head in, squinting, able to make out an empty hallway that led down to a flickering light.

Hayley silently made her way down the hall toward the light until she came upon a small room that reminded her of a bunker where someone might hide to wait out the apocalypse. The light was from a couple of burning candles. There was a small, lumpy-looking cot in the corner. A rifle hanging on the wall. A few boxes of canned goods and supplies. And as she had expected, paper plates with a few of her Mummy Meat Sliders and Pepperoni Pizza Pockets jack-o'-lanterns.

There was no one in the room.

Whoever had been here was gone.

Or was he?

Hayley suddenly felt a rush of air against her neck.

As if someone was standing behind her, breathing.

She spun around.

A scream caught in her throat as she found herself face-to-face with Pennywise the Clown!

Chapter Eleven

As the creepy Pennywise, with his grotesque, distorted, evil smile and beady menacing eyes, advanced upon Hayley, she bolted forward, trying to push past him and out the door of the bunker.

But Pennywise anticipated the move and forcefully shoved her back as she tried ducking around him. Hayley stumbled and fell back on the cot as Pennywise slammed the door shut and locked it, effectively trapping her inside with him.

"You might as well take off that mask, Lenny. I know it's you," Hayley said, eyeing him warily, not sure what she would do in the event of a frontal attack.

Pennywise didn't say a word, but she could see his eyes blinking nervously behind the clown mask.

"I found the wedding ring you stole from Clara Beaumont's house in the pantry. I knew you had to be somewhere close by," Hayley explained matter-of-factly, desperately attempting to remain calm and not let on to Pennywise that she was seconds from fainting dead away from sheer fright.

Pennywise stood frozen by the door for a few moments, still refusing or afraid to say anything.

Hayley sighed. "Lenny Bash, take that mask off right now!"

The scary clown glared defiantly at Hayley some more, but then his white-gloved left hand slowly reached up and pulled the mask off, revealing Lenny's sweaty, troubled face.

He tried wiping the sweat off with the puffy arm of his clown costume, but the bunker was so hot, he didn't stay dry for long before more sweat beads rolled precipitously down his forehead.

"You shouldn't have come back here, Hayley," Lenny growled before picking up the sledgehammer from Randy's Annie Wilkes costume that had been leaning against the wall next to the door. "Everything would have been fine if you all had just gone home after cleaning up from the party."

"No, Lenny, no one was going to go home. Not until we figured out what was going on around here."

Lenny swallowed hard and raised the sledgehammer. "I don't want to hurt you . . . But I will if I have to . . ."

Hayley, sitting on the cot, leaned back against the wall, wanting to put as much distance from him as possible. She carefully eyed the door.

"Don't try to yell. This room is basically soundproof. No one out there will hear you," Lenny warned.

Hayley glanced around, taking in the shelves of canned food, a generator, a first-aid kit in the corner—all the supplies you would need for an underground bunker during a nuclear blast or zombie apocalypse. "What is this place? How did you find it?"

"I came across it by accident when I used to work here, back when Chef Romeo owned the place," Lenny said. "One night, after the restaurant closed and the boss thought everyone had gone home, I stayed behind because I was pumping myself up to ask Romeo for a raise. I went to his office, and he wasn't there, and that's when I saw the pantry wall was open, and there was this secret passage. It was the craziest thing! I thought things like this were only in the movies! I was curious, so I followed it down here to this room, where I found Chef Romeo stocking it with some canned goods! I surprised the hell out of him! At first, he was mad at me for snooping, but then he made me swear I'd never tell anybody about it!"

"How did Chef Romeo find it?"

"He didn't. He was the one who built it. The pantry and storeroom used to be three times the size they are now when he first bought the building, but Chef Romeo added the secret back wall and turned the rest of it into an escape room."

"But why? Was he worried Bar Harbor was going to be the target of an alien invasion or get hit by an asteroid? Normally, the biggest threat we have to face is an influx of obnoxious summer tourists and too many black flies."

"Chef Romeo told me when he moved here from New York, he left behind a few enemies, and so he wanted to know he had a safe hiding place in case they somehow found him up here," Lenny said.

Hayley knew the kid was speaking the truth.

She had been acutely aware from investigating the mysterious circumstances surrounding his untimely death that the colorful, gregarious and loud Chef Romeo Russo had suffered a few financial crises back in Brooklyn, using mob money to open a restaurant that went belly-up, raising the ire of his lenders when he couldn't pay it back as the interest skyrocketed every single day. Then, there was the astoundingly bad decision to get romantically involved with a mafia kingpin's wife; that certainly did not bring down the temperature of the already scalding-hot situation. It all resulted in the chef skipping town and starting anew in Maine, where he had hoped he would never be found. Unfortunately, a couple of adversaries from a very long list of individuals out to get the chef eventually did locate him, which resulted in his untimely demise. That's when Hayley took over the lease of the restaurant, changed the name to Hayley's Kitchen, and started a whole new business.

But at the time, she had no clue about any secret room.

Not until now.

"How did Chef Romeo convince you to keep quiet about what you had found?"

"With a big wad of hundred-dollar bills," Lenny snorted. "He told me there was more where that came from if I stayed loyal to him and kept my mouth shut. I figured why not; I'd do anything he wanted as long as he kept throwing cash at me. But just my luck, he died right after that, and then you took over . . ."

"I always wondered why you didn't stay on, why you just up and quit . . ."

Lenny shrugged. "Big mistake, in retrospect. But at the time, I was just a dumb lug with money to burn. Why should I work when I could party, drink beer, smoke weed, chase girls? I even got myself a brand-new Harley David-son, which I crashed into a telephone pole trying to do a wheelie three days after I bought it."

"And then you found yourself broke again," Hayley guessed.

"Who knew I could go through so much money that fast? I'd never had two cents to my name, so how was I ever going to be responsible with that kind of cash? My parents had already kicked me out; I had nowhere to go. I couldn't afford rent, so a couple buddies took me in for a while, but I couldn't stay with them forever, I got desper-ate . . ."

Hayley stood up from the cot. "So you began robbing houses for spare cash and jewelry you could pawn."

"I promised myself I was only going to do it once. Just once. So I would have enough to put down a deposit on a room to rent. I knew the Clements on Arata Drive up by the golf course were going to be out of town. I overheard Mrs. Clement talking to a friend at the Shop 'n' Save. It was so easy. I was in and out in no time. I had enough for rent and food for a whole month. But then, there was more partying, the money disappeared again, so I thought to myself, one more time, just one more time . . ."

"But it wasn't one more time. You kept going . . ."

"Like I said, it was always so easy . . ."

"Until it wasn't," Hayley said sharply.

Lenny's eyes flicked to the floor.

Hayley folded her arms. "Clara Beaumont was not supposed to be home tonight; she was supposed to be out of town visiting her sister, but she caught a cold and canceled her trip at the last minute, and that's when the two of you came face-to-face in her house . . ."

"I was coming up the stairs when I looked up and saw her standing there at the top of the landing, holding a baseball bat in her hand. She had heard me break in through the kitchen window downstairs and was coming to investigate. I wasn't expecting to see anyone . . ." Lenny mumbled. "I swear, Hayley, I was more scared than she was . . ."

"What happened next?"

"Mrs. Beaumont started screaming and yelling, and the next thing I knew she was coming at me with the bat and taking whacks at me! You should see the nasty bruises I got on my arm. I was just trying to defend myself . . ." His voice quivered. "But . . ."

Hayley's heart sank as she anticipated what was coming next. "But what, Lenny?"

He looked up at Hayley, his face full of shame. "I was

just trying to grab the bat away from her, but when I yanked it out of her hand, she somehow lost her balance, and that's when . . ."

"She tumbled down the stairs and hit her head on the hardwood floor at the bottom!"

"I didn't mean to hurt her! It was an accident!"

"But you didn't call for help; you just ran away and left her there!" Hayley snapped accusingly.

Lenny nodded. "Yes, I panicked. I didn't know what to do! This was the only place I knew where I could lie low for a while until the heat died down and I could sneak out of town without getting caught."

"But how did we not see you come in? We had eyes on the front door all night, and the back door was locked from the inside."

"I showed up when you were still setting up for the party; you had the back door open while you and Liddy and Mona were bringing in all the food. I waited until you went back to Mona's truck for another load, and then I was able to slip in, without any of you noticing, and hide back here in Chef Romeo's secret room."

That was why Lenny never showed up on Randy's video at any point during the party.

"I didn't think anyone would ever be able to find me," Lenny continued. "I didn't know I had dropped Mrs. Beaumont's wedding ring." Lenny sniffed and wiped his nose with his index finger, tears pooling in his eyes. "I swear on my life, Hayley, I never meant to kill Mrs. Beaumont!"

"You didn't."

Lenny's eyes widened in surprise. "What are you talking about? I saw her fall down the stairs and hit her head! There was blood!"

"You didn't kill Clara Beaumont, Lenny. She's recovering in the hospital. She may have a concussion, but she is going to live."

A wave of relief washed over Lenny's face. "Oh man, oh wow, I can't tell you how much better that makes me feel . . ."

"Yes, you can rest easy. But what about Boris Candy?"

Lenny's face went pale.

Hayley bravely took a step forward. "Did you murder him?"

Lenny began to slowly shake his head. "No . . . I . . ."

Hayley's eyes zeroed in on the sledgehammer at Lenny's side. She could make out traces of blood on it. "I can buy Mrs. Beaumont accidentally tripping and falling down the stairs, and I'm sure the police will as well. But explain to me how Mr. Candy *accidentally* ran his head into the flat edge of that sledgehammer, Lenny, because that one has me stumped."

Lenny glanced at the sledgehammer, noticing the blood for the first time. He knew he was caught. He raised his eyes, staring at Hayley, his face full of alarm and desperation, like a scared rabbit suddenly trapped in a hunter's cage.

That's when he menacingly raised the sledgehammer over his head.

Chapter Twelve

"What are you going to do, Lenny, bash me in the back of the head too, just like you did to poor Boris Candy?" Hayley cried.

Gripping the sledgehammer and waving it around in the air, Lenny vigorously shook his head. "No, no, you make it sound like I *wanted* to kill him, but I didn't. I had no choice!"

"Everyone has a choice, Lenny, and you made the wrong one," Hayley said. "And right now you have another choice to make. What are you going to do with that sledge-hammer?"

Hayley held her breath.

Lenny stopped waving the weapon around threaten-ingly but kept holding it above his head, staring up at it. Then he slowly lowered it to his side.

Hayley felt relieved that she had been spared for now, but she was not going to take anything for granted. Her mind raced, desperate to come up with some kind of plan to escape this secret locked room.

"I can pretty much guess what happened next, Lenny," Hayley said softly, trying not to sound too aggressive, which might set him off again. "You were hiding out here after running away from Clara Beaumont's house, but you were hungry, you needed something to eat, and you probably didn't want to use up your food supply so early on," Hayley said, pointing to the shelf of canned goods above them. "On the other side of the wall, there was a party in full swing with lots of food, so you snuck out and snatched some pans of appetizers I had prepared when no one was around."

Lenny nodded. "The food smelled really good, and I was starving so bad, I decided to take the risk. And it worked. Nobody saw me. But then I got thirsty, I had a limited supply of bottled water back here, so I decided to grab some sodas from the coolers in the storeroom. But I couldn't get to them because those two little girls were pretending to be witches right next to the pantry. They would have spotted me the second I came out. So I stood behind the pantry wall, listening, waiting for them to finish up with their silly witch spells and return to the party. That's when I heard Mr. Candy come in to see the girls playing, and he yelled at them and upset them. After he left, they cast some kind of nasty spell on him. Then finally, I heard them leave. They never had a clue I was right behind the pantry wall listening to them the whole time."

"You figured it was safe to come out at that point to get your drinks, but then unexpectedly Mr. Candy returned . . ."

"Yeah, he came rushing in, like he was in a big hurry," Lenny said.

"That's because Mona's son, Chet, had just spiked his hot chocolate with Ex-Lax," Hayley explained. "He was running back here to find the bathroom since the two out front were occupied."

"At first, I didn't know who he was, in that evil clown getup."

"But Mr. Candy recognized you, and you could not have him telling anyone you were here, because the police might find out and surround the place, and you'd be trapped—"

"He tried to get past me; he looked so frantic, I didn't know he was rushing for the bathroom; I thought he was scared of me, knew what I had done, so I tried to stop him. There was a scuffle, and Mr. Candy started yelling. I wrestled him to the floor, tried to keep him quiet, begged him to stop making so much noise, but that just got him more upset and louder, and then he managed to squirm free. He tried to run, and that's when I saw the sledgehammer someone left in the kitchen leaning up against the wall . . ."

"So you grabbed it and chased after Mr. Candy and hit him in the back of the head to stop him from alerting anyone to your presence," Hayley said solemnly. "But Mr. Candy had no clue you had just robbed Clara Beaumont's house, or injured her, or were on the run from the law. Nobody did, not until Bruce showed up after the party was over with the news that Clara Beaumont had regained consciousness and identified you. So you killed the poor man for no reason."

"I . . . I didn't know that . . ."

"You dragged his body into the walk-in freezer to hide it, but then you got an idea. Why not put on Mr. Candy's Pennywise costume so no one else would recognize you. You could walk around the party undetected and stock up on more food for your extended stay."

"I had no idea how long I would have to be holed up here; it could be weeks, maybe months. I couldn't risk leaving too early when everybody was still looking for me . . ."

All the pieces were finally coming together.

"That's why Mr. Candy was acting so strange around Sergio, after purposely trying to scare him earlier in the Pennywise costume, because it wasn't Mr. Candy. It was you," Hayley deduced. "After loading up and returning to this room, you were confident you had gotten away with it; nobody else saw you poking around. When Mr. Candy's body was found, there would be no witness to point the finger at you. The focus would be on the other party guests. You were home free."

"Until you found that damn ring," Lenny spit out. He took some time collecting his thoughts, figuring out his next move before he spoke again. Finally, his eyes flicked back to Hayley. "I'm sorry, Hayley, you've always been real nice to me, but I can't let you leave here and tell anyone where I am."

He took a menacing step toward her. He was even more intimidating in the frightening clown costume. He backed her up against the wall, then reached out with his white-gloved hands and shoved her down on the lumpy cot. Then he sprang across the room, grabbed some rope off the shelf and began binding her hands and feet as Hayley frantically searched the room for some means of escape. Unfortunately, she was trussed up before she had the opportunity to formulate any kind of workable plan.

She was now Lenny's prisoner.

"How long do you plan on keeping me here? My husband, my friends, they're just on the other side of the pantry wall; they're going to be searching for me."

Lenny picked up a roll of duct tape and pressed a piece across Hayley's mouth. "That's why you're going to stay nice and quiet here in the secret room. They call it that because nobody knows about it; it's a secret. And I'm going to make sure it stays that way."

Lenny bent down and lifted Hayley's feet up on the cot so she was in a prone position. "Why don't you get some rest? You're going to be here a while. But I swear, Hayley, when I do leave here and get out of town, I promise I will send word to your family where they can find you."

Hayley tried to say something, but her words were muffled underneath the duct tape.

"Since there's going to be two of us living here, we're going to need more food than what I've got stacked on the shelf. I think I saw another box of canned beans and vegetables in the storeroom. Wait here, I'll be right back."

He unbolted the lock on the door and hurried off.

Wait here?

Was he joking?

Where on earth could she go?

Hayley cranked her head around desperately.

There had to be some means of freeing herself.

Her eyes scanned the room, settling on the two burning candles bathing the room in a flickering orange light.

The flame.

It could burn through the ropes that tied her hands.

Hayley struggled to stand up, which was made all the more difficult with her hands bound behind her back and her feet tied together, but she managed, after a couple of tries, to remain upright without falling back down on the cot. She hopped over to one of the candles and spun around, dropping to her knees so her hands were on the same level as the burning candle. She stretched her arms out as far as they could go, wincing in pain, wishing she had paid more attention in the stretch class she had taken with Liddy that one time. The flame touched her outstretched finger and scalded her skin, causing her to emit a muffled yelp. She closed both hands into fists and prayed the flame would make contact with the rope and not her flesh. One of her fists accidentally bumped into the candle, nearly knocking it off the small table and onto the floor.

She patiently tried again, and again, finally succeeding on the fourth attempt. She began to smell the smoke from the flame as it slowly burned through the ropes. She wrenched her wrists in opposite directions, feeling the rope start to loosen.

She was seconds away from freedom when Lenny suddenly appeared in the doorway of the room. "I smell something burning!" His eyes settled on Hayley trying to free herself. "What are you doing?"

He lunged across the room and roughly grabbed Hayley to stop her. Her hopes of escaping were dashed as he shoved her face-first up against the wall so he could inspect her hands, tied behind her back, to insure they were still secure.

Hayley craned her neck to see that, during the mêlée, the candle had been knocked off the table and onto the floor, where it rolled over on its side over to the cot, stopped by the army-issue gray blanket hanging down the side. The flame ignited the fabric, and the blanket caught fire, which quickly spread to the sheets and the mattress.

Hayley screamed through the duct tape over her mouth and made frantic gestures with her head toward the fire, trying to warn Lenny.

Satisfied Hayley was bound to his satisfaction, Lenny finally became aware of black smoke in the air and spun around to see the cot on fire. With Lenny distracted, Hayley seized the opportunity to propel herself away from the wall, crashing into Lenny's body, which sent him flying across the room, tripping over his own two feet. He tried to grab the shelf to keep himself from falling, but the weight of his body dislodged the whole shelf from the wall. Stacks of canned food came raining down on him, smashing against his head until he was stretched out onto the floor, dazed and half-conscious.

As the flames grew, dancing up the wall above the cot, Hayley frantically tried screaming for help, but to no avail, not with the tape over her mouth and her hands and feet still tied.

She tried to wildly hop out of the room, but now the thickening black smoke threatened to overcome her. She felt light-headed, close to passing out. The whole building would soon be up in flames and destroyed.

She glanced down at Lenny.

He was still disoriented, rubbing his head, not fully aware that he too was about to succumb to smoke inhalation.

Then, suddenly, through the black smoke, Hayley saw King Kong burst through the room, look around, and then fling his massive, hairy body on top of the burning cot, effectively smothering the flames until they were snuffed out, except for a few burning pieces of fake fur left on the gorilla suit that he pounded out with his giant paws, like an ape in the jungle emulating Tarzan's cry by beating his chest.

Mona appeared in the doorway brandishing a fire extinguisher, which she used to spray white foam on the cot as well as Bruce's gorilla costume, just to be safe.

Sergio rushed in and pulled the tape off Hayley's mouth, then quickly began untying the ropes.

"Are you all right?" Sergio asked.

Hayley nodded as she coughed, waving away the last remnants of black smoke in the room, managing to choke out, "Yes, how . . . how did you find me?"

"We smelled smoke out in the dining room," Sergio explained. "And then we all fanned out to see where it could be coming from. Bruce noticed the black smoke billowing out from underneath the pantry wall. That's when he realized it was a door and not a wall. He followed the smoke down here to find you!"

"Thank you, King Kong!" Hayley gushed as she hugged Bruce, who was still inside his gorilla suit. "I always knew you were misunderstood."

"Come on, let's get you out of here," Bruce said gently as he guided his wife toward the door, his eyes falling to Lenny, who was writhing and moaning on the floor. "We'll leave Sergio to deal with him."

Sergio gave them a wink, then marched over and hauled Lenny to his feet, snapping handcuffs onto his wrists.

As Bruce escorted Hayley back up the narrow passage to the pantry, he turned and grinned. "I'm resisting the urge to pick you up and carry you out in my arms like Fay Wray."

"You are my hero, Bruce, but let's not push it. I can walk just fine."

He chuckled and leaned over and gave her a sweet kiss on the cheek. As they emerged from behind the pantry wall to the kitchen and storeroom where everyone else—Liddy, Randy, Dr. Reddy, Jodie, Pia, and Chet—all waited anxiously for them, Hayley turned to Liddy and remarked, "I have to admit, Liddy, you were right about one thing."

"What's that?" Liddy asked, perplexed.

Hayley turned to her husband, sizing him up, and then said with a smile, "Bruce does look oddly sexy in his gorilla suit."

Chapter Thirteen

Lenny Bash sat glumly in a chair, his hands cuffed behind his back, when Lieutenant Donnie finally arrived at the restaurant.

After reading Lenny his rights and calling the station to have Donnie come over and escort Lenny to jail, Sergio had finally dismissed Dr. Reddy, who grabbed her daughter firmly by the hand and huffily fled the scene, much to everyone's enormous relief. Hayley announced that Dr. Reddy would definitely not be invited back for next year's Halloween party at Hayley's Kitchen.

"Are you seriously considering doing this again after what happened this year?" Liddy asked.

"I'm an eternal optimist," Hayley explained. "Besides, what are the odds that another fugitive will be hiding behind the walls of my restaurant this same time next year?"

"Given your track record, I'd say they're pretty good," Bruce cracked.

Donnie sadly shuffled over to Lenny, took him by the arm, and hauled him to his feet, muttering, "Okay, Lenny, let's go."

Sergio instantly noticed his young lieutenant's dispirited demeanor, and walked over and pulled him aside. "Everything okay, Donnie?"

"Yeah, Chief, I guess," Donnie shrugged.

No one in the dining room believed him for even a moment.

"Come on, Donnie, you can tell me. I know something's bothering you," Sergio said, patting him on the back.

He turned and lightly shoved Lenny back down in the chair before confiding to the boss, "I'm just a little bummed I wasn't the one to catch the perp. I really wanted to prove to you that I'm worthy of that promotion you gave me."

Sergio smiled warmly. "Donnie, there is no doubt in my mind I made the right decision about making you a lieutenant. You're one of my best officers. You're smart, loyal, a real good chicken."

Donnie looked up at Sergio, confused. "Sorry, Chief, what?"

"Chicken. A good chicken. It's another way of saying nice person, right?" Sergio said, turning to the others, who had no idea what he was talking about.

"Egg," Lenny mumbled from his chair.

Sergio spun around to Lenny. "What did you say?"

"Egg. The saying is, you're a good egg," Lenny sighed.

"Chicken. Egg. It's practically the same thing," Sergio snapped.

"No, it isn't," Lenny argued, shaking his head.

"Nobody asked you! You're under arrest! So just sit there and be quiet!" Sergio yelled, before turning his attention back to Donnie. "You're a good egg, Donnie. I'm real proud of you."

Donnie lit up. "Thanks, Chief. I'm going to work hard and be the best lieutenant this town has ever seen. I know I can do it because I've got a great role model in you to look up to. I can only hope to be as upstanding and trustworthy and, most importantly, brave as you . . ."

Someone came up behind Sergio and tapped him on the shoulder. He cranked his head around, and at the sight of Pennywise the Clown hovering close to him, Sergio let out a terrified high-pitched shriek so loud, Hayley thought her wineglasses might shatter.

Everyone burst out laughing, even Lenny, who wisely got himself under control and quickly clammed up after Sergio shot him a stern look of warning.

Sergio then grabbed the evil clown mask by the red hair and ripped it off, revealing Mona's son, Chet, who was giggling hysterically.

"Very funny, kid!" Sergio roared. "You want me to arrest you, too?"

"For what, making an officer of the law scream like a little girl?" Chet howled.

"That's enough, Chet; show the Chief some respect," Mona barked, attempting to be serious before she lost it all over again and guffawed, unable to catch her breath.

Lieutenant Donnie, trying his hardest not to join in on the raucous laughter and tick off the boss, hurriedly escorted Lenny out of the restaurant to his police cruiser.

"Come on, everybody. I'll finally put that pot of coffee on, and we'll have a late-night snack of leftover Halloween treats," Hayley offered.

"I can't be drinking caffeine this late at night," Liddy said. "I won't be able to sleep a wink."

"There's hot chocolate left, if anyone wants some," Chet said with a mischievous grin.

"Thin ice, mister man," Mona growled, pointing a finger at her son. "You are on thin ice!"

Island Food & Cocktails
by
Hayley Powell

Another Halloween is finally behind us! This year, however, will definitely stand out as one to remember, especially given the sad passing of Mr. Candy, the school's music teacher. I hear his students are going to put on a band concert as well as a bake sale in his memory so they can purchase some new music stands for the band room, something that Mr. Candy had been requesting for some time.

It's no mystery that Mr. Candy had quite a sweet tooth, and the irony of his last name was not lost on anyone. Anyway, I thought I would make a candy pie as my own personal tribute and drop it off at the bake sale. This is the perfect recipe to share with you at this time of year because it will help you use up some of that leftover candy you may still have piled up from Halloween.

Speaking of a sweet tooth, I also have a pretty big one, and the other night, I found myself sitting in the living room scarfing down a bag of candy that I had bought for Halloween, but perhaps may or may not have forgotten to leave out on the front porch for the trick-or-treaters. As I munched on a Kit Kat bar, I flashbacked to a memory from many years ago, when my brother, Randy, and I were little kids. It's a Halloween story he loves to tell this time of year at cocktail parties.

Randy was about eleven years old and had been planning for weeks to go out trick-or-treating with his friends to load up on candy, especially since Halloween was the only time of year that our mother would allow us to indulge; she did so for a week straight before she started worrying about our weight and cavities, and then she would confiscate whatever candy was left and donate it all to Housing for the Elderly, where she worked.

Randy and his buddies had been plotting their trick-or-treat route for weeks with military precision because they were expecting to each score a pillowcase full of sugary sweets. This year, Randy was secretly planning to hide at least half his haul where our mother wouldn't find it, so he could gorge himself well beyond the typical allotted week of inhaling our stashes, and Mom wouldn't be the wiser.

Unfortunately, Randy was so caught up in preparing for Halloween, he neglected all his household chores and responsibilities, and needless to say, our mother was growing increasingly frustrated. She warned Randy that he better stop dragging his feet or else. Of course, Randy promised he would get to the chores, but he never did.

So when Randy's math teacher called the house and informed our mother that he hadn't turned in two homework assignments and failed a pop quiz that week, well, that was the proverbial straw that broke the camel's back.

With one day to go before Halloween, Randy waltzed through the door that night for dinner, only to discover our mother standing in the middle of the room with her arms crossed and tapping one foot on the floor with her pursed-lipped, narrow-eyed expression that said, "You are in a world of trouble!"

Randy took one glance at her and knew he was in a code-red situation. He expected her to rant on and on about how irresponsibly he was acting. What he did not expect was for her to ground him for the whole week, allowing him to only go to school, and then he had to come straight home. He was also banned from all extracurricular activities and social events— including trick-or-treating!

Well, you can imagine there were elephant tears, lots of pleading, endless promises to bring his grades up, but this time, Mom didn't budge. I honestly thought she would. I over-heard her on the phone, telling her friend Jane about it, and how she would have expected this kind of behavior from me, but not her normally well-behaved Randy. I should have been in-sulted, but as they say, when the shoe fits . . .

Anyway, Halloween arrived, and much to my surprise, Mom was still sticking to her guns. As I left with my friends, a crestfallen Randy had lost all hope of her changing her mind and stomped upstairs after dinner, slamming the door to his room not once, but twice, to make a point.

I met up with my posse, but after only a half hour going door to door with our plastic pump-kins, I decided to head home because I had been sniffling all day and wasn't feeling too well. I was walking down our street and could see a steady stream of kids going up and down the steps of our front porch as my mother handed out fistfuls of candy.

That's when I noticed a group of kids milling about around the back of our house. Curious, I snuck around to the other side and peeked around the corner to see what they were up to.

Somebody had brought a ladder and had leaned it up against the house right under Randy's bedroom window. I could see him climbing down, his empty pillow case in hand. Somebody gave him a Frankenstein mask, and he put it on and zipped around to the front, where he joined a group of kids approaching our house to get some candy. After our mother dropped some candy bars in his pillow case, Randy broke off from the group, ran back around to his friends, returned the Franken-stein mask, and then borrowed a Harry Potter mask. Then he did the same thing all over again. Our mother was loading her own son up with candy and didn't even realize it!

Randy repeated this trick at least six more times, using a number of different masks, in-cluding Thor, Batman, Minnie Mouse, Lurch from *The Addams Family*, the Creature from the Black Lagoon, and the blue My Little Pony.

I had to admit, it was a genius plan. So clever, in fact, I was actually proud of his inge-nuity, and so I decided not to rat him out.

But just when you think you've pulled one over on your parent, there always comes a sur-prise. Two days later, as I was coming down-stairs for dinner, I heard Mom on the phone again with Jane.

"I know, Jane, I actually couldn't believe it was him. He must have come to the door four or five times before I finally figured out it was Randy. The mask was different every time, but I don't know of any other boy in the neighbor-hood who had a Pink Power Ranger patch on the front pocket of his jacket! I knew right then and there he was trying to pull a fast one."

I never did have the heart to break it to

Randy that our mother knew all along what he had done that night because it has been his favorite story to recount over the years at Halloween parties.

Of course, I guess now, if he reads this column, he will finally know the cat is out of the bag.

So Happy Halloween, dear brother, and here's to many more!

With the arrival of fall, you can count on three things to never change.

• A drop in temperature, ushering in the colder months ahead.

• The annual return of the Pumpkin Spice latte.

• Store shelves stocked with bags and bags of candy corn.

Over the years, candy corn has become highly controversial; to me, there only seems to be two sides of the fence. You either love it or hate it! There really doesn't seem to be any middle ground, and I am definitely on the side of those who do *not* love it. That said, however, I thought that, for this column, instead of just ignoring it, for those of you who do love candy corn, I have an extra special cocktail recipe just for you!

So drink up, enjoy, and Happy Halloween!

Candy Corn Martini

Ingredients
2 ounces vodka
3 ounces sour mix
2 ounces pineapple juice
1 ounce Grenadine
Whipped cream for topping

Combine vodka, sour mix, and pineapple juice in a shaker with ice and shake well.

Strain into a martini glass and slowly pour the grenadine in so it settles on the bottom.

Top with whipped cream and enjoy.

No-Bake Candy Pie

This is a quick and simple, no-bake pie recipe that you can customize to your own personal preference with candy bars or loose candy. I love Heath Bars, so I freeze them, then smash them with a rolling pin to put in my pie. But I have a friend who loves Butterfingers, so she uses those instead. I have also used M&Ms, Reese's, and Snickers for variety. You name it, I have probably used it. Give it a try with your favorite leftover Halloween candy, and I know your kids will thank you!

Ingredients
1 8-ounce package cream cheese, at room temperature
1 8-ounce container of whipped topping, thawed
5 Heath Bars broken in pieces (save some to sprinkle on
   top of the pie or crunch more candy)
1 pre-made chocolate or graham-cracker pie crust

In a bowl, beat the cream cheese until smooth. Fold in the whipped topping. Add in your crushed candy, minus the candy for the topping. Spoon into the pie crust and smooth over, then sprinkle the reserved candy over the top. Refrigerate for 2–4 hours. Slice and serve!

SCARED OFF

Barbara Ross

Chapter One

"Aunt Julia, can you come and get us?" My thirteen-year-old niece, Page, was on the line, barely holding it together, a quivering voice with a sniffle at the end.

"I can hardly hear you." There was some kind of commotion in the background. "Are you still at Talia's?"

Another sniffle. "Yes."

"What's wrong?"

"Some older kids came. They brought some beers." More sniffles.

"I'm on my way."

I turned off the TV, shoved my feet into a pair of flats, grabbed my keys, and headed for the stairs. I hoofed it down the harbor hill toward my mom's house, where my car was stored in her garage. I was nervous, curious, but not panicked. Page was a sensible kid, mature for her age. Surprised as I was by the call, I was confident she could handle herself until I got there.

As I went, I turned back to look at my place. My studio apartment was dark, as I intended, to discourage trick-or-treaters. Gus's restaurant on the first floor of the building was closed up tight. For two off-seasons, I had run a dinner restaurant in Gus's space with my boyfriend, Chris. But Chris and I were no longer, and neither was the restaurant. We'd talked about trying to carry on despite the change in our personal status and decided it would be too hard.

Mom's porch light was on and welcoming, even though it was almost ten o'clock and no one would still be trick-or-treating except the hardiest of teenagers. She was babysitting for my three-year-old nephew, Jack. I didn't stop to go inside but hurried around to the three-car garage at the back.

My sister, Livvie, and brother-in-law, Sonny, were in Portland, attending a Halloween party at a friend's house and then staying overnight in a hotel. It was the first time they'd been away without the kids since—honestly, it may have been the first time they'd ever been away without the kids. Livvie had been pregnant with Page when she and Sonny got married, so their domestic life started with a bang, like two teenagers shot out of a cannon. I really, really hoped whatever was going on with Page wouldn't require me to call them.

Page had declared herself too old for trick-or-treating. She and her best friend, Vanessa, were supposed to be having a sleepover at their new friend Talia's house. It had all been arranged by my sister. I was merely backup to the backup.

Busman's Harbor was quiet as the grave. As I drove down Main Street, the stores that were still open in the off-season had brightly lit windows displaying Halloween or harvest scenes, but no one was about. I drove cautiously nonetheless, wary of stragglers in costumes jumping out from between parked cars.

I saw the flashing blue lights of all three of Busman's Harbor's patrol cars as soon as I turned off Main onto Talia's street. Adrenaline surged, tensing my body and causing my heart to thrum in my chest. Whatever was going on was way more serious than I'd assumed. Every light in Talia's big Victorian house was on, which made it look like a demented jack-o'-lantern from the street. I screeched to the curb and jumped out, pelting toward the steps.

My friend Jamie Dawes, in his police uniform, opened the front door. "Whoa, Julia. The girls are fine."

I two-stepped, catching my breath. "Then why are you here? And why did Page call me to pick her up?"

"C'mon in, and see for yourself."

Jamie led me into a large front hallway, open to the third floor with a staircase winding along the walls. An enormous brass chandelier hung from the ceiling three stories above. The curtained French doors that presumably led to the front room were closed. I followed Jamie toward the back of the house.

The granite countertops and hardwood floor in the big kitchen were sticky with spilled, smelly beer. Potato-chip crumbs were dusted across the room, like feathers from a particularly vicious pillow fight. Most of the cabinet doors hung open. One had obviously served as Talia's parents' bar. It was empty except for a single, quarter-full bottle of gin tipped on its side.

"Did the other kids take off when you pulled up?" I asked.

"No. Something spooked them before we got here. We drove up the street to waves of teenagers, half of them in costume, running in the opposite direction. It was like the zombie apocalypse."

I laughed and relaxed. Jamie wouldn't be joking if Page was hurt.

Jamie flashed his familiar, comforting grin. He was a cop in this situation, but he was also an old friend. His mom and dad's yard backed onto my parents' property. Now he lived in the house alone. His parents had moved to Florida to be near his older sister. For three years, he'd been the newest member of Busman's Harbor's six-person police force, until a retirement had led to the hiring of a new "new guy" the previous spring.

"There wasn't a soul to be seen as I drove over," I told him. Through the back window I spotted flashlight beams bobbing in the backyard.

"Pete and the other guys are looking for stragglers," Jamie reassured me. "The girls are in the living room."

Chapter Two

Page, her best friend, Vanessa, and their hostess, Talia, were huddled on the formal, burgundy-colored couch, sobbing quietly. The tears unnerved me all over again. Page wasn't a crier. I ran to them and hugged each one, even Talia, whom I'd never met. "What on earth happened?"

Page was the brave one who spoke up. "We were having a sleepover," she said, and then stopped. I let the silence fall heavy between us and waited for the rest of the story. "We texted some girls in our class and invited them over," she finally admitted.

"Did you have permission to invite anyone else?" I could guess the answer.

"No." Page hung her head, her bright red curls falling across her freckled cheeks. A single tear fell from the end of her nose.

"It was just three girls," Vanessa added loyally. She would defend Page in any situation. They'd been best friends since Vanessa had moved to town three years earlier. Physically, they couldn't have been more different. Page was tall, taller than me already. She'd probably already attained her full height and had a swimmer's powerful body. Vanessa had long, tawny brown hair and improbable green eyes. She'd always been the shortest kid in their class and was still awaiting her growth spurt. But woe to anyone who was tempted to intimidate her based on her size. She was also, probably, my ex-boyfriend Chris's niece, but that mess was no longer my problem.

"Girls we know, our own age," Vanessa added.

I nodded. I was more than two decades older than these girls, but I remembered how these things went.

"They must have told other kids, even though they swear they didn't." Page was a little feistier than she'd been at first. Looking for scapegoats. "And then kids started coming."

"Boys," Vanessa said. "Big boys, with beers. And girls, like from the high school."

"Before we knew it, the house was full," Page continued. "Kids were everywhere, even in Talia's parents' bedroom." She made a gagging face. "The music was really, really loud, and they wouldn't turn it down, even when we asked them. And there was a fight."

"Not really a bad fight," Vanessa clarified. "Two boys were shoving and shouting in the backyard."

"Where are your parents?" I asked Talia. Livvie never would have agreed to a sleepover if she'd known no adults would be at home.

"At a party," Talia said. It was the first time she'd spoken. She was brown-eyed and brown-haired. Her height split the difference between Page and Vanessa. She looked like she'd been a good-looking child who was now passing through a mild, adolescent rough patch on her way to being a good-looking adult.

"Then who's in charge?" I asked.

"Mrs. Zelisko," Talia volunteered. "She lives upstairs."

"Oh." I had a passing knowledge of Mrs. Zelisko, a short, round, older woman I'd seen around town.

"We tried to find her," Page said, "when things got out of control, but we couldn't. We went to her apartment on the third floor, and she wasn't there. Like anywhere."

I looked at Jamie, who stood in the archway between the living and dining rooms. He held his arms out, palms upward. The cops hadn't found her either.

"And then the ghost came!" Talia said the words with maximum thirteen-year-old drama, and the other two squealed.

"The ghost?" I looked at Jamie. The slightest hint of a smile played on his lips.

"The ghost of Mrs. Zelisko!" Vanessa yelled.

"She was all dressed in white! Like a bride with a veil!" Talia screeched.

"Her face was white, like a clown, and she was flying," Page insisted.

The girls' eyes were bright, their voices high. "And all the kids who saw her screamed and ran." Vanessa was breathless.

"And then all the other kids, who didn't even see her, were screaming and running out the doors, too," Page added.

The girls went silent, staring at me through three sets of big, teary eyes.

"I think that brings us up-to-date," Jamie said. "I've called Talia's parents. They're on their way."

"Where's your overnight stuff?" I asked Page and Vanessa.

"Upstairs in Talia's room," Vanessa answered.

I glanced at Jamie, who nodded it was okay. "Why don't the two of you go and pack up? Talia, you go with them. I want to talk to Officer Dawes for a moment."

"There's no one up there," Jamie reassured them. "We've checked."

The girls rose from the couch. Faces strained, clinging together, they headed for the stairs. I followed Jamie back into the kitchen.

"How much trouble are they in?" I asked as soon as they were out of earshot. "Do I need to call Livvie and Sonny? I hate to interrupt their weekend if I don't have to."

Jamie surveyed the disaster of a kitchen. "This is clearly something that got out of hand. From what they told me, they didn't even know most of the kids who showed up." He put his palms down flat on the granite countertop and then jerked them away, rubbing the sticky stuff from his fingers. "They may be in huge trouble with their parents, but I don't think we'll be involved after tonight."

My shoulders relaxed, and I exhaled noisily. "Thanks," I said, meaning it. One of the great benefits of small-town life is knowing the local police.

"What's up with the flying?" I was tempted to change my assessment of my niece as a mature, level-headed kid.

"Darned if I know." Jamie drew his dark eyebrows together. He was one of those blue-eyed blonds with black brows and lashes and tannable skin. It was, as my sister said, *not fair.* "I don't know what they saw, but something frightened those kids into running out of here."

Jamie's partner, Pete Howland, entered through the kitchen door, his flashlight still on. His normally jovial face was twisted in a grimace. "You need to come see this," he said to Jamie.

"Excuse me." Jamie disappeared with Howland into the dark backyard.

Chapter Three

I looked around the big front hall while I waited for the girls. The three broad streets that climbed the hill in Busman's Harbor were lined with houses similar to this one. My mother lived in one. They were sea captains' houses, built in the days when ships and shipping dominated coastal life. The houses were designed to impress, even to intimidate. I'd never been in this one. The layout was different from the others I knew, but the feeling was the same.

Typical of these old houses, the ceilings on the first and second floor were high, maybe fourteen feet on the first floor and twelve on the second. The third-floor ceiling was lower, the space originally intended for servants. Added together, the ceiling of the open entrance hall towered almost forty feet above me. A staircase wound around the space. From a two-step landing to the left of the front door, the stairs turned and climbed up the wall. When they reached the second floor, there was another turn, and a balcony ran across the wall. I could see a doorway and a long hall off it. The girls' voices floated down from somewhere up there.

At the end of the balcony, there was another turn, and the stairs continued along a third wall to a small landing and a door on the top floor. The door was narrow and flat, obviously added long after the house was built to provide the tenant of the auxiliary apartment with privacy.

Where was the tenant? The girls' wild story aside, Mrs. Zelisko must have gone out, even though she'd been put in charge by Talia's irresponsible parents. My irritation rose.

The girls trooped down the stairs, Page and Vanessa each carrying a backpack and a bed pillow. Page's was in a pink pillowcase I recognized. Vanessa's was a teddy-bear print. They were still little girls in a lot of ways.

I was about to tell them to put their stuff in my car, but I hesitated. I didn't want to leave Talia alone with the police until her parents got home. Jamie was an old family friend to us but a stranger to her. She was clearly a nervous wreck, like the other two girls. I felt we should stay for moral support.

As I stood in the hallway, debating what to do, the back door opened, and Jamie reappeared, a flashlight in his hand, his mouth set. He beckoned me over. "Take Page and Vanessa home. This property is a crime scene. We're calling in the state police Major Crimes Unit."

From unfortunate experience, I knew what that meant. I looked into his eyes. "Please tell me it's not a kid."

Jamie shook his head. "Mrs. Zelisko."

At my mother's house, after consultation with Mom, I called my sister. No matter how discreet the cops were, word would certainly be flying around about the wild party. It wouldn't take long for news of the body to get out. We wanted to reach her before someone else did.

Livvie said they'd each had a couple of drinks at the party they'd attended and would drive back first thing in the morning. Even though I hated cutting their weekend short, I didn't protest.

The girls were either asleep or pretending to be in the "pink princess" bedroom Mom had decorated for Page when my dad was dying and Livvie and Page stayed over so often Mom thought Page needed her own room. Under intense questioning by Mom and me, Page and Vanessa had been polite, contrite, but not forthcoming. They knew they were in a whole lot of trouble.

Vanessa often stayed over when her mother, Emmy, worked the late shift at Crowley's, Busman's Harbor's nosiest, most touristy bar. At this time of year, the leaves were gone, and so were the tourists, so Crowley's was only open on Friday and Saturday nights. I'd texted Emmy to let her know Vanessa was at Mom's. She'd immediately sent a hurried thumbs-up. But small-town life being what it was, by the time she'd arrived at Mom's house two hours later, wild-eyed, she'd heard the whole story.

"What do we know about Mrs. Zelisko?" I asked Mom and Emmy. We were seated at Mom's kitchen table, and even though there was silence from upstairs, I kept my voice low. I knew from my own childhood that sound traveled up the back stairs.

"Not much, I'm afraid." My mother matched my hushed tone.

"I think," Emmy ventured, "she goes to Star of the Sea?" Star of the Sea was the local Catholic church.

Emmy was still in her Halloween costume, so it was hard to take her seriously. She was dressed as a cat. Not a sexy, cat-woman type cat, which would certainly have enhanced her tips. Instead, she wore something that looked like furry footie pajamas in what might have been a leopard, or tiger, or even calico print. The outfit had a hood with cat's ears on it, which Emmy wore up for warmth. My mother, true to the code of the thrifty Yankee housewife she'd become, never turned on the heat until Novem-

ber 1. The minutes were ticking rapidly toward that mo-
mentous date. Since I ran the family business, the Snowden Family Clambake, out of my dad's old office on the
second floor of Mom's house, I could hardly wait for heat
day to arrive.

"I think Mrs. Zelisko moved here five years or so ago,"
Mom ventured. "She's always rented the apartment on the
third floor of that house."

"What did she do?" I asked. "Is she retired?" My hazy
picture of Mrs. Zelisko included steel gray hair, an oval
face with a prominent nose, and an extra chin. She had a
hairy wart on one cheek near her ear. The perfect face for
scaring children. She was short and cylindrical and wore
black dresses so tight they looked like sausage casings.
Though I could picture her, I couldn't guess her age.

"She's a bookkeeper," Mom said. "She takes care of the
books for a lot of small businesses here in town. After
your dad died and before you came home to run the clambake, I considered hiring her. Your dad always took care
of the books, and I didn't think it was a strength of
Sonny's."

My parents had founded the Snowden Family Clambake to keep the private island my mother had inherited in
the family. From mid-June to mid-October, we loaded
three hundred visitors on our tour boat, showed them the
islands, lighthouses, seals, and eagles of Busman's Harbor,
then took them briefly into the North Atlantic until we
docked at Morrow Island. There we served an authentic
Maine clambake meal; twin lobsters, the soft-shelled
clams called steamers, corn on the cob, a potato, an onion,
and a hard-boiled egg, all cooked under seaweed and salt-
water-soaked tarps and over a roaring hardwood fire.

My brother-in-law had run the clambake for a few years
after Dad died—and had nearly run it into the ground. It

wasn't entirely his fault. There had been a recession, bad weather, and an ill-advised bank loan. The less said about those unhappy days the better. I had been called home to run the business. Four years later, I was still here. I'd thought I would marry Chris and make a life. Now, I had no idea what I was doing.

Mom, Emmy, and I talked about Mrs. Zelisko. What would bring a single woman in her . . . fifties? . . . to Busman's Harbor? If she wasn't in the tourist trade, if she didn't have friends or family locally, perhaps she simply liked living by the sea.

Eventually, Emmy took off. She lived on Thistle Island in a trailer parked on her old gran's property. Her four-year-old son, Luther, was a little too much for the elderly woman to handle when he was awake, so Emmy had to get some sleep and pick him up early in the morning.

Mom suggested I spend the night in my old room. I thought about my apartment, empty and dark, and agreed.

Chapter Four

In the morning, I was awakened by familiar sounds floating up the back stairs. Forks scraped across plates, water ran in the sink, and the murmur of adult voices, punctuated occasionally by the loud, querying voice of my nephew, Jack, came from the kitchen table. The sky visible through the windows was gray. Gusts of wind rattled the old, wooden frames. I snuggled under the covers for a few minutes before I got up.

Sort of dressed, in sweatpants and a T-shirt I found abandoned in my old bureau, I made my way down to the kitchen. Livvie and Sonny were already there. Someone, probably not my mom, had made a batch of scrambled eggs, and there was buttered toast on the counter. Everyone sat around the kitchen table except Jack, who had been excused and was careening around the circle formed by the dining room, living room, front hall, and kitchen. "Jack, don't run," Livvie cautioned in a voice that sounded robotic and distracted.

Mom, Sonny, and Livvie ate and talked in subdued tones about all the construction in Portland. "Cranes everywhere," Sonny complained, but the traffic on the way home was, he said, "Light. Easy." Page sat at the table, silent and bent over, the eggs on her plate untouched.

"Good morning." Mom forced a tight smile. *Nothing to see here. Perfectly normal breakfast*, her expression said.

"I'm sorry you had to come home," I said to Livvie and Sonny, not sure how close to the elephant in the room I was supposed to get.

Sonny shrugged his big shoulders. "No problem. We'll do it a different time."

They wouldn't. "Did Emmy already pick up Vanessa?"

"First thing this morning," Mom confirmed.

I took some eggs from the pan, picked up a couple of pieces of toast, and sat down, still unclear on what I should or shouldn't say about the previous night.

"Mom, can I be excused?" Page asked.

"You didn't eat a thing," my mother said.

Livvie put a hand up, "It's okay."

"Can I go see Talia?"

"Talia's across the street," Mom explained to me. "The state police asked the Davies to stay somewhere else since their home is . . ."—she hesitated—"unavailable."

"You can say it," Page grumped. "I know there's a dead body there. I'm not a baby."

"So they've checked into the Snuggles," Mom finished.

The Snuggles Inn was run by Fee and Vee Snugg, neighbors, family friends, and honorary great aunts. I could see how the Davies family's situation would have appealed to Fee and Vee's big hearts.

Livvie answered Page's original question. "Lieutenant Binder and Sergeant Flynn have asked that you don't talk to Talia or Vanessa, even by phone or text, until they've taken your statement. Besides, your father and I haven't decided on your punishment yet."

The girls had looked so bedraggled the night before that I was tempted to say they'd been punished enough, but I kept my mouth shut. This was none of my business.

"I'm sorry about what happened," Livvie continued. "But you, Vanessa, and Talia invited those other girls over, something you were expressly forbidden to do."

Page looked wildly from one parent to the other and then made puppy-dog eyes at my mother, willing her to intervene. When Mom didn't take the bait, Page folded her arms across her chest but didn't leave the room.

I finished my eggs and gulped down a second cup of coffee. "I'm going across the street to talk to the Davies," I said.

"I'll come with you." Sonny pushed back his chair. "I have some questions. First up, how do they get off leaving the house when these girls are having a sleepover?"

"Dad!" Page shrunk into herself even further.

Livvie put a cautioning hand on her husband's arm. "Let's leave that discussion for later. We have more important things to deal with."

Sonny hesitated, but pulled his chair forward again, back under the table. "Okay, but these people have some explaining to do."

"Dad!"

Livvie walked me to the front door. "Are you going like that?"

I looked down at the sweatpants and T-shirt. "Casual visit," I said.

She followed me onto the porch. "Binder and Flynn said they'd come around ten to take Page's statement. Can you be here? You know those guys better than Sonny and I do, and you've been through this before."

"Of course," I said. "Anything you need."

Vee answered the door at the Snuggles, dressed as she always was in a skirt, blouse, hose, and heels. Today, appropriate to the season, the skirt was a wool plaid of deep oranges, browns, and yellows, and she wore a cardigan in the same deep orange over her crisp, off-white blouse. Her snow-white hair was in the neat chignon she always wore. I wondered if, after all these years, it grew that way. She was perfectly made up, which made me even more self-conscious about the sweats and T.

"Julia, what a delight. You've come to visit."

"Yes," I hesitated, "and no. I'm actually here to see the Davies."

Vee didn't miss a beat. "They're in the dining room. Or at least the adults are. I think Talia's in her room."

"Perfect. Thanks." I stepped through the door into the big front hallway and made for the swinging door to the dining room. I'd been in and out of that house so often since I was a child, I felt as comfortable there as I did in my mother's home or my own.

Talia's parents sat at the Snugg sisters' polished mahogany table with their backs to the door. They turned and rose at the sound of my footsteps.

"Howard Davies." He extended a hand.

"Blair Davies," she said and then offered her hand as well.

"Julia Snowden."

"You're Page's aunt," Blair said. "You came to the girls' rescue last night. We can't thank you enough."

My first impression was that Blair Davies was much older than her husband. He wore his brown hair long, with not a hint of gray. He had a youthful body, loose-limbed and lean. Her hair was completely white and fell to her shoulders. Her body was soft and pleasantly round. But as I looked from one face to the other, I saw the same lines around the eyes, the slight softening of skin at the chin. They were probably quite close in age. Late forties or early fifties, I guessed.

"Nice to meet you both. Unfortunately, I was too late for an actual rescue. I'm sorry I had to leave Talia alone with the police. They wouldn't let me take her."

"We pulled into the driveway moments after you left with Page and Vanessa. Talia was happy to see us, but of all the things that happened last night, I don't think spending a little time waiting with Officer Dawes was the traumatizing event," Howard said.

"How's Talia doing?" I asked.

"She's quiet and withdrawn," Blair answered. "It's a lot to process."

Howard Davies blew out air. "Sit, sit," he said, gesturing toward the dining table. "There's still coffee in the carafe."

I helped myself to coffee and cream in one of the Snugg sisters' china cups with the delicate pink roses painted on it, and sat across the table from the Davies. "Have you spoken to the police this morning?"

"They called to ask us to be available since they plan to come over later to interview Talia," Howard said. "They have crime-scene techs working at our house and in our yard. That's all we know."

"They asked if we knew who Mrs. Zelisko's next of kin would be," Blair added. "Unfortunately, we don't."

"We inherited her as a tenant," Howard explained. "She rented the third-floor apartment from the previous owners. We had no immediate use for the space, and it was nice to have a little cash coming in to help with the moving expenses. We welcomed Mrs. Zelisko staying on." He paused. "It's not like we interviewed her or selected her. The previous owners vouched for her. They told us she paid the rent on time, kept the place neat, didn't intrude in their family life. Her apartment didn't have a separate entrance, so she had to go through our living space to get to hers. It was a little awkward, but as the previous owners told us, she did her best to respect our privacy, and we respected hers."

"Did you get to know her at all?" I asked.

"A little," Blair answered. "We have a traditional Sunday meal, usually a roast or a casserole, served earlier than our normal workday dinner time. We invited her a few times. But our conversations tended to the general. Plans for the house, town events. She never talked about her past. We asked a few times. That accent." Blair paused and looked around the room, as if the source of the accent might be hiding in a corner. "She was polite, but not expansive."

"Where is the accent from?"

"Slovenia, she said," Howard answered.

"Talia is at an awkward age," Blair said. "She wasn't happy about the move. Thirteen is a terrible age to move a kid. She's too old for a babysitter, but we were concerned about leaving her at night or for several hours on her own."

"So we would ask Mrs. Zelisko to keep an eye on her"—Howard picked up the story—"and tell Talia she could go to Mrs. Zelisko if she needed anything when we weren't home. It seemed to suit them both."

"Believe us"—Blair Davies looked straight at me, begging for what? understanding? forgiveness?—"we never, ever would have left your niece and her friend at our home for a sleepover without adult supervision. We thought it was three girls who'd be watching movies and eating snacks. We're so thrilled Talia has made friends."

"I work at Emerson Laboratory," Howard said. "We accepted an invitation to a Halloween party at the home of one of my colleagues. We had lots of friends in Massachusetts, but moving here, especially during the season when everyone is so busy, has been challenging. I have work, and now Talia has school, but it's been hard on Blair. So I jumped at the chance to go to this party. I shouldn't have."

"We never imagined . . ." Blair's voice broke, and she stared into her lap. "We are so sorry. Please tell your sister and brother-in-law how sorry we are."

Chapter Five

I shivered my way back to my apartment to shower and change into my fall uniform of jeans, a flannel shirt over a T-shirt, and work boots. On the way out the door, I grabbed my quilted vest off a hook by the staircase. The day was gray and chilly, a harbinger of the weather the rest of November would bring, if it wasn't worse.

As I walked back over the harbor hill, I saw the unmarked state police car belonging to Lieutenant Jerry Binder and his partner, Sergeant Tom Flynn, pull to the curb in front of my mother's house. I met the detectives on the front walk.

"Julia." Under his ski-slope nose, Jerry Binder's mouth turned up in a genuine smile. "You can't seem to stay out of trouble."

"Coincidence. I picked up my niece and her friend because Sonny and Livvie were out of town."

"Uh-huh." Tom Flynn didn't seem to find the fact that I kept turning up in their cases nearly so funny.

I led them to Mom's house and opened the front door. "Livvie has asked me to sit in on Page's interview, if that's okay."

Binder stepped across the threshold. "The more the merrier."

"Just keep quiet and let us drive," Flynn added. Completely unnecessarily in my opinion.

"We'll need to talk to you after," Binder said. "Since you were there when the body was discovered."

"I'm not sure what I can add to whatever Officers Dawes and Howland told you, but I'm happy to help in any way I can."

Livvie was in the kitchen. Mom had gone to work, and Livvie had sent Sonny and Jack home. I wasn't sure how she'd talked Sonny into not being present for his daughter's interview, but I was relieved. Things would go much more smoothly without Sonny's simmering temper and Jack's kinetic energy.

"Page!" Livvie called up the back stairs to her daughter. "Lieutenant Binder and Sergeant Flynn are here."

Page walked down the stairs, staring carefully at her feet. She was dressed in blue jeans and a nice shirt, and she'd made an attempt to tame her red curls, pulling them back in a ponytail.

"Hello." Page addressed the policemen.

"Shall we sit here?" Binder gestured to the kitchen table.

"Of course," Livvie said. "Anybody need anything? Coffee? Water?"

"Coffee would be nice," Binder said.

Flynn added, "Water, thanks."

I doubted they were thirsty. They probably wanted the atmosphere to appear more relaxed. Page was plainly miserable.

Livvie distributed the drinks, including a glass of water for Page, who hadn't requested it. Binder, sitting across from Page, leaned forward and put the elbows of his tweed sports coat on the table. Next to him, Flynn took out his notebook. Livvie sat next to Page. I took the chair at the end of the table.

Binder's sports coat looked comfy and lived-in, like Binder did. He was in his late forties; sandy hair ringed his bald head. He had two boys a little younger than Page. He was normally the good cop in these interviews, patient and understanding, while Flynn pushed aggressively for the details.

I hoped Flynn wouldn't push Page too hard. The cops were on the trail of a murderer, but Page was a kid. She'd met both detectives before, but in passing and never in a situation like this. Flynn, with his buzz-cut hair, military bearing, and gym-toned body, could be intimidating even when he didn't mean to be.

"Page," Binder said in his nice-dad voice, "we're going to ask you some questions about last night. It's very important that you're honest, even if you think your answer might get you or a friend of yours in trouble. Can you do that?"

Page nodded, face solemn.

"Nothing she says can get her in more trouble than she's already in." Livvie saw what Binder was doing.

"Okay," Binder said. "Let's begin. What time did you arrive at the Davies' house?"

Page looked at her mother, who nodded, encouraging her. "Vanessa's mom, Emmy, picked me up here before her shift started at Crowley's. It was around five o'clock, I think." Her voice had a soft, little-girl quality I hadn't heard in years.

"Sonny and I had left for Portland," Livvie said. "So Page was already here at Mom's."

Binder gave her a curt nod and turned his attention back to Page. "Who did you see at the Davies' house when you arrived?"

"Talia and her parents." Page continued in the same,

barely audible tone. "And Vanessa, who came with me, of course."

"Both of Talia's parents were present when you arrived," Binder confirmed.

"Yes."

"Then what happened?"

"Mrs. Davies went over the rules. She said we could watch whatever we wanted on the TV, even if it was scary. She said there was pizza and salad for dinner and soda, which Talia was excited about because normally she's not allowed. Mrs. Davies said we could go into the family room; she'd take care of the trick-or-treaters."

"Did you see Mrs. Zelisko at any time when Talia's parents were still there?" Flynn asked.

"No. I never saw her at all, until . . ." Page's eyes again darted to her mother. Livvie nodded, her expression serious.

"We'll get to that." Binder steered the conversation kindly but firmly. "For now, let's keep talking about the time before the Davies left."

"We watched a movie, not a scary one. We could hear the doorbell ring, and Mrs. Davies complimenting all the little kids on their costumes while she gave out the candy. Then she heated up the pizza and called us to the kitchen to eat." Page drew a deep breath. "That's when she told us she and Mr. Davies were going out." Page picked up her water glass and took a long drink. "I was worried because I knew my parents wouldn't like that. But then Mrs. Davies explained that Mrs. Zelisko was upstairs, so I felt fine about it. A little later, Mr. and Mrs. Davies came into the back room to say goodbye to us. They said Mrs. Zelisko would be keeping her ears open, and we should go to her if we had any problems. And then they left."

"What time was that?" Binder asked.

"We'd been there maybe two hours?" Page didn't sound too sure.

"What did you do when they left?" Binder continued.

"At first, we started another movie, but we got bored, so then we started texting with some friends."

"Are these texts still on your phone?" Flynn asked.

"Yes."

"We'd like to see it, if that's okay."

"My mom has it."

Livvie retrieved the phone from her oversized pocketbook in the back hall. The rest of us were silent while we waited, though I had a million questions. Livvie entered the password and held out the phone. Flynn reached across the table and took it.

While Flynn examined the phone, Binder went on with the interview. "Who did you text with, Page?"

"Different friends from school. We were asking what they were doing. Some went trick-or-treating; some handed out candy. Then we found out Jenna Warren was having a sleepover at her house with Kennedy and Lucy."

"I don't see that text here," Flynn said.

"It isn't on my phone. We were all on our own phones, checking in with different people. Talia was texting with Jenna and invited them over." Page paused, looking again at her mother. "I told her not to. But she said as long as we were quiet, Mrs. Zelisko wouldn't come downstairs, and no one would ever know."

Livvie looked at me, an amused squint to her eyes. Only a thirteen-year-old girl could believe six adolescent girls could remain quiet enough not to attract attention.

"And the three girls did come over," Binder said.

"Yes. Right away. Jenna only lives around the corner from Talia."

Flynn asked the girls' full names and wrote them down.

I wondered if their parents knew they'd been at the Davies' or if the girls had snuck out and the parents were in for an unpleasant surprise.

"Then what happened?" Binder leaned farther forward and lowered his voice. We were getting to the hard part.

"Jenna did a group text to the whole world saying there was a party at Talia's and her parents weren't home." Page's voice quivered. "And then people started coming from everywhere, bringing beer. Big kids. High school kids. Jenna let the first group in, and after that we couldn't keep them out. They kept letting each other in."

"Did you know these kids?" Flynn asked.

"Some I know, like from swim team." Page had been on the Y swim team since she could dog-paddle. High school kids served as assistant coaches and lifeguards. "Some I recognized from school." Busman's Harbor had a combined middle and high school in the same building. The kids would pass each other in the halls. "Some were in costumes with creepy masks or makeup. Some I'm sure I've never seen before."

"How many kids would you say were there at the peak of the party?" Binder asked.

"Maybe a hundred?"

I doubted that was the actual number, but however many it was, it had seemed overwhelming to Page.

Binder didn't have to prompt her to continue.

"The party went on and on. Kids started wrecking the house. The music was really loud. There was a fight in the backyard. Someone threw up in the downstairs bathroom and didn't clean it up. People were in the bedrooms." Page shuddered. "Talia was crying. She knew she was in so much trouble. We didn't understand why Mrs. Zelisko didn't come downstairs and throw those kids out. Talia and I went up to get her."

At this point, both Binder and Flynn got very interested. They leaned in toward Page, whose eyes opened wide. She pushed her chair back a little.

"Did you see Mrs. Zelisko?" Flynn asked.

"There was no one in her apartment," Page said. "It was empty. We looked in every room that we could get in. Talia said maybe she forgot she was supposed to watch us and went out."

"Were there rooms up there you couldn't get into?" Binder asked.

"One door was closed. I thought it might be the bathroom. Talia wasn't sure. Mrs. Zelisko already lived there when Talia's family moved in, so Talia had never been in the apartment. We knocked and knocked. I tried the knob." Page's skin, already flushed behind her freckles, reddened more. "Normally I would *never*. But we were really scared. I couldn't open it."

"The door was locked from the inside?" Flynn tried to keep his normal bark in check.

"I don't know. The knob turned, but the door was stuck."

"Then what did you do?" Binder prompted.

"We went back downstairs. We couldn't find Vanessa. We shouted for her, but the house was so noisy. I got really nervous, so I called Aunt Julia." Page looked at me. "I didn't know what else to do."

"It's okay, sweetie," I said. "That's what I'm here for." Not only had Livvie and Sonny specifically asked me to provide backup in this instance, I thought it was generally the job description of an aunt to take those kinds of calls. I never wanted Page to hesitate to call me.

"What time did you call your Aunt Julia?" Binder asked.

"I don't know." Page sounded weepy, like not knowing the time was a personal failing.

Flynn scrolled through her phone. "Does nine forty-three sound right?"

"Yes," I said.

"Go on," Binder said to Page.

"The house was so crowded. There were people everywhere. There was a big group in the front hall, where Talia and I ended up when we came down the stairs from the apartment. Finally, I spotted Vanessa through the archway to the kitchen. I called out to her. A girl screamed and pointed up. And then everyone was screaming and pointing. Mrs. Zelisko flew down from the ceiling! She was all dressed in white like a bride! Her face was white. She was a ghost! That's where she was when we were in her apartment. She was *dead*." Page burst into noisy tears. Livvie put an arm around her. The poor kid. The fanciful flying ghost story aside, whatever had happened had clearly been traumatizing. And something had happened. Mrs. Zelisko *was* dead.

"When you say she flew—" Flynn was at least making an effort to hide his skepticism.

"Flew like a bird," Page insisted, "from her apartment to the first floor."

"What happened when she reached the bottom?" Flynn asked.

"I don't know. There were too many people. Everyone was screaming and running out of the front door and the back door. I screamed too and pulled Talia outside. We ran to the corner of the block. That's where Vanessa finally caught up to us."

Binder kept moving Page forward in the story. "What happened when you reached the corner?"

"Everyone else kept running, but Vanessa, Talia, and I stopped. We could see that the front door of Talia's house was wide open. Vanessa and I couldn't leave Talia. We could hear the police sirens. Besides, I'd already called Aunt Julia. So we went back."

"That was brave," Binder said.

Or foolish.

"Did you call the police?" I asked Page.

Flynn shook his head. "Neighbors. Multiple neighbors."

"Did you ever see Mrs. Zelisko or her ghost again?" Binder asked.

"No. Never. She wasn't in the hall when we got back to the house. The police came, and Aunt Julia came, and Vanessa and I came back to Grammy's house, and that was it."

Binder sat back in his chair. "Thank you, Page. You have been very, very helpful. Can you write down the names of everyone you remember seeing at the party?"

Livvie fetched a pad and pencil from beside Mom's landline, and Page labored, tongue sticking out through her lips. In the end, she had about twenty first and last names, ten more first names or nicknames. Binder and Flynn accepted it gratefully. It was as good a place as any to get started.

Flynn scrolled through Page's phone as she worked. "Did you take any photos of the party?"

Page looked at him like he was crazy. "Are you kidding?"

"Page, that's not the way we talk to Sergeant Flynn, or any grown-up," Livvie scolded.

"Are you on any social media? Could some of your friends have posted photos?"

"Instagram," Page answered. "I follow a lot of kids from school."

Flynn looked at Livvie, who nodded and then went back to the phone and scrolled. "There are lots of photos of the party." Flynn held the phone out to Page. "Take a look to see if it helps you remember anyone else."

Page took the phone and diligently scrolled. She added three names to her list. When she was done, she handed the phone back to Flynn.

Flynn tried to give it back. "It's okay. If we need it again, we'll ask."

"Give it to my mom," Page said, resigned. She handed the list to Flynn and allowed herself to be hugged by her mother. I walked the detectives out to the front porch.

Chapter Six

"Do you have anything to add?" Binder asked me.

"No. Page did a good job on the parts where I was involved. Was she helpful?"

"Very. Especially the names she was able to provide." Flynn folded Page's list and put it in his notebook.

"Have you had any luck finding Mrs. Zelisko's next of kin?" I asked.

"Zero," Binder answered. "We can't find anything about her before she fetched up on your particular peninsula five years ago."

"Really? The feds must know something about her. When she immigrated, for sure."

"We're waiting to hear back from them. You're sure she was an immigrant?"

"She had a pronounced accent. Eastern European. She told the Davies she was from Slovenia."

Binder nodded. "We'll ask them about it. We're off to see them next. Across the street." He paused. "Of course, it's possible she immigrated years ago under a maiden name and Mr. Zelisko was someone who came and went subsequent to her arrival here."

"True. I don't think there's been a Mr. Zelisko since she arrived in town. I've heard she was a parishioner at Star of the Sea. It could be that someone there is a closer friend and knows more about her."

"Thanks," Binder said. "We're still searching her apartment, computer, and phone. Maybe there's some correspondence that will lead us in the right direction. In the meantime, we have to talk to Talia and Vanessa, and then get started on this list your niece gave us. Somewhere, there's an eyewitness."

"How did she die?" I asked.

"Awaiting autopsy results." Flynn was abrupt.

"But it definitely was murder?"

"No question," Binder answered.

"Was her body just lying in the backyard?"

"It was in the shed," Flynn said. "The killer had taken the trouble to hide it."

"What do you think about this whole crazy ghost thing?" I asked.

"I was going to ask you the same question." Binder wasn't amused. Murder was serious business.

The door of the Snuggles Inn opened, and Blair Davies strode onto the wide front porch. "Detectives?" she shouted in our direction.

"That's us," Binder called back. "Lieutenant Jerry Binder and Sergeant Tom Flynn. We're finishing up with Ms. Snowden, and we'll be right over."

"That's why I came out," Blair shouted. "I just got off the phone with Livvie. She told me Julia was present during Page's interview. I wondered if Julia could do the same for Talia. Livvie tells me Julia has some experience in these situations, and at least Talia knows her a little bit."

Binder looked at me and sighed. "I can't think of a reason why not. Julia, do you have time to join us?"

"Absolutely."

*   *   *

Blair led us through the inn to the dining room. Talia sat, slump-shouldered, next to her dad. Blair went around the table and took the chair on the other side of her. The detectives and I arranged ourselves across from them.

Vee Snugg bustled in from the kitchen. "Anyone need anything?" She knew Binder and Flynn from previous investigations, and neither Snugg sister ever missed a chance to check out Flynn's sports-jacket clad biceps.

"Miss Snugg." Binder rose and gave Vee a hug. Flynn also rose but stuck out a hand in self-defense. "Maybe some tea," Binder suggested. "And something for Miss Davies."

"Water, thank you," Talia said miserably.

While we waited for the tea, Binder steered the conversation toward the Davies' background. They had moved from Medview, Massachusetts, in June, right after school got out, so Howard could take a management job at Emerson Lab. These were prestigious, good jobs in Busman's Harbor, the kind Maine communities had too few of. The kind that could attract people from out of state to shore up our dwindling population.

Back in Massachusetts, Blair had been an elementary school teacher, but she hadn't found a position since they'd relocated. "It's been challenging to make friends," she said. "Everyone here seems to know everyone already." She spread her hands out in front of her, a gesture taking in the whole town and all the people in it.

"That's why we accepted the Halloween party invitation," Howard explained, "so Blair could get to know some of my colleagues and their partners. We never should have." He shook his head with regret.

"We'll get to that," Binder said.

Vee and Fee and Fee's Scottish terrier, Mackie, arrived with the tea, Talia's water, and a plate of Vee's pumpkin cookies. "In case you're peckish."

If Vee was unsparingly glamorous, no matter the occasion, Fee was her opposite. Bent over from arthritis, she kept her steel-gray bangs out of her face with a pink plastic barrette. She never used makeup, and today she wore a brown corduroy skirt, a tan sweater, and the very footwear you picture when you hear the words "sensible shoes." Like her sister, she was smitten with Flynn. He had never done anything to encourage them, except for his daily, lengthy trips to the gym. I was convinced he toiled there for his own satisfaction and not for anyone's admiration of the results.

"Thank you," I said. Vee's pumpkin cookies had been a favorite since I was a kid. Fee bustled to the corner cabinet and distributed six small plates around the table. The heavenly smell of the big cookies was getting to me. They were shaped like pumpkins, and Vee had delicately decorated them with a lacey tracing of orange frosting to indicate the pumpkin shell and a green leaf peeping out from the stem.

"They're gluten-free," Vee said.

What the what?

"So you can eat one, Sergeant." She beamed at Flynn. "Or two."

Ohhh. Light dawned. Binder and Flynn had stayed at the B&B a number of times when they'd been in town on previous cases, and it had been source of endless frustration for Vee that Flynn never touched the goodies she painstakingly baked for their breakfasts. She had tried to tempt him with muffins, scones, and coffee cake, and he'd bypassed them all. Evidently, she'd decided that the only possible explanation was that he was gluten-intolerant.

I suspected he would object as much, if not more, to the light and dark sugar, chocolate chips, and sticks of butter that were in the delicious cookies. His body was a temple. But I had to give Vee points for trying.

I grabbed the cookie plate, took one to set a good example, and then started it around the table. At a minimum, the food would serve as an icebreaker. Talia was plainly miserable. She'd disobeyed her parents and gotten their home trashed. The senior Davies felt horribly guilty about leaving the girls to go to the party. And all of that and more had combined to set the stage for the murder of their tenant and the transformation of their home into a crime scene.

Everyone took a cookie until the plate made its way back around to Flynn, who was seated next to me. He held the plate in mid-air in front of him while Vee stared him down. Finally, he took the smallest cookie, which wasn't small, and the sisters withdrew.

My cookie was exactly as I remembered them from my youth—pumpkiny, and spicy, chocolatey and cakey, yet moist with a crunch from the walnuts that were in it. It perked me up considerably, and I thought Talia and Blair looked less droopy. Flynn's cookie sat untouched on his plate.

Binder got down to business. He asked first about the deceased. Mr. and Mrs. Davies gave the answers I already knew. Slovenian. Lived in the house when they bought it. Faithful attendee of Star of the Sea Catholic church.

"How about the previous owners?" Flynn asked. "The people who rented to her originally. Maybe they know more."

"They moved to Buffalo," Howard said. "I'll send you their contact information."

"Please." Flynn slid his business card across the table.

"Did Mrs. Zelisko tell you anything about Mr.

Zelisko?" Binder asked. "If she was widowed or divorced?"

"Never," Blair answered. "Honestly, I wondered if there had been a Mr. Zelisko. I thought the 'Mrs.' might be more of an honorific."

A dead end. Binder appeared unperturbed. "Did she ever happen to mention what year she arrived in this country?" he asked. "Or maybe where she lived in the States before she moved to Busman's Harbor?"

All three Davies shook their heads.

"Or maybe where she lived immediately before coming to Busman's Harbor?" Flynn asked.

"No, nothing like that," Blair said.

"She didn't talk about her past," Howard added.

"Which was weird," Talia said, "because we talked about the past and where we moved from, like, all the time."

"I never really thought about it that way," Howard said, "but you're right, sweetheart."

Talia physically shook off the "sweetheart" with a flick of her hand, as if it was an annoying gnat.

"Did she pay rent by check or electronic transfer?" Flynn asked. "Our team has her laptop, and we'll find her bank account, but a check or account number could help us."

Howard colored slightly. "She paid in cash."

It wasn't an unusual arrangement for tenants in these auxiliary apartments to pay in cash. They usually got a discount for doing so, and the homeowner rarely reported the income to the IRS.

Binder steered the conversation to the previous night. Blair narrated the first part, up until the older Davies left for the party. Howard apologized again, profusely, for their bad judgment.

Talia took up the tale from there. In response to Binder's patient questioning, her telling of events matched Page's. Not so much so that it sounded rehearsed, but in all the important areas, their stories were the same. Even more than Page had, Talia grew more miserable as the story progressed and she described the party at her family home growing wilder and more out of control. As she talked, tears slid down her nose and fell onto the pink rosebuds on the china plate in front of her.

"It's okay." Blair rubbed her daughter's back. "We all make mistakes. No one could have foreseen everything that happened last night. The detectives just want to know about Mrs. Zelisko."

On the other side of Talia, Howard shifted his chair, his mouth turned down at the corners. He didn't seem inclined to let his daughter off so lightly. Perhaps no one could have foreseen a murder, but the gathering of teenagers once word was on the street that the Davies weren't home was entirely foreseeable.

Talia described the search for Mrs. Zelisko in more detail than Page had. She told how they'd looked in the sitting room and the bedroom, and had knocked at the bathroom door.

"You're sure it was the bathroom," Flynn confirmed.

"Not sure, but it was right over my bathroom on the second floor, and we hadn't seen one anywhere else in the apartment."

"Makes sense," Binder said.

"We knocked and called, and she didn't answer," Talia continued. "Page tried to open the door but couldn't."

"Did you look in the closets or under the bed?" Binder pressed.

"No!" Talia sat up sharply. "I would *never*. It's her privacy."

"It's okay that you didn't," Binder assured her. "We just want to be thorough."

Talia took a deep breath and continued. She described the jammed-up gathering in the front hall. "And then Mrs. Zelisko floated down the stairs!"

Floated, not flew, as Page had said. Flynn caught it too. "She came down the stairs slowly?"

"She floated across the room," Talia explained as if to someone not bright.

"I don't understand," Flynn persisted. "Did she come down the bannister?"

Talia shook her head. "She was *old*." As if being old made it impossible to consider that Mrs. Zelisko might have slid down the bannister, but not impossible to consider that she might have floated through the air.

"How was she dressed?" Binder asked.

"She was all in white."

"Like a white dress?"

"No. Like white robes and a white veil. Like a nun. More like a nun in a white whaddyamacallit."

"Habit," Blair supplied.

"Habit," Talia repeated.

It didn't take long to wind up the rest of the story. The teenagers running out of the house. The police arriving. Me arriving and then leaving with Page and Vanessa. The Davies coming home. Flynn examined Talia's phone while Binder led the family through the denouement with business-like precision.

The detectives thanked the family and stood. I did, too.

"I imagine you're anxious to get back to your home," Binder said to them. "We'll move as quickly as we can."

Blair shuddered. "To tell the truth, we're not in any hurry. Take your time."

Before they left, I watched Lieutenant Binder quietly fold a paper napkin around Flynn's uneaten cookie and slip it into the pocket of his sports coat.

I followed the detectives to their car. "What do you think?" I asked them.

"Those girls saw something in that hallway," Binder said. "But did they see a live woman or a dead one? That's the question."

Chapter Seven

Binder and Flynn got in their car and drove away. I suspected they were off to lunch at Gus's, but my strategy of standing in the street looking like I had nothing in particular to do didn't earn me an invitation.

I headed in the opposite direction, toward the Star of the Sea Catholic church. I walked down to the waterfront and crossed the wooden footbridge that connected the two sides of the inner harbor. In the summer, I might have lingered on the bridge to look out at the islands and the pleasure boats, but the November wind cut across the water. I stuck my hands in my vest pockets.

The inner harbor was the touristy part of Busman's Harbor, as opposed to the back harbor, where the lobster boats were moored. The east side was lined with fancy hotels and more recently built condo complexes. Above them loomed the bright white central steeple of the Star of the Sea.

The original, modest church had been built for the Irish servants of the wealthy "rusticators" who summered in Maine in the late nineteenth century, my mother's ancestors among them. When the town had been flooded with French Canadian immigrants, who moved here to work in the canneries, the current church was built. Now it served all the town's Catholics, from locals to snowbird retirees to summer families. They worshipped upstairs in the nave of the big church during the tourist season. In the off-season, when the summer people were gone and the snow-birds fled daily for warmer climes, services were held in the much more economically and successfully heated basement.

When I was young, there had been two full-time priests assigned to the Star of the Sea year-round. They lived in a house on the grounds, indulged by a devoted housekeeper. Now there was one part-time cleric, who rotated among three churches. He lived two towns away and seemed to show up in Busman's Harbor only when duty called, much to the disgruntlement of his more vocal parishioners.

But if their clerics registered as indifferent, the hard-core laity at the Star of the Sea did not let that affect their dedication. If anything, the priestly neglect revved them up. Which is why, as I approached the building, I was certain I would find the people I sought in the church hall on a Saturday afternoon.

Sure enough, I spotted Clarice Kemp across the big room, diligently pricing donated items for the church's main fundraiser, an auction that was nine months in the future. Clarice was the biggest gossip in Busman's Harbor. She'd recently retired from her job at the front desk of the Lighthouse Inn, a job that had put her at the nexus of town gossip, with sources ranging from the tourists staying in the rooms, to the locals eating in the dining room, to the yachters pulling up their boats outside. Now that Clarice had moved on from her life at the crossroads, I had heard she was spending her time at the Star of the Sea, another gossip hotbed, though it did confine her mostly to firsthand information about the town's Catholics.

There were a few other people in the room. Mike Parker—the "pipe charmer," as my family called him, since he somehow was able to keep the ancient plumbing at my mother's house up and running—and his wife, Doreen, were also pricing items. The half a dozen or so other people looked familiar, but I didn't know their names. I gave a wave and a smile to all and headed for Clarice.

"Julia, would you say this is mid-century modern?" She held out an enormous table lamp with a bulbous, over-sized base inlaid with teal disks that might have been ceramic or plastic. The rest of the lamp was an unconvincing gold, except for the teal shade that spiraled from a wide bottom to a curlicued top.

"It sure is—" I groped for words.

"Ugly?" Clarice suggested.

"I was going to say grotesque."

"But is it *so* grotesque that it's somehow trendy or beautiful? I don't want some hipster from Brooklyn sweeping in here and thinking he's putting something over on us."

I laughed. "I haven't lived in New York City for going on four years. I'm afraid I can't tell you what the hipsters will go for."

Clarice put the lamp back on the table. "I'll have Bev from Bev's Antiques take a look at it before I price it. What brings you here today?" Like a reporter, she moved us straight to the heart of the matter.

"I heard that Mrs. Zelisko was a parishioner here."

"Oooh," Clarice said. Her dreams of an original source had been realized. "I heard you were there when Pete Howland discovered the body."

The others in the room moved in closer. Needless to say, Mrs. Zelisko's murder was the number-one topic of conversation around town.

"Only tangentially," I assured her. "I happened to be at the Davies' house picking up my niece and her friend at the time."

"I heard there was a wild party," a woman said. "My friend lives on the street. Lots of college kids in revealing costumes having sex on the lawn and"—she lowered her voice—"*doing drugs*."

"I don't think it was as wild as all that," I protested. It didn't discourage them. The group closed in tighter. "The state police Major Crimes Unit is having trouble finding Mrs. Zelisko's next of kin," I continued, revealing my insider knowledge, which might or might not be a mistake in this situation. "And I thought maybe she had a close friend or friends here who might be able to help."

I let the suggestion sit while they looked at one another.

True to her role as a leader, Clarice spoke first. "Mrs. Zelisko was an absolute stalwart of the church. She was a professional bookkeeper, as you may know, and she gave generously of her time and talents. For example, she managed the books for this auction. At the end of the day, we sell over three thousand items—the big stuff in the main tent, the silent auction items, and the items we sell outright; sometimes we combine them into pretty baskets or boxes. It's a lot to keep track of, and I'm always so proud when we present the check with the proceeds to Father every year."

"Very admirable," I said. "But what I'm after is, did Mrs. Zelisko have any particular friends? Someone she may have confided in? The police need information about her family."

Clarice looked around the group and shook her head. "I never heard of any family. I had the impression she came to this country on her own."

"Then she'd have family back in her old country," I pointed out. "Or maybe even her husband's family. Someone who should be told about her death."

"She wasn't a person who made friends," a white-haired woman said. "She didn't have a car, and I offered to drive her to Hannaford several times. She never accepted."

That jibed with a memory I had of Mrs. Zelisko, climbing the harbor hill, string bags of groceries swinging at her sides.

"She was a little deaf," Doreen added. "I thought that might be why she avoided conversations."

Clarice nodded. "It took me a long time to catch on to that. She read lips quite well, but I'm sure it was tiring for her."

"I would say the people she was closest to were her clients," Mike the plumber said. "She kept the books for a lot of parishioners here."

"She approached us about her services," his wife added. "But I've always kept the books for the business."

"Who were her clients specifically?" I asked.

"Gleason's Hardware was one of the biggest," someone said, "and the most recent."

"Walker's Art Supplies," added another. "Barry Walker has been with her for a long time. I think he was one of her first clients."

"Gordon's Jewelry, for sure," Mike said.

"All owned by church members," Clarice said.

"Okay. I'll talk to them." A thought occurred to me. "Do any of you know her first name?"

"Uhm, Ellen?" Doreen ventured, though she didn't sound sure. "She didn't really use it."

"Helen?" Clarice suggested. "She always said it very quickly. And there was the accent."

"Or Eileen," someone else said.

"Irene," Mike put in. "It was definitely Irene."

"No, it wasn't," Doreen objected. "It definitely wasn't."

Chapter Eight

I said goodbye and thank you to the assembled group and made my way back downtown from the church, crossing over the footbridge.

There was no escaping the conclusion that Mrs. Zelisko valued her privacy. But why? Was it a natural reticence, perhaps caused by her hearing loss, or did something about her past make her reluctant to share personal information? Something about her past that was dangerous enough to get her killed.

It was very much the Maine way to let people keep themselves to themselves. Even Clarice Kemp, who would pass along any personal tidbit that came her way, wouldn't pry to get it, at least not with her subject directly. Our peninsula was, in a literal sense, the end of the road. It wasn't all that unusual for people to roll into town hoping to leave the past behind.

The footbridge left me off on the town pier right by the Snowden Family Clambake ticket kiosk. The little building always looked forlorn during the off-season, sitting alone on the concrete pier. I looked through the window to make sure no mail had been mistakenly put through the slot, but the tiny space was exactly as we'd left it when we'd cleaned up one last time and locked the door after Columbus Day.

From the pier, I walked a block to the corner of Main and Main, where Main Street crosses over itself after circling the harbor hill. On the first weekend in November, with Halloween over and the holiday season not yet begun, the street was deserted. The stoplight at the corner, the only one in town, was set to blinking yellow. Gordon's Jewelry was on the left-hand corner and Walker's Art Supplies and Frame Shop on the right. Unlike many of the shops on Main Street, both were open year-round. I went up the steps and opened the door of the jewelry shop.

Mr. Gordon, chubby and white-haired, was at his desk, bent over a velvet tray, a jeweler's loupe in his eye. The sound of the door opening caused him to sit up and turn in my direction.

"Julia, my dear. What brings you in on this chilly day?"

"Hi, Mr. Gordon. I've come to talk to you about your bookkeeper, Mrs. Zelisko. I'm sure you've heard."

He took the loupe off and replaced it with a thick pair of glasses. He gestured for me to sit on the wooden chair across from him. "I have indeed. Terrible tragedy. She was a fine woman." He looked genuinely saddened by the death.

I sat down. "Do you know much about her?"

"She's a member of Star of the Sea." He offered the one piece of information everyone seemed to have.

"I mean personally."

He hesitated. "Not really. When she came here, she was all business, no chitchat. I thought maybe she struggled with the language and that's why she avoided small talk. Then I realized she understood and spoke perfectly; she just didn't want to chatter. I didn't want to pry."

"How did you come to hire her?"

"When she first arrived in town, she joined the church. During a church auction committee meeting soon after she arrived, she introduced herself, said she was looking for clients." He took off his glasses and cleaned them rigorously with a soft cloth. "Alicia did the books for the business back then, but when it became too much for her, I remembered Mrs. Zelisko."

Mr. Gordon's wife, Alicia, had been very much his partner in life and in the jewelry business. She'd been a warm presence in the store, helping nervous boyfriends pick out engagement rings, sweethearts find something for their valentines, and happy tourists discover souvenirs that would remind them of their visit to the Maine mid-coast. But a couple of years earlier, her mind had started to wander, not a good thing in a business that traded in the careful display and tracking of expensive goods. When Alicia was unable to help at all, Mr. Gordon still brought her to the store every day, where he could watch her and she could interact with people. Since the summer, even that had not been possible, and he'd hired someone to watch her at home. Mrs. Zelisko's interest in doing his bookkeeping must have seemed like a lifeline.

"It's all become so complicated," he was saying. "We used to keep our books in a paper ledger. But now it's all QuickBooks and this and that. We have to keep very close track of the sales tax, of course. We sell some high-end items here."

Sales tax, I knew from my own experience with our little gift store at the Snowden Family Clambake, was money a retailer collected and kept in trust on behalf of the state of Maine. The money didn't belong to the retailer and had to be passed on, along with a filing that accounted for it, in a timely manner. It was a simple process, but an important one.

"Mrs. Zelisko was wonderful," Mr. Gordon continued. "She took care of everything. I never worried a day about that aspect of the business when she was on the job. Which reminds me," he squinted over the top of his glasses. "I'll need to get my records back. I wonder when that will be."

"The police have Mrs. Zelisko's laptop," I told him. "They're trying to find her next of kin. Plus solve her murder, of course. I'm sure they'll make arrangements with her clients to get the information they need when they're done with it. You don't know, by any chance, who her next of kin might be?"

"No," Mr. Gordon answered slowly. "Like I said, we never discussed anything personal."

I stood up. "I figured. Do you know her first name? You paid her. I thought it might be on a check or a bank account."

"She had me pay her in her little company's name," he said. "I don't remember it. It's all automated, so I haven't looked at it since we set it up. Do you want me to look it up for you?"

"No, please don't trouble yourself." The police would have that information and more.

"As you please, "Mr. Gordon responded. But he had already drifted back to the gems on his desk, the jeweler's loupe in his eye.

I crossed the street to Walker's Art Supplies and Frame Shop. Empty parking spots lined Main Street. During the season, a single empty space could spark a fistfight.

Walker's had been there as long as I could remember. Every June, when the school year was over and we prepared to move to Morrow Island, where our clambake was held, my mother brought Livvie and me to pick out colored pencils, pipe cleaners, tongue depressors, pot-holder loops, and clay for molding. Anything to keep us busy on rainy island days when the clambake didn't operate. Our morning at Walker's was like a second Christmas, even better because you got to pick out your own gifts. We loved it. None of the crafts took long-term with me, but Livvie spent her winters working at a pottery studio in town. She made the plates, lamps, and serving pieces the shop offered and painted them, too, with a delicate, controlled hand. It was a talent I envied.

I opened one of the double doors and entered Walker's familiar space. It was as different from Gordon's as possible. Gordon's was a tidy jewelry box, each piece displayed individually, uncrowded and locked up tight. Walker's was a double storefront. The long shelves that lined its walls were dusty and disheveled. Barry Walker claimed to know exactly where everything was, but he did not. Part of the fun of going to Walker's was hunting for the stuff of your dreams and finding a few things you hadn't thought about or even known existed but absolutely had to have the moment you discovered them.

Barry was on the right side of the big floor, the part of the store he used as his studio. In the off-season, he always painted like a frenzied squirrel. One canvas stood on his easel, while others, in various stages of completion, were scattered around that side of the shop, leaning against shelves and preventing patrons from getting near whatever goods were hidden behind them. Barry's paintings were angry abstract slashes in vibrant colors, the last thing most tourists wanted to purchase as a reminder of their mid-coast vacation. He would have done better with lobsters and lighthouses, which he was more than capable of painting, but Barry's only artistic interest was in pleasing himself.

He looked up when I stepped into the store. "Julia Snowden, as I live and breathe. What brings you here? Have a hankering to make your mom some new potholders?" He was a big, shambling man with long gray hair. He'd sported a day's growth of whiskers long before that look became fashionable. On the street, he was often mistaken for a homeless person, which didn't seem to bother him in the least.

I smiled at the tease. "That's Page's department now." Though Page had probably outgrown the task as well. "I wanted to talk to you about Mrs. Zelisko."

"Oh." Barry rubbed his brush with a cloth and then popped it into a jar of smelly liquid. "Darn shame."

"Yes, it is. I understand you were a client."

"A happy one. She was a lifesaver. I tried to keep up with the paperwork after Fran went to work at the home, but then it got ahead of me. I couldn't manage the quarterly filings with the IRS and the state. Five years ago, when Mrs. Zelisko joined our church and said she was available, I hired her on the spot. She started the next day. I'd gotten things in a terrible mess. It took her a while, but she untangled it."

Like Gordon's Jewelry, Walker's had started off as a mom-and-pop operation. But, in their case, revenue had dwindled during the recession and never completely returned. Fran Walker had taken a full-time job as an aid at a rehabilitation facility up the peninsula. It didn't surprise me that Barry had made a mess of their books.

"The police are looking for a next of kin. Did Mrs. Zelisko ever talk about her personal life?"

Barry shook his shaggy curls. "Never. Kept herself to herself, she did. I was always working when she was here, either tending to customers or painting. She respected my work and got down to hers. From time to time, she'd ask me about an expense or a particular sale we made, but that was it."

"Do you know her first name?" I asked him.

"Mrs.," he answered with a twinkle in his eye.

"Did you ever have any problem with the work she did? Anything at all?"

"In the beginning, it took us some time to get used to one another. I got a notice from the IRS that they hadn't received a quarterly payment. I asked Mrs. Zelisko about it. She said my payment had crossed in the mail with the notice and not to worry about it."

A tiny pit of concerned opened in my belly. "And it never happened again?"

"Never," Barry said. "She said I shouldn't be bothered by those types of concerns, so after that, we used her address for any IRS correspondence. State of Maine, too." He gestured toward the counter behind the cash register that functioned as his desk. It was piled high with mail, papers, catalogs, and art supplies. "It was better if the paperwork went to her anyway."

I thanked Barry and went on my way, taking a last look at the rambling, shambling mess as I closed the door.

Gleason's Hardware was a large store and a going concern, busy from early in the morning, when contractors arrived to pick up their materials, until late into the afternoon. It was an old-fashioned store where the employees knew the stock and were always happy to provide helpful advice on any project you might be tackling.

There was a big-box store in Brunswick, but it was forty minutes away, too far for a plumber, electrician, or carpenter working on the peninsula to travel in the morning before going to a job. Too far for a handy homeowner or an unhandy one who simply wanted a drain cover for the kitchen sink or new blinds for the bedroom. Almost every-one in town had an account at Gleason's.

Gleason's had been run by the same family for five gen-erations, and the only difference from then to now was that some of the goods had changed and you could no longer tie up your horse and buggy outside. The current proprietor was Al Gleason, a man in his mid-sixties who made even the work apron he and his employees wore look dapper. His son and daughter worked alongside him. Whenever I interacted with either of them, I had the im-pression they were thrilled to be in a position to carry on the family legacy.

The store was busy by Busman's Harbor off-season standards. I counted four employees and half a dozen cus-tomers wandering around in the big space. It took a while to find Al, but I kept asking. It turned out he was in his of-fice at the back of the main floor.

"Julia." He peered over his reading glasses and the paper he'd been studying. "Can I help you find some-thing?"

"I'd like to talk about Mrs. Zelisko."

"Ah." His smile disappeared. "I heard you were there when the body was found." He gestured to a stool in a corner of the office. "What can I tell you?"

"Anything at all. The police are looking for her next of kin. Did she ever speak about her family, or maybe a hus-band?"

"Never. We've only worked together for nine months or so. My brother-in-law Frank used to work here in the back office. He did all our bookkeeping. I hired Mrs. Zelisko when Frank retired."

I remembered Frank, a short, round man with a perma-nent squint. All he was missing was the green eyeshade.

"Once we got things set up," Al continued, "we didn't

speak often and then mostly over the phone. The information she needed—employee timesheets, sales, inventory records—went to her electronically. Occasionally, she'd walk over with a document I needed to sign, but that was it."

"Did you ever have any trouble with her work?" I was thinking about Barry Walker's notice from the IRS.

"Never," he said, and then reconsidered. "Nothing except maybe the occasional timing thing. Let me put it this way, I had a lot more trouble with my brother-in-law when he did our books."

"Did you know Mrs. Zelisko's first name?" I asked.

"No. She did me the honor of calling me mister. I returned the respect."

Chapter Nine

O ur ugly, modern town-hall-fire-station-police-head-quarters was on my route home from Gleason's. The parking lot out front was full. Several sullen teens, accompanied by a glowering parent or two, were entering or exiting. I couldn't imagine Lieutenant Binder and Sergeant Flynn were having a good day.

I decided to stop in and tell them what I'd learned, which admittedly wasn't much. Still, I thought every little bit might help. While some of the teens might turn out to be good witnesses, it was hard to believe one of the students at Busman's Harbor High had killed Mrs. Zelisko. What possible reason could they have? Unless the town was nurturing a budding serial killer.

As I'd guessed, Binder and Flynn were more than happy to squeeze me into their busy schedule. The civilian receptionist nodded that I should enter the multi-purpose room the detectives used as an office when they were in town. It was a cavernous space intended for large meetings and assemblies. The pair sat together at a plastic folding table on the far side of the room, Binder pecking at his laptop, Flynn bent over his notebook.

"Tough day so far?" I asked.

Binder wiped a hand from his chin up over his ski-slope

nose and onto his bald head. "Brutal. The kids are mostly useless. They were drunk, or making out, or otherwise distracted. And the parents are *so* mad. About the party, about the drinking, and about having to take time out during their Saturday to come down here and sit through this."

"Have you interviewed all the kids who were at the party?"

He shook his head. "We still don't know who most of them are."

"People are terrible at estimating crowd size, and kids are notoriously worse," Flynn said. "The texts have been flying around all day, and now it's like Woodstock. Every kid in town was there or is saying they were there. We're going to be looking for these kids and taking statements for days."

"We ask each kid who else was there. But they're with their parents. They don't want to get their friends in trouble." Binder leaned back in the folding chair. "So while 'everyone' was there, we have the names of precious few."

"And we can't quit until we've found everyone."

"Because one of them might be the killer," I said.

"Yes, that, and we need some reliable witnesses."

"I've been talking to some people around town," I started. "Trying to find out what I can about Mrs. Zelisko's personal life."

Flynn sat forward. "And did you?"

"Absolutely not," I said. "She was active in the Star of the Sea Catholic church, as you've already heard. It seems she found most of her clients there. I've talked to a few at small businesses on Main Street. They all speak very well of her but know nothing about her next of kin, her husband's name, or even her first name."

"Ah." Binder picked up an envelope from his desk. "Apparently, it's Helene. If the billing department at her cell phone provider is to be believed. But that's as far as we've gotten. No next of kin yet, though we have her laptop and phone in the lab back in Augusta, so I hope we'll know something soon."

"Barry Walker at Walker's Art Supplies told me he has all his financial mail from the IRS and the state of Maine sent directly to Mrs. Zelisko," I said. "Did you find a lot of client mail?"

Flynn looked at Binder and then spoke. "Not so far. The crime-scene folks are still at the apartment. I'll tell them to be on the lookout, though I imagine most of it is electronic nowadays. I'm sure either the crime-scene people or the tech people will find it."

"Barry is particularly disorganized. It may have been something she did only for him," I told them.

Binder looked at his laptop and then back at me, anxious, I could tell, to get on with their busy day.

"Was Mrs. Zelisko really wearing a wedding dress or a nun's habit when she died?" I asked.

"She was dressed in a white nightgown and wrapped in a white sheet," Binder answered, "when Pete Howland found her in the shed."

"Is the autopsy final? How did she die?" Sometimes they would tell me, depending on their mood and whether they thought I was helpful or in the way.

"Not final, but pretty definitive," Flynn said. "She was strangled. Though the body was pretty banged up. We should hear today whether that damage was pre- or postmortem."

Would all those kids have heard nothing? I wanted to ask, but both men had stood.

"Thanks so much for coming in, Julia," Binder said, slowly and deliberately.

"Anytime," I said. "See you soon."

*   *   *

I looked around the cubicle wall that separated the reception area from the bullpen that all six of Busman's Harbor's sworn officers shared to see if Jamie wanted to grab lunch. There was no one in the room. I wasn't surprised. The local police had no doubt been drafted to help with the murder investigation, in addition to their usual duties. I was headed out the glass door into the cold when Emmy Bailey and Vanessa hurried up the walk.

"Julia, I'm so glad we ran into you." Emmy sounded mega-relieved. "Can you be present while Vanessa has her interview? Livvie said you were there for Page, and it really helped her stay calm. You have so much more experience with this."

I looked at Vanessa to see if this intrusion was welcome. She gave a tight but encouraging smile.

"Sure," I said. "Let's do this."

We walked along the corridor toward the multi-purpose room. "It's not hard, and the detectives won't be mean like they sometimes are on TV," I told Vanessa. "You're a witness, not a suspect. Tell the truth and be as accurate as you can, and you'll be fine."

Vanessa's shoulders, which had been somewhere in the vicinity of her ears, dropped visibly.

"We're here to see Lieutenant Binder and Sergeant Flynn," I told the civilian receptionist. "Emmy and Vanessa Bailey."

She glared at me. "And Julia Snowden," I added.

"Just a moment."

Binder and Flynn stood as we came in. "Ms. Bailey, Vanessa." Binder squinted at me in a way I hoped signaled amusement. "Ms. Snowden."

We acknowledged who we were. Binder and Flynn shook hands with Emmy and a flustered Vanessa and indicated they should sit on the other side of the plastic table. I dragged a chair over from the opposite side of the room and sat, too.

"I hope you don't mind I asked Julia to come," Emmy said.

"The more the merrier." Then Binder went through the same speech with Vanessa that he had given the other girls. She sat, unmoving, and looked him right in the eye.

Her story was the same as Page's and Talia's. The sleepover, the invitation to the three girls, and then the party spiraling out of control. Unlike Page and Talia, who were taller, Vanessa was tiny. In a house crowded with older kids drinking, dancing, and horsing around, she'd been buffeted by the crowd and had ended up pushed into the kitchen. That's why she hadn't been with Page and Talia when they went upstairs looking for Mrs. Zelisko.

"Did you see anyone go out the back door?" Binder asked.

"Lots of people." Vanessa didn't hesitate. "People were going in and out the whole time. The backyard was, like, part of the party. Two boys were fighting out there, too."

Flynn read her a list of the kids they'd identified already and asked her if she'd seen them at the party. Vanessa answered, "yes," "no," or "I don't know who that is" in about equal measure.

Binder leaned forward, the fond father. "I get that you didn't know all the kids, but did you recognize them all, like from the hallways at school or around town?"

Vanessa shook her head. "I'm sure there were kids there from other schools." For the first time, she paused. "Maybe even, like, older kids. Not in school anymore."

Binder glanced at Flynn. "You think there might have been kids there who were beyond high school age?" It seemed like this was the first he was hearing this.

"Uh-huh. I think so. Some of them looked older."

What did that mean? Kids were terrible at judging ages.

"Did you recognize any of these older kids? Like maybe from working around town? Hannaford? The convenience store?" Binder's tone was still gentle.

Vanessa shook her head.

"Were they mostly boys or mostly girls, these older kids?" Flynn asked.

"Boys, I think. But I couldn't say definitely. There were a lot of people there."

"What happened after you ended up in the kitchen?" Binder asked.

"I heard Page calling from the living room. I couldn't reach her and Talia through all the people. They were in the archway between the living room and the front hall. I should have gone through the kitchen door into the hall, but I didn't know, so I-I . . ." Vanessa's speech slowed down, her confidence deserting her.

"It's okay," Binder said.

Emmy, who'd been silent and still during the interview to that point, laid a hand on her daughter's arm. "It's okay, sweetie. Nothing you say here is going to get you into trouble. More trouble," she amended.

"What happened then?" Binder brought her back to the point where she'd left off.

"Then Mrs. Zelisko fell down the stairs."

"She *fell* down the stairs?" Flynn attempted to clarify. Page had said "flew"; Talia had said "floated." Heaven knew what the other kids they'd spoken to had said, if they'd even been in the hallway when it happened.

"Not fell exactly," Vanessa said. "Everyone was screaming and shoving and running. When I got pushed into the hallway, Mrs. Zelisko was tumbling down that last set of stairs. Then she was at the bottom in a heap."

"What did she look like?" Binder asked.

"At the bottom of the stairs, she was all wrapped up like a mummy."

"What did you do then?" Binder kept the interview moving.

"I screamed and ran out like everyone else. I ran until I found Talia and Page at the end of the block. We decided to go back. There were still kids running in the other direction. Kids who probably weren't in the hallway when it happened. One kid knocked me over, right on my bum. It still hurts. But I got up and kept going."

"And when you got back to the house?" Binder prompted.

"The door was wide open."

"And Mrs. Zelisko?"

"Wasn't there." Vanessa's brave façade crumbled. Her voice quivered. Tears weren't far away.

"Did you see, at any time, either before you left the house or when you got back, anyone approach Mrs. Zelisko at the bottom of the stairs?" I could tell Binder was trying not to push her, but he needed to know.

"No!" Vanessa wailed. "I told you. I ran out as fast as I could. When I got back, she wasn't there. Nothing was there at all!" And then the tears did come.

Chapter Ten

Emmy and I had a hurried conference on the sidewalk in front of the police station. Page, Vanessa, and Talia were supposed to be grounded, but Emmy had to get to work. It seemed cruel to leave Vanessa, who was red-eyed and shaky, on her own. Page was still at Mom's house. I called Livvie, who'd gone home. She listened patiently and agreed the girls could be together now that they'd all had their interviews.

"Do you think they'll work each other up into a lather?" she asked me.

I glanced down the block, where Vanessa stood, awaiting a decision, her big, green eyes trained on me. "I don't know, but I think it's good for them to be together. They've had this traumatic experience. Not just Mrs. Zelisko, but the party. In some ways, they're the only ones who understand what they've been through."

"Okay," Livvie said. "I'll call Mom and let her know." She paused. "I'll call Blair Davies and invite Talia, too."

Emmy took off for Crowley's and her waitressing shift after giving Vanessa a fierce hug. "Promise you'll be good. I'll have my phone in my apron pocket, on vibrate. Here's yours." She reached into her bag and gave Vanessa her phone. With permission, Flynn had scrolled through it, as he had with Page and Talia's phones. "Call if you need me," Emmy said.

By the time Vanessa and I made it to Mom's house, Page was on the porch. Vanessa ran to her, and they hugged each other so hard Vanessa squealed. Across the street, the front door of the Snuggles Inn burst open. Talia flew out and ran across the street, pausing to look both ways, but otherwise her feet barely touched the ground. Page and Vanessa opened their arms to embrace her, and then all three of them went into the house.

Blair Davies came out the Snuggles front door and watched them go inside. She raised a hand in a dispirited wave and sat heavily in one of the two Adirondack chairs the sisters had left on the porch for late-season guests. I felt bad for her. It had been poor judgment to leave three girls with Mrs. Zelisko in charge, sure. But the Davies hadn't thrown the party or bought the beer. The whole thing had spiraled beyond their wildest imaginings. I crossed the street and sat down next to her.

Blair smiled, a small, tentative smile. Despite the events of the last day, we didn't really know each other.

"I appreciate your sister asking Talia to be with the other girls. She's been like a caged animal. I want to be mad at her. Inviting those friends over was clearly out of line. But all I can do is worry." As if to underline her concern, Blair rubbed her hands together, the universal sign for worry. And for being cold. Either was possible. "Howard's gone to work," she said. "Talia's with her friends. I don't know what to do with myself."

I tried to come up with ideas for her, though I suspected "helpful suggestions" wasn't what she was looking for. She was new in town, barred from her home, her tenant murdered. I opened my mouth to respond a few times but, on reviewing every possibility, thought better of it.

"Howard loves his work at the oceanographic lab," she said. "He's happy as a clam. Which is what he studies, by the way, clams. Talia had a hard summer. Seventh grade is a tough time to move a kid, particularly one who's lived in the same house and hung out with the same kids for almost her whole life. Particularly an only child. But now that she's settled into her new school and has found Page and Vanessa, she's much happier. Or she was until last night."

The cold seeped through the slats on the bottom of the chair. I would have loved to go home and get warm, but Blair clearly needed to talk.

"I'm the one who can't make the change," she continued. "The summer was great. Buy a big house in Maine and you'll discover friends you never knew you had. All summer people from our old hometown visited. And relatives we hadn't seen in years. The house was full and noisy. We went to the beach, took harbor cruises, toured the lighthouses and the botanical garden. We went out to your family's clambake once and loved it. Visiting friends gave us an excuse to learn about our new home."

The door opened, and Fee appeared on the porch, two folded blankets in contrasting plaids in her arms and Mackie at her heels. Wordlessly, she tucked a blanket around Blair and then one around me. I thanked her. Blair gave Fee a wan smile, and she and the dog disappeared back inside.

"It felt so strange not to go back to school. I miss it terribly," Blair said when the door to the inn had closed. "But I'll have to wait for someone to die to get a job around here." She stared into the middle distance. "Sometimes I would hear Mrs. Zelisko walking around in her apartment upstairs. She didn't have a separate entrance. She had to come and go through our house. Somehow that made it worse. I was alone all day, but I felt I had no privacy. She was there all the time. I couldn't forget her presence. It drove me crazy. That house, which I loved at first sight, has never felt like home. They say a house is not really your home until you've been alone in it. I never felt like I was."

"I've heard Mrs. Zelisko was deaf," I said. Maybe Blair had more privacy than she thought she did.

Blair shook her head. "Not deaf. A little hard of hearing. Sometimes I would call to her from across a room, and if she wasn't looking in my direction, she wouldn't hear me. And she kept her phone and TV up *loud*. But in conversation, face-to-face, she understood every word you said."

Blair shifted in her chair and drew the blanket tighter around her. "I wanted to tell Mrs. Zelisko to leave. I begged Howard. But he liked the money, even though we didn't need it. Our house in Massachusetts sold for way more than we paid here. And"—she paused—"he was concerned about where she would live."

Howard wasn't wrong. At this time of year, there would be plenty of places for Mrs. Zelisko to move, even at the rent I suspected she paid for a third-floor apartment without exterior access. But come June, she might well be out of luck. Every space would be rented to tourists for top dollar or used to house summer help.

"I'm glad Howard disagreed with me and we never asked her to move. I'm ashamed of myself for being so selfish." Blair put her head in her hands. "I'm sorry I wasn't nicer to Mrs. Zelisko. Maybe we could have been friends."

Mrs. Zelisko apparently hadn't had friends. Not in the way Blair meant. But it didn't seem like the right time to point that out.

I sat with Blair Davies for a long time, comfy under the

Snuggles Inn blanket. I steered the conversation away from everything Mrs. Zelisko. I prattled on about all the fun things the town had planned for the rest of the season. The festival of Christmas trees. The lights at the botanical garden. The day we all got up at dawn to Christmas-shop in our pajamas.

Blair allowed herself to be jollied along. I could tell it was an effort to climb out of her gloom, but she made it, and we ended up laughing a lot. The sun grew dimmer. We wouldn't revert to standard time until that night, but on the eastern edge of the time zone, dark came early even before daylight saving time ended.

Eventually, it was too cold to sit even with the blankets. We stood and folded them, working together. Then we hugged. She went inside, and I trudged home to my apartment.

Chapter Eleven

It had been six months, but I still wasn't used to returning to an empty house. It wasn't so much that it was empty. Chris worked long hours during the season, like I did, and I often got home first. It was more that I hadn't gotten used to coming home to a house where nothing had been moved unless I moved it. Nothing had been eaten unless I ate it. The bed hadn't been made unless I made it. No wet towels in the bathroom. No size-eleven work boots piled by the stairs. When Mrs. Zelisko had been alive, Blair Davies had longed for an empty house. Increasingly, I longed for a full one.

My mother had offered Le Roi, our Maine Coon cat, to keep me company. He had belonged to the old caretakers on Morrow Island. When they left, I took him, but he'd regarded Chris as an interloper, and a battle of wills ensued. Which is to say Le Roi had done everything he was capable of to get rid of Chris, including, memorably, spilling my shampoo, spreading it all over the bathroom floor and then jumping repeatedly from the headboard onto Chris's head until he got out of bed, wandered into the bathroom, and nearly killed himself on the slippery floor. Attempted murder.

Finally, when Chris was unable to put his boots on in

the morning without checking inside them, Le Roi had been removed to my mother's. It was an arrangement that suited all of us. I still got to see him every day when I went to work in the Snowden Family Clambake office on the second floor of my mother's house. In the summer, Le Roi lived with my sister on Morrow Island, where he wandered freely and begged for clams and pieces of lobster from any clambake customer with a soft heart.

I'd refused Mom's offer to return him. I could tell Le Roi loved it at her house and she loved having him. I didn't have the heart.

I grabbed my laptop, sat down on my beat-up old couch, with its view out the window to dusk settling over the back harbor, and searched for any sign of Mrs. Zelisko on the web. There was no website for her business and nothing about her online. She wasn't even in the photo of the Star of the Sea auction committee that appeared after their successful fundraiser year after year.

I snapped the laptop shut. What did I think I was doing? The police would have done this and more. But I felt so deeply curious about, and sorry for, Helene Zelisko. How did someone end up so isolated that even her "friends" at church didn't know her first name?

It wasn't like I was a social butterfly or given to deeply intimate relationships beyond my family and, formerly, my boyfriend. But this woman who lived alone, worked alone . . . It seemed to be a choice, but I couldn't help but wonder, was she hiding from someone? Someone who had found her and killed her?

My stomach rumbled. I hadn't eaten lunch. In the tiny kitchen alcove of the studio, I opened the refrigerator door. Light spilled onto the dark linoleum floor. A can of bacon fat, a limp bunch of celery, and a piece of cheddar cheese with mold on all sides stared back at me.

Chris was a wonderful cook, and when we'd run the dinner restaurant together, I'd never had to worry about my next meal. Or what to do with my time. I was busy every moment of every day, and I loved it.

The long winter loomed. The clambake business would be wound up when I closed the books on the season and divided the profits among Mom, Sonny and Livvie, Quentin Tupper, our silent investor, and me.

Hannaford closed at six o'clock in the off-season. If I was going to eat, I had to shop. I grabbed my keys and quilted vest and headed down the stairs. I walked through the dark restaurant to the back door and was surprised to see Page in the glow from the outside light, huddled in a sweatshirt that couldn't be keeping her warm enough.

"Page! You scared me. You shouldn't be out alone at night." I didn't elaborate. Murderer on the loose, Page a potential witness. But she understood what I meant. "Where are Vanessa and Talia?"

"I left them at Grammy's." She didn't wait for me but led me back to my own apartment.

"What's the matter?" She was pale and shaking. My stomach clenched as I wondered, after almost twenty-four hours of awful revelations, what could be upsetting her so much.

"I remembered something. Something I didn't tell the police."

I moved toward her. "That's okay, honey. Lieutenant Binder and Sergeant Flynn won't be mad. We'll go in the morning, and you can explain that you forgot."

"It's important." She paused. "And it's bad."

I waited for her to work up her nerve.

"Mr. Davies came home during the party. I saw him."

Now I was alarmed. "Howard Davies was at the house while the party was going on?"

"Yes." She squeaked out her answer. Then she found her voice. "I saw him going up the stairs from the first to the second floor. The hallway and staircase were filled with kids, and I thought it was so weird he didn't say anything. I called out to him, but it was so noisy. And then after it all happened, with the ghost of Mrs. Zelisko flying down from the ceiling and the police coming, it went right out of my head, and I've only just thought of it."

"What time was this?"

"I can't remember. The party was full-on, though."

"Was it before or after you and Talia went to look for Mrs. Zelisko?"

"Before." Her voice was stronger. "I'm sure before. Like, fifteen minutes before."

"If he was climbing the stairs, was his back to you?"

"Yes."

"Did you see his face?"

"No."

"Then why do you think it was him?"

"It looked like him from the back. And he had on the same clothes he was wearing when he left for his work party. Dad clothes, not kid clothes."

"Dad clothes?" I wasn't sure what Page thought that meant.

"A navy-blue sweater and those pants. Those tan pants."

"You mean khakis?"

"Like Quentin wears." She was losing patience with me. Quentin Tupper, the silent investor in the Snowden Family Clambake, was probably the only man Page knew who wore khakis. Kids didn't wear them, unless it was part of a school uniform or under duress.

"Are you sure it was Mr. Davies?" I asked.

"No." And then she burst into tears.

* * *

I called Flynn to find out if the detectives were still in town. He and Binder were finishing dinner at Crowley's. They would meet us at the police station in fifteen minutes. I called Livvie to tell her what was going on. Then I called Mom to tell her Page was with me. We agreed she should keep Vanessa with her since Emmy was at work, but she should send Talia back to the Snuggles.

I hoped the walk to the police station would calm Page down, but she fretted the whole way. "What if it wasn't Mr. Davies? I could get him in so much trouble. I'm not sure."

"Lieutenant Binder and Sergeant Flynn are good at their jobs," I told her. "They'll talk to Mr. Davies. They'll interview the other guests who were at the work party to find out if he left at any time. They won't charge him with murder on your say so."

She stopped walking. "Maybe I shouldn't tell them. Won't Mr. Davies be so mad?"

"No. Mr. Davies wants to get to the bottom of this as much as anyone. He'll be happy to clear this up with the police." *Unless he was the murderer.* My voice was firm, though I wasn't one hundred percent sure of what I was saying. I didn't know Howard Davies from a hole in the wall. "Maybe he's already told the detectives he went home during the party. We don't know everything people have told them."

Page looked doubtful but started walking again.

Binder and Flynn did their best to make Page comfortable, even though the high ceiling and meeting-room-sized space of the multi-purpose room was intimidating. Responding to Binder's patient questions, she told the story to them exactly as she had told it to me. She was clear that she couldn't identify Howard Davies, though, "It really looked like him from the back. I was sure it was him at the time. He was wearing the same clothes."

When they were done, Binder took Page to the adjacent firehouse to find a treat in the firefighters' always well-stocked kitchen.

"What do you think?" I asked Flynn, as we stood in the dark hall waiting for them to return.

"She saw someone she thought was him, for sure. Davies is a young-looking guy, but he's in his early fifties. Would he look like a teenager from behind?"

"Probably not," I said. "Which means . . . ?"

"Which means if it wasn't Davies, there was a grown man mixed in among the teenagers at that party," Flynn concluded.

"Exactly what I was thinking. Have any of the other kids mentioned an adult male in the house?"

Flynn shook his head. "No. But they've been terrible witnesses. No one saw anything until Mrs. Zelisko flew through the air. Which every one of them claims they saw, by the way, even though not all of them were in the front hall when it happened."

"So she flew a few laps around the house and yard?"

He laughed. "So we've been told."

Binder and Page returned, then she and I walked back to Mom's. By the time we got there, the detectives' unmarked car was parked across the street, and Binder and Flynn were on the Snuggles Inn porch, asking to speak to Howard Davies.

Chapter Twelve

I woke up early, woolly-headed and confused. Then I re-alized the time had "fallen back" and my phone and laptop clocks had reset themselves overnight. The weather was still gray. I was tempted to stay in bed.

From downstairs at Gus's came the sounds of conversations, the scrape of the spatula across the grill, and the rattle of dishes being dumped into Gus's ancient dishwasher. Gus usually had three distinct crowds on Sunday. The before-church crowd, the no-church crowd, and the after-church crowd. I could tell by the amount of car-door slamming and yelling going on in the parking lot that other people were as messed up by the time change as I was.

I decided to see what I could discover about Howard Davies on the web. I found exactly what I would have expected before Page had revealed what she had seen. There was an announcement in our local paper about Howard's new job at the oceanographic lab. Before that, in Med-view, Massachusetts, Howard had played in a lot of tennis tournaments at a local club. Blair taught school, as she'd said. Talia was frequently on the honor roll at her old middle school and had had a lead in the school play.

A perfectly normal family. But how many normal families end up with a body in their shed?

I was about to give up when my cell phone buzzed. I didn't immediately recognize the number.

"Julia? Barry Walker." He was gasping, like it was hard to breathe.

"Barry, what is it?"

The sound of a deep inhalation followed by the slow release of breath traveled through my phone. "When we were talking yesterday, I got to worrying about my taxes. I left a message for the police that I needed my documents, but no one called me back. So this morning, I called the IRS. They have an emergency number, and I thought this was an emergency. I was on hold forever, but then an agent came on the line. He told me my federal taxes haven't been filed for years! Since the Zelisko woman took over my account. He couldn't tell me what I owed, of course, since he didn't have any of the paperwork, but he said the interest and penalties could really be piling up. I could owe more than the business is worth, even if I sold my building!"

The hysterical edge had crept back into his voice. I could understand why.

"You need to tell the state police about this," I said.

"*Why*?" Barry yelled through the phone. "If I tell them, they'll think I murdered her! If she wasn't dead, I'd be contemplating it right now."

"If Mrs. Zelisko was mismanaging your account, that's important information."

"Mismanaging? She wasn't failing to pay the taxes, like some kind of mistake or neglect. She was taking money from me, telling me she paid the taxes and then not paying them. She was stealing!"

Walker's always seemed to be barely hanging on. How much could Barry owe? It seemed more likely Mrs. Zelisko had been lying to him about the amounts and then pocketing the money. Even then, it couldn't be a lot of money, hardly worth risking your reputation for. Unless she was doing it to a lot of clients.

"I'm coming over," I said. "Give me half an hour."

But the time I opened the door of Walker's Art Supplies and Frame Shop, Al Gleason was already there, leaning against the high counter Barry used to cut the mats for his picture frames. Al's arms were crossed over his chest, and he was listening to an agitated Barry Walker.

Mr. Gordon scurried in behind me.

Al Gleason unfolded his arms and turned to me. "You were right on in what you guessed, Julia. My employees' withholding hasn't been paid in four months. Neither have their insurance premiums. I'd been getting notices, lots of them from the insurance company, but Mrs. Zelisko had changed the contact info, even the phone number. She was getting the calls about our non-payment."

"You were right about our store, too," Mr. Gordon said. "Sales tax hasn't been paid in months, even through the busy season." Christmas and Valentine's kept Gordon's Jewelry afloat in the winter, but the busy season was tourist season."

"Ugh," Mr. Gleason said sympathetically. "I'm guessing all that money isn't sitting in your bank account."

Mr. Gordon shook his head. "Not one penny of it. The money has disappeared."

"Maybe not." They all looked at me. "She's been stealing from Barry for five years." I didn't add that he was the most disorganized, the most trusting, and the most susceptible of the three of them. "I'm guessing she's been stealing long-term from others. I'd love to get a look at the books for the Star of the Sea auction. But if she started stealing from the hardware store and the jewelry store in the last four months, that means something has changed. Maybe she thought she was on the verge of being caught and she was planning to run somewhere. Or looking for a big hit so she could retire someplace warm. Maybe the police will find some of the money. It's not like she spent it on an extravagant lifestyle."

"Unless she had a gambling problem." Mr. Gordon looked miserable.

"If the money doesn't turn up during the police investigation, because they find out she was murdered for another reason, we can hire a forensic accountant to track it down," Al Gleason said.

I turned to Barry. "You see now that you have to talk to the police, right? There's safety in numbers. Lieutenant Binder and Sergeant Flynn won't suspect you specifically, because Mrs. Zelisko robbed a lot of people. More than the three of you in this room, I'm certain."

"Okay, okay," Barry said. "I agree. We talk to the police."

Chapter Thirteen

I called Binder and Flynn, who came right over. As the shop owners told the cops what they knew, I could see Flynn's eyes grow bigger. There must be dozens of people in town who had a motive to kill Mrs. Zelisko.

Binder asked the three men to come to the station to give formal statements after they closed up their shops for the day. Gleason had employees at the hardware store, who could cover him, so he said he'd be over in the afternoon. Mr. Gordon and Barry Walker would come by later.

Out on the sidewalk, Binder, Flynn and I stood in a tight circle against the wind, processing what we'd heard.

"This case gets weirder and weirder," Flynn said.

"And more and more complicated," Binder agreed. "By the way," he looked at me, "Howard Davies didn't leave his work party. It's not just his wife who vouches for him; we easily located plenty of witnesses. There were two cars in the host's driveway parked behind the Davies' car. The house where the party was is way out in East Busman's Village, too far to walk and make it back without his absence being noticed. No one can see how he could possibly have gotten home, even if he'd left."

Flynn stepped away from us to make a phone call.

Binder looked at me. "The crime-scene techs are finished with the Davies' house. We're about to let the family move back in. Tom and I are going over for a last look while it's empty. Want to come?"

Flynn ended his call, and both men started down the sidewalk toward the Davies' house without waiting for my answer. They knew what it would be.

We stood on the big front porch while Flynn turned the key in the lock. Inside, the house was the same temperature as outside. If the Davies did that thing of not turning on the heat until November 1, it hadn't been on when they left Halloween night, and it still wasn't.

I knew it wasn't the job of the crime-scene techs to clean the house, but I was unprepared for the mess we found when we walked in. It felt like time had stopped and the party had just ended. It had only been two days earlier, yet it felt like weeks. This disheveled house with the Halloween decorations was from another time. It was terrible that the Davies had to come home to this.

We walked into the chilly hallway, then through the kitchen, which smelled so strongly of dried beer I had to hold my breath, and out into the yard. Flynn paced off the number of steps from the back stairs to the shed, coming up with twenty both times he did it.

Back inside, I followed the detectives as they roamed the first floor. The party had obviously raged principally in the kitchen and family room. The dining room was in less disarray, though there were overturned bottles and cans on the surface of the cherry dining table. The living room was in the best shape.

From there, we went back into the big entrance hallway. A glance around and then up to the ceiling confirmed my impressions of two days earlier. It was a towering space, made more dramatic by the staircase that ringed it and the large brass chandelier that hung down from the ceiling high above.

I stood on the second-story balcony while the detectives looked around the family bedrooms. I wasn't an officer of the law, so it felt like it would be a terrible invasion of the family's privacy for me to go in.

Then we climbed the stairs to Mrs. Zelisko's apartment. Evidence of the police search was all around us. In the sitting room, the top of the desk had been cleared, and the empty drawers hung open. The seat cushions of the love seat and easy chair were askew. In the tiny kitchen, the cupboard and all four drawers were empty, their contents left on the small table and the only chair, and in piles on the floor.

In the bedroom, the covers had been removed from the bed and left in a heap on top of the twin mattress. The bureau drawers hung open, Mrs. Zelisko's white underthings left in plain sight. I thought that, little as I knew her, Mrs. Zelisko would have been mortified. The small closet door was open. Inside hung five black dresses, two black jackets, and two black cardigans.

"Notice anything strange about this place?" Flynn asked me.

"There's nothing personal," I answered. The blank walls held no artwork or photos, and no empty hooks or light spots to indicate there had been any. "Were there any family photos on the tables or shelves that maybe your guys took?"

Flynn shook his head. "Zero."

"It's strange, because she spent so much time here," I said. "She worked at home, except at the rare times she went to her clients' businesses. Blair Davies said she heard Mrs. Zelisko moving around up here all day. She almost never went out except for errands and to services and meetings at the Star of the Sea."

"The papers we took from the desk and the laptop will help untangle some of this mess with her clients, but there was nothing personal there, either," Binder said.

"Weird," I said.

"And unhelpful," Binder added.

The last place we looked was the bathroom. "Mrs. Zelisko and her killer were hiding in here when Page and Talia came to look for her," I said.

"Yes, that's what we think, too," Flynn confirmed.

"Was she alive or dead at that point? Was she killed here or in some other room?"

Flynn shrugged. "Not clear."

"Why was she in her nightgown?" Binder wondered. "And why didn't she go downstairs when she heard all the noise?"

"She was hard of hearing," I told him. "I've heard differing accounts about how deaf she was." I peered through the doorway. "This bathroom looks so ordinary." The room was narrow and white. A clawfoot tub stood against one long wall. It had been fitted with a shower and a shower curtain holder. "Did you guys take the shower curtain?"

Binder walked into the room, looked around, and exited quickly. "We have it."

We returned to the landing at the top of the stairs. It was so small the three of us could barely fit on it together. The railing height was barely up to my hip, and I'm short. It wouldn't be code in a modern house. I had an uncomfortable feeling as I looked over the edge. However she'd gone down—flew, floated, or fell—Mrs. Zelisko had a long trip.

Something small and fluttery on the elaborate chandelier far below caught my eye. "Wait, what's that?" Then more excited, I pointed. "I think I know what happened." I gave one little jump, then immediately stopped. The landing was precarious enough without any sudden moves.

I took a deep breath and rolled out a scenario. "Mrs. Zelisko is dead when the girls come upstairs. The killer hears them and drags the corpse into the bathroom. Then he's trapped. He has to get out of the house, and he decides he has to get Mrs. Zelisko out, too."

"Why?" Binder asked. "Why not sneak out himself and leave her for the Davies to find?"

"He must think the girls will be back, possibly at any moment. He can't risk them finding her while he's still making his escape."

"He's not a practiced killer," Flynn surmised. "He's panicking."

"He grabs the top sheet off her bed and ties it around her," I said. "He's going to pretend she's a ghost, a drunk ghost, and carry her out."

"He Weekend-at-Bernie's her!" The look on Binder's face was priceless.

"Except it doesn't go so well. She's small, but probably heavier and certainly more awkward to carry than he assumes," I continued.

Flynn got into the spirit of it. "He trips or loses hold of her, and she goes over the railing."

"And down into the front hall." Binder was buying it, or at least admitting the possibility.

"Not quite," I said. "She's hurtling down. Any kid who happens to be looking up, maybe talking to someone on the stairs above them, is going to see her and start screaming. Soon they're all screaming and running out the door. But Mrs. Zelisko doesn't make it to the floor. She catches on the chandelier, and the momentum swings her back and forth across the room. She falls off onto the stairs from the second to the first floor. She tumbles down from there, rolling the sheet back around her, and ends up on the landing. Depending on when a kid looks, she flies, floats, or falls."

"In a swirl of white fabric," Binder said.

"The kids have run off." Flynn continued the story. "The killer walks down the stairs, picks up the body, goes out the back door, and sticks her in the shed. He's bought a lot of time. The local cops don't find the body until after ten-fifteen. He could have been home by then."

"Or in a bar creating alibis," Binder said.

"Or off the peninsula and halfway to Route 95, if he wasn't from around here," I said.

"Wasn't from around here?" Flynn was surprised. "Based on our conversation with your shop-owner friends, there were probably a dozen people in town who may have wanted her dead. She couldn't cover her tracks forever."

We finally left the little landing and trooped down the stairs. "Something changed," I said. "Four months ago, she went from skimming a little extra from Barry Walker, a perfect mark, and probably some others like him, to embezzling sales tax from Mr. Gordon and employee withholding and insurance premiums from Gleason's. That was a much more dangerous game. She was bound to get caught."

"A much more lucrative game, too," Flynn said.

Binder stated the obvious conclusion. "She was preparing to run."

"Yes." We were downstairs in the hallway by then. "The question is, what changed four months ago?"

"The Davies moved to town," Flynn answered.

"The Davies moved to town, and Mrs. Zelisko no

longer felt safe," Binder said. "The question is, why? We need to talk to them again."

Flynn fetched a ladder from the shed. He put gloves on, climbed up, and pulled the piece of fabric I'd spotted from the chandelier.

"Sheet fabric?" Binder asked from the ground.

"Uh-huh." Flynn climbed down.

"We need to get it to the lab to see if it matches the sheet the body was wrapped in, but I think Julia's solved a piece of the puzzle." Binder smiled at me. "Thank you."

Chapter Fourteen

I walked with Binder and Flynn back to the police station. As they were going in, Jamie came out.

"Julia! Great to see you. Want to have lunch?" He smiled like he was genuinely excited by the prospect.

"Sure. Do you have time?" Earlier in the fall, we had gone to lunch occasionally. I suspected Mom put him up to it, as a part of some "Dine with Poor Lonely Julia" program.

"I have to eat," he answered. "We're still rounding up kids who either were definitely at or were rumored to be at the party. And then, an hour ago, we got a list of Mrs. Zelisko's bookkeeping clients. We're calling all of them to set up meetings as well. I'm afraid they're getting some not great news."

"I heard."

He laughed. "I figured."

We walked toward Gus's, though we hadn't discussed where to eat. We entered via the front door, something I almost never did, and climbed down the stairs into the big room, where the open kitchen, counter and stools, and candlepin bowling lane were. Beyond it was the dining room with its booths, fake leather banquettes, and stunning views of the back harbor.

The restaurant was moderately busy with the Sunday lunch crowd, and I hurried through to an empty booth. I still felt really weird at Gus's. It wasn't like I was afraid of

running into Chris. When you break up with someone in a
town this small, you know you're going to run into them.
Frequently. It was that the restaurant held so many memories. Chris and I had run the dinner restaurant there and
eaten oh-so-many breakfasts. It was the place where we'd
re-met when I'd moved back to town. The memories were
in every corner of the space, and I couldn't shake them off.

"Howdy, stranger." Gus approached, order pad at the
ready. No one in town except his wife knew how old he
was, but he opened at the restaurant at five in the morning
to feed the fishermen and stayed open until after three,
seven days a week, eleven months a year.

"I live upstairs," I pointed out.

"I give you your privacy." He sounded indignant. Gus
did a great indignant. "You've been scarce down here."

"Busy," I said, which was a total lie. Without the dinner
restaurant to run in the off-season, I wasn't busy enough.

"What'll you have?"

For lunch, Gus serves Maine hot dogs, which are bright
red for some reason, hamburgers, grilled cheese, BLTs, and
PB&J. In other words, things you could make for yourself
at home. He accompanies them with the world's best
French fries, and you can't do that at home.

"BLT," I said.

"Burger." Jamie didn't add rare, medium, or well-done.
He was too experienced a diner to attempt to tell Gus how
to cook a burger. You got 'em the way he made 'em, and
you didn't complain.

When Gus left, I looked around to make sure we wouldn't
be heard. Then I leaned toward Jamie. "I don't get it. I mean,
you know how Mrs. Zelisko lived. Third floor walk-up, no
car, five black dresses, and a couple of sweaters. There is no
way she spent the money she'd been conning people out of all
these years."

"For some thieves, the thrill is in the stealing," he said. "Not in spending the money. Not in the money at all."

I shook my head. "What I don't get is how it happened. She'd just gotten to town when Barry Walker hired her. Barry's disorganized, but she was handling his money. Why didn't he check her references?"

"The Star of the Sea Catholic church," Jamie answered. "She met people there, and they trusted her. Barry Walker was the perfect early mark. He was desperate for help. He didn't ask a lot of questions. With each new client, it got easier to get the next one. These people all knew one another. Each of them expected that *someone* had done the due diligence regarding references and such. If no one actually had, how would they know? After a while, it was embarrassing to ask."

"That's disgusting."

"Yup. It's called affinity fraud. The original Ponzi's victims were Italian-Americans from his own community. Bernie Madoff devasted Jewish foundations and charities. It's how con artists gain trust. We get notices at the station all the time. Scam going through the evangelical community. Someone pitching fraudulent investments at Elk's clubs. It's how it's done."

Gus arrived with our food, and the conversation turned to more cheerful topics. Jamie was going to Florida to see his parents for Thanksgiving. We made a plan to maybe see a movie sometime.

Gus came back, and we paid him in cash, the only tender he accepted as legal.

"Headed upstairs?" Jamie asked as he rose to leave.

"No. I'm going to Mom's. Page is still there. But before I do, I have an errand to run."

Gus waved as we walked back through the front room. "Don't be such a stranger."

Chapter Fifteen

On my way to Mom's, I stopped at our neighbors, the Goldsmiths. "Harley graduated from high school last year, right?" I asked June Goldsmith after we said hello. She'd been surprised to find me on her porch.

"She did. You would have been invited to the party, but I knew you'd be working out on Morrow Island."

I swiped with my hand to let her know not to stress about it. "Was Harley at that big party here in town on Halloween?"

"The one where Mrs. Zelisko was murdered? No, thank goodness. Harley's at UMaine Portland. She decided to stay on campus for Halloween weekend." June looked at me expectantly, wondering where the conversation was going.

"Did Harley leave her yearbook home, do you know? Could I borrow it overnight?"

Whatever June Goldsmith had expected me to say, that wasn't it. "I'll quickly check her room."

She returned within minutes with the book, bound in "Busman's High blue" faux leather, and handed it to me.

"I'll get it right back to you," I said.

"No hurry. I don't expect Harley home until Thanksgiving."

When I got to Mom's house, Page was at the kitchen table, textbook open, worksheet in front of her. School again tomorrow.

I sat down next to her. "Do you have a lot to do?"

She bit the eraser on her pencil. "Almost done." There was a sheet of math problems in front of her, and she appeared to have a couple left.

"Great. When you're finished, come find me."

Mom was in the sitting room off her bedroom, watching Sunday programming on PBS. "Julia, what are you doing here?"

"How come you still have Page?"

"She's upset. Sonny and Livvie both have work tomorrow. It's hectic in their house in the mornings. They thought it might be better if Page had some quiet time here and a little space before she had to go to school and see all those kids. There's bound to be a lot of chatter about the party and the murder. Livvie dropped clothes and her schoolwork off earlier. "

I thought about mornings at Livvie's house. Sonny would be long gone, off to help his father pull his lobster traps. Lobsters were scarce in November, and the weather would make work on the boat miserable, but the price the co-op paid was commensurately higher. Livvie would have her hands full getting Jack dressed and delivered to daycare before she went to her job at the pottery studio. She wouldn't have time to give extra attention to Page.

Livvie's busy life contrasted starkly with my own. Empty apartment. No restaurant to run. Empty. Dark. Still. What was I doing with my life?

"You didn't answer my question." Mom brought me back into the moment. "What are you doing here? You know you're always welcome, but you weren't expected."

There was never any point in trying to tiptoe around my

mom. "The police still haven't identified all the kids who were at the party. I got a yearbook from June Goldsmith. I want to go through it with Page to see if she recognizes any of the photos as people who were there."

My mother pursed her lips and squinted at me. "Is that a good idea? I'm supposed to be letting Page settle down and get ready for the week."

"I think it is!" I left the room before she could object further.

Page and I met in her room, behind a closed door. I wasn't doing anything wrong, and Page seemed a whole lot happier about this activity than doing her homework, but I didn't want my mother to feel the need to interrupt.

I explained to Page that she hadn't seen Howard Davies at the party. "But," I said, "you did see someone. Someone dressed like they were older going up the stairs not long before you and Talia went to look for Mrs. Zelisko. I thought we could look through this yearbook to see if it was someone who's already graduated. Did you see his face at all?"

"I'm not sure. I may have seen it earlier, you know, before I saw his back going up the stairs."

We went slowly through the pages of the yearbook containing the senior photos. Page shook her head, no, no, no, with each turn of the page. It didn't mean none of the kids had been at the party. It only meant she didn't recognize them, but it didn't represent progress. We looked at the rest of the book, including the photos of teams, clubs, performances. Page did recognize lots of those students and said some of them had been at the party. But in every case she'd already given the kid's name to Binder and Flynn.

When we closed the book, I sighed.

"Don't be sad, Aunt Julia," Page said. "Even if the man I saw wasn't Mr. Davies, he was a grown-up. He isn't going to be in this yearbook." Her face brightened, "Let's see if we can find anyone on my Instagram."

"Do you have your phone?" I was surprised.

"No." She rolled her eyes. "But I can sign onto my account from yours."

"Didn't Flynn ask you go through your social media on that first morning?"

"Yes, but I didn't know what I was looking for."

Page expertly signed onto her Instagram account from my phone and scrolled back in her feed to Friday night. The photos from her friends, taken in the thick of the action, were even more horrible than their leftover mess had caused me to imagine. Kids in gory, scary-looking costumes swilled from big liquor bottles, no doubt the ones stolen from the Davies. They danced in the dining room, made out in the corners, and threw up on the lawn.

There were no photos of the actual moment Mrs. Zelisko fell from above. It must have happened too fast. The kids had been stunned, and then they'd run.

Lots of the photos were pretty dark. It was hard to make out faces. Squeezed in next to Page, I squinted at the screen, looking for a man in a navy sweater and khakis.

Then finally, she stopped scrolling. "Look!" She pointed to the edge of an image on her phone. "It's him!"

"How can you tell?" Only about a quarter of the figure was visible. The sliver of his face we could see was in profile. His hair was the same medium brown as Howard Davies's. The man in the photo gestured into the frame with a hand and an arm covered in a navy-blue sweater. One long khaki pant leg ended in a blue sock and brown loafer. Definitely not a kid, unless he'd come in costume as his father. I peered at what I could see of the man's face. He did look older, out of his teens. But it was hard to be sure with so little visible.

We scrolled quickly after that, looking for better photos of the same man. We switched to the profile page of the girl who had taken the original photo. Nothing turned up anywhere.

"We need to tell Lieutenant Binder and Sergeant Flynn about this," I told Page. "Maybe this girl has more photos on her phone she didn't upload."

"Okay." Page was losing steam.

"Text the photo to me along with the name of the girl who took the picture, and I'll send the info along to the detectives. They'll probably want to talk to you again."

"Sure."

Page did as I asked, but seemed deflated. Whether she was worried about about talking to the detectives again or school in the morning, I couldn't tell. I forwarded the text with a brief explanation to Binder and Flynn.

"I'm sorry all this happened," I said.

Page looked even more miserable. "It was our fault. If we hadn't texted those other girls . . . If there hadn't been a party . . ."

"You didn't murder Mrs. Zelisko." I was firm.

"But if we hadn't—"

"Aw, honey." I hugged her. "I don't know what happened to Mrs. Zelisko, but it's clearer and clearer she wasn't murdered by a kid at that party."

Page sniffled and nodded into my shoulder. I hoped Binder and Flynn would get back to me soon. We needed to get this case solved.

Chapter Sixteen

I didn't hear back from the detectives that night, but they were at Gus's restaurant when I came down from my apartment the next morning. For months, I'd been scuttling in and out through the back door, but in the spirit of desensitizing myself to the restaurant, I walked boldly through it.

Gus, unusual for a restaurateur, was not a fan of out-of-towners. But the state-police detectives had eaten there frequently enough that they'd wormed their way into his good graces, such as they were.

Binder called to me. "Julia, join us!" They already had their food in front of them, Binder, a western omelet, Flynn, as always, two soft-boiled eggs. Gus had also provided Flynn with two pieces of heavily buttered white toast. Flynn wouldn't eat it, but it came with the order, and Gus duly brought it. Flynn's abstemious ways bugged Gus as much as they bugged Vee Snugg. The detectives would probably be finished before I got served, but I sat down anyway.

"Thanks for the photo," Binder said. He pulled his phone from his jacket pocket and opened my text. He put on his reading glasses and squinted. "Not much to go on, but more than we had before."

Flynn also had his phone out. "Unknown victim, unknown suspect. This case gets better and better."

"We have an expert going through Mrs. Zelisko's laptop, trying to figure out how much she stole, who she stole it from, and how she did it," Binder said. "We sent the fabric we took from the chandelier to the lab. And we described what might have happened to the medical examiner. She's going to let us know if the injuries to the body are consistent with that scenario. We're making progress, but it feels like we're not."

"Too many possibilities," Flynn said. "Was it someone Zelisko stole from here in town, or maybe in her past life? But since we don't know anything about her past life, we don't know who that might have been. And then there's this guy." Flynn tapped the photo on his phone.

"Page says she's never seen him before, if that helps," I offered.

"It would have been more helpful if she had," Flynn groused.

After breakfast, I went back upstairs to my apartment. Flynn was right. We didn't know who Mrs. Zelisko was. And we didn't know where she'd come from.

Why had she stepped up the stealing four months ago? The answer had to be that the Davies had arrived in town and become her landlords. What about the Davies had scared her to the point that she started planning to run, if that was what she was doing? Howard worked at the oceanographic lab. Blair was an elementary school teacher. Talia was thirteen. They were the opposite of scary.

The most logical answer was it had something to do not with who the Davies were, but where they came from.

I got out my laptop and settled onto my couch for a good search. Luckily, Medview, Massachusetts, had a local paper, and the local paper had put ten years of its archives online. That seemed like a fruitful avenue. I paid a little money, and I was in.

First, I tried searching for "Zelisko," though that was almost certainly not her name. "Embezzled" got me an article about a local manufacturing company whose treasurer had disappeared with millions. A compelling story, but not the one I was looking for. "Bookkeeper" got me a lot of links to old help-wanted ads.

I searched the edition for New Year's Day, five years back. Everyone agreed Mrs. Zelisko had arrived in Busman's Harbor around then. There was nothing of note in that day's paper, so I scrolled one week back, to December 25.

The format of the online paper immediately changed. Rather than a fully searchable online version, the archives from five years earlier and before were images of the actual paper that had been digitized and put online. This format, which I could skim, might be more useful.

Even though the paper was weekly, that still left a lot of pages to go through. I figured if Mrs. Zelisko had disappeared from Busman's Harbor, having stolen from a dozen town merchants, it would be a huge story in our *Gazette*. So I decided to read backward through the issues of the Medview paper, examining front pages only.

By the time I finished looking at three years' worth, 150 front pages, I began to wonder if I was crazy. But I couldn't think of what else to do. Page was hurting, as were Vanessa and Talia. Barry, Mr. Gordon, and Al Gleason were angry, confused, and scared. And somewhere out there, there was probably a family, maybe a distant one, that deserved to know that Mrs. Zelisko, or whatever her name was, was dead.

I stood and stretched, rolling my head around on my

shoulders to release the tension in my neck. Downstairs, Gus's was quiet, in the lull between breakfast and lunch. I got a glass of ice water from my kitchen and settled back onto the couch.

I was nine years back when I found it. A Mrs. Irene Chumley, who worked as a bookkeeper for many small businesses in Medview, had disappeared into the night, taking with her money that belonged to her clients and leaving them with a mountain of debt. Several former clients were quoted in the article—the owners of an appliance store, a shoe repair shop, a small dry-cleaning chain, and a delicatessen. None of those interviewed knew anything about Mrs. Chumley, except that she spoke with an Irish accent and was a devoted member and enthusiastic volunteer at St. Theresa's Catholic church in Medview.

My heart hammered in my chest. Finally, progress. Irene Chumley and Helene Zelisko had to be the same woman. They had the same M.O.

Now that I'd spotted the front-page article, I scrolled forward in time, examining the inside pages of the paper. There were follow-up stories about Mrs. Chumley. The local police had coordinated with the FBI. Tragically, several of the businesses she'd stolen from had failed, including the appliance store and the shoe repair shop.

Hands shaking, I called Flynn.

He didn't bother to say hello. "We're about to talk to the Davies about that photo you found. Do you want to come along? They're still at the Snuggles."

"I'll be right there. I have some information that may be helpful when you talk to them."

Binder and Flynn were already inside when I arrived at the Snuggles Inn. The Davies' bags, two carry-on-sized suitcases and a backpack, waited in the front hall. The family was packed and ready to go home.

Everyone was in the inn's formal living room. The Davies sat on the antique couch. The detectives were seated in straight-backed chairs across from them. Vee and Fee hovered in the background, dying to know what was happening. There was a fire going in the hearth. Mackie snoozed on the oriental carpet.

Howard Davies held a photo in front of him, a blown-up version of the one I'd texted to the detectives. Blair and Talia sat on either side of him. All three squinted as he turned the photo from side to side.

"I don't recognize him," Howard said. "I can certainly see why someone would think it was me. We were dressed almost identically."

Blair took the photo and brought it closer to her face. "He does look older. Too old to be at a teenage party, though I can't really tell how old."

"Talia, did you see this man at the party?" Binder asked.

"I don't think so."

"Page saw him going up the stairs fifteen minutes or so before you both went up to find Mrs. Zelisko," Binder said. "Does that help you remember?"

Talia shook her head. "No."

I cleared my throat. "I think I know something about Mrs. Zelisko. She worked in your old hometown of Medview as a bookkeeper." Binder and Flynn whipped their heads around to stare at me, but they didn't stop me, so I continued. "She called herself Mrs. Irene Chumley. She disappeared nine years ago, after stealing from her clients. Several businesses closed due to their losses. Does any of this sound familiar?"

"Well, I'll be." Howard sat back on the couch, clearly surprised by the news.

"We didn't live in Medview nine years ago," Blair explained. "We were still living in Boston then. We moved to Medview for the schools when Talia started kindergarten."

"You said you had a lot of visitors from Medview over the summer," I said. "Could any of them have been victims of Mrs. Zelisko—or Chumley, as she was? Were any of your guests small-business owners?"

"I don't think so." Blair spoke slowly, thinking. "Our visitors were neighbors, fellow teachers, parents bringing friends of Talia's." She stopped. Her eyes opened wide. "Howard, what did Warren and Sue Littlefield do before they retired?"

Howard sat up straighter. "I think they owned an appliance store in town. They don't talk about it. I gathered it ended badly."

"When they visited, did the Littlefields see Mrs. Zelisko?" I asked.

"Maybe," Blair said. "Yes. I remember it now. We were in our car, returning from the botanical garden. Mrs. Zelisko came down the front walk as we pulled into our driveway. I called out to her so I could introduce them, but she didn't hear me."

"Did the Littlefields see her?" Binder asked.

"I'm sure they did." The memory was coming back to her. Blair's words came out in a rush. "They asked about her. I explained she was our third-floor tenant. The strange thing was, Warren and Sue left soon afterward. I had thought they would stay for dinner. Warren said they didn't like to drive after dark. It wouldn't be dark for hours."

"When was this?" Flynn asked.

"The end of June," Blair said. "They were our first summer visitors."

"I hate to disappoint you, but they're not who you're looking for." Howard smiled a little. "They're in their late seventies."

The energy drained from the room like water from a bathtub when the plug was pulled. Flynn shut his notebook. "Probably not then." We sat silently for a moment.

"Wait," Howard said slowly. "I remember they had hoped their son would run the business after them. When it went belly-up, he went to work selling appliances in a big-box store."

"How old is the Littlefields' son?" Binder asked.

Chapter Seventeen

Two days later, I had coffee with Binder and Flynn at Gus's. The Massachusetts State Police had picked up Peter Littlefield at Maine's request, and the detectives had traveled the two hours south to interrogate him.

"He confessed instantly," Flynn said before I sat down.

"He couldn't wait to get it off his chest. He'd clearly been suffering since the night of the murder. I almost felt sorry for him," Binder said. "Almost."

"We interviewed the parents as well," Flynn said. "Warren and Sue Littlefield recognized Mrs. Zelisko—or Mrs. Chumley, as they knew her—when they visited the Davies. They were stunned speechless, made their excuses, and left."

Gus came over and took our order. Coffees for Binder and me, tepid water for Flynn. As always, Gus took Flynn's dietary regime as a personal affront. "Drink something brown and strong, man," he said. "Put some hair on that puny chest."

Even while sitting, Flynn managed to puff out his anything-but-puny chest. "Doing fine in that department," he said.

Binder waited for Gus to leave before he spoke. "On the way home from the Davies' house, the Littlefields agreed to do nothing. They were sure they'd never see a penny of their money. Losing the business had been a horrible ordeal. They wanted the past to remain in the past.

"But as the weeks went by, Mrs. Littlefield worried Mrs. Zelisko might be at it again. She fretted about all the people who would be hurt. She was desperate to call the authorities. Mr. Littlefield absolutely refused. They reached an impasse. Last week, Mrs. Littlefield decided to confide in their son, Peter, and ask him to help persuade his father."

"Telling Peter was a mistake." Flynn picked up the tale. "He went home and stewed. He'd expected to take over his parents' business. The store had been holding its own. The Littlefields had a reputation as people who really knew their stock, made great recommendations, and provided quality, timely installation and service. Peter saw a future where he'd make a nice living, be his own boss, and be a respected business owner in the community. He thought he was set."

"Then it all ended," Binder said. "He went to work in a big-box store selling the same appliances but for twelve dollars an hour."

"The more he stewed, the angrier he got," Flynn said. "On Halloween night, he worked himself up into a state where he was determined to confront the woman he believed, not without reason, had caused his unhappiness."

Gus delivered the coffees, but not the despised glass of tepid water. Flynn would have to wait.

"Peter Littlefield swears he didn't plan to kill her," Binder continued when Gus turned and left without a word. "He wanted to talk to her, let her know what she'd done to his life. He thought it might get heated, but that was as far as it would go."

"Laying the foundation to avoid a first-degree-murder charge." Flynn was unimpressed by Littlefield's claim.

"So it was a complete coincidence he showed up on Halloween?" I asked.

"He was shocked when he pulled up to the Davies' house to discover there was a wild party in progress." Binder said. "But then he thought it might be a good cover if he was going to be yelling at her. He had some idea he would force her to return the money.

"He slipped into the house, which wasn't hard, given what was going on, and went up the stairs. Mrs. Zelisko was in her living room in her nightclothes. The television was on full blast. She didn't hear him come in. She seemed oblivious to the noise coming from downstairs. When he confronted her, she cut him dead, told him he'd never see a penny of the money she'd taken. She didn't try to deny what she'd done. She was calm, disdainful. He said that's what set him off. Before he knew it, he had strangled her."

"That's when Talia and Page came up the stairs toward the apartment, calling out for Mrs. Zelisko," Flynn said. "Mrs. Zelisko had turned off the television when she and Littlefield started their conversation. He said he almost had a heart attack when he heard the girls coming. He dragged the body into the bathroom and locked the door. He heard Page try to open it."

I shuddered, thinking how close my niece and her friend had come to a murderer. What would have happened if they had been able to open the bathroom door?

"The rest happened pretty much as you figured it," Flynn said. "The girls left, and he was stuck in the bathroom with a body. He did try to Weekend-at-Bernie's her. He wanted time to get as far away as possible. He tied the bedsheet around her and fireman-carried her out onto the landing. Mrs. Zelisko was tiny, but she was a dead weight.

As he turned to close the apartment door behind him, he lost his footing, and she slipped off his shoulder and went over the low railing. He almost did, too. He watched in horror as she fell, got caught in the chandelier, and was swung over onto the staircase. He was sure he was done for."

"But by the time he got downstairs," Binder finished the story, "the house was empty. He picked her back up, slung her over his shoulder, and executed his original plan. He went out the back door and stuffed her in the shed. He was off the peninsula before Officer Howland discovered the body."

"It almost worked." Flynn shook his head. "He had no record, wasn't in any system, and had no apparent connection to 'Mrs. Zelisko.'"

"It might have worked if Julia hadn't found the connection," Binder said.

"And the photo," Flynn added.

My coffee was cold. I'd been so engrossed in the story, I'd forgotten to drink it. "Is there any hope my friends will get their money back?" I asked.

"Above our pay grade," Flynn answered. "Now that we know she was the target of a previous investigation, that part of the case is back at the FBI."

"The money is probably abroad," Binder said. "It will take a long time to get it back, if that ever happens. Your friends should get attorneys. The IRS and the state of Maine will negotiate some kind of terms for payment."

Not encouraging. "But her victims will have to pay."

"Yes."

"Where was Mrs. Zelisko in those four and a half years between when she left Medview and when she arrived in Busman's Harbor?" It was hardly relevant, but I was dying to know.

"The FBI believes she was in Exeter, New Hampshire, running the same old game. They have cases there. They're connecting the dots," Flynn answered.

"Who was she, really?" I asked.

Binder shook his head. "That we don't know yet."

So there might never be any notification of a next of kin. No one might ever know she had died. The murder was solved, but it didn't feel great. "So many victims," I said. "Three towns worth."

"That we know about," Flynn reminded me.

"And Warren and Sue Littlefield," Binder said. "When Sue realized her conversation with her son had started a chain of events that would end up with him in prison . . . You should have seen her reaction. It about broke my heart."

Chapter Eighteen

Ten days later, Mom gave a dinner party. She invited the Davies and the Snuggs, Emmy Bailey, Vanessa and Luther, Livvie, Sonny, Page and Jack, and me. "A way to fend off the dark," she said. "A welcome to new neighbors. It can be hard to make friends here."

Thirty-five years on, Mom was still the outsider, the summer person who lived on a private island who'd married the son of a local lobsterman. Blair's loneliness had captured her heart.

Sonny went over early to help Mom cook the chicken. Livvie brought a delicious pumpkin soup. I made a fall salad composed with pomegranate seeds and mandarin oranges. Vee turned up with one of her delicious apple pies. The Davies brought the wine.

Page and I set Mom's long dining room table. "How many?" I wondered aloud.

"Fourteen, plus Jack's booster seat," Mom called from the kitchen.

I counted and recounted. "Are you sure?" I shouted back.

"Yes!"

I shrugged and did as she asked.

A few days earlier, Barry Walker had called me. "Julia, can you help me out with the business?"

"Barry, I'm neither a tax attorney nor an accountant. You need an expert."

"I don't mean with that part of it," he said. "I mean with the business itself. You see how things are here. One more season, and I'll go under even without trying to repay the tax bill. You turned your family's clambake around. Come help me. I'll find some way to pay you something."

"Maybe you've found your winter job," Livvie said when I told her about it.

I laughed. "I don't think so. I took Barry's offer to pay as a statement of good intentions, not a promise I can take to the bank."

"Not just Walker's," Livvie said. "There are lots of businesses you could help in town. You went to school for it. You saved the Snowden Family Clambake."

"With a lot of luck and an investor," I pointed out.

"An investor was what we needed." Livvie put her fists on her hips, a sure sign I shouldn't bother arguing. "Think about it."

I smiled. She was relentless. "I will."

The three girls were thrilled to see one another and disappeared into Page's room. They were still on semi-lockdown. Page had to give her phone to Livvie every day when she got home from swim-team practice and didn't get it back until the next morning. I had heard the others were on similar restrictions.

When we finally gathered around the table, I had an intense longing for Chris to be beside me. But then I looked at the remarkable women surrounding me. My mom, a widow who'd rebuilt her life after a devastating loss. Fee and Vee, never married, running their own successful business. Emmy, divorced, making it work with two kids. And Blair and Livvie, married, raising children who were entering into their teenage years. Blair had left a job she loved for the sake of her husband's career. I hoped it would turn out to be worthwhile. I hoped she would find a place in Busman's Harbor.

There was still an extra place at the table. The back door opened, and Jamie came in, calling out, "Sorry I'm late." He entered the dining room as he shed his coat. "Thanks for inviting me."

Mom looked at me. "I hate the idea of him rattling around in that big old house all alone," she whispered.

It was the dark time between Halloween and Thanksgiving. The sun set at quarter past four in the afternoon. It was like entering a long tunnel.

But the candles burned brightly on the dinner table, and the conversation flowed easily. Mom raised her glass. "To old friends." She looked at the Snuggs and Jamie, who offered their glasses. "And new." She clinked with Howard Davies, who sat beside her. "Always remember the Snowdens are here if you need us."

"And we for all of you," Fee Snugg said.

"And we for all of you," Blair Davies added.

"And me for all of you." Jamie caught my eye and brought his glass to mine.

"Cheers!" Jack yelled and winged his sippy cup across the table, where it bounced off of Jamie's head.

"Whoa! That's not how we do it!" Sonny glowered, and Jack's face fell. "You'll get it, buddy," Sonny said more softly. "You'll get it soon."

RECIPES

Vee's Gluten-free Pumpkin Cookies

In the story, Vee Snugg makes her traditional pumpkin cookies gluten-free in an attempt to entice Sergeant Tom Flynn. In reality, you can make them either way. Vee's recipe is a twist on one that used to appear on the Libby pumpkin can. Lots of people make versions of these cookies, but I think Vee's are particularly delicious.

Ingredients
3½ cups Bob's Red Mill Gluten-Free All-Purpose Baking Flour (or standard all-purpose flour)
2⅓ cup old-fashioned oats
1¾ teaspoon baking soda
2 teaspoons pumpkin pie spice
1½ teaspoon salt
3½ sticks butter, softened
1¾ cup sugar
1¾ cup packed brown sugar
1 15-ounce can of pure pumpkin
2 large eggs
1¾ teaspoon vanilla abstract
1¾ cup chopped walnuts
1¾ cup chocolate chips
Decorator icing (optional)

Instructions
Mix flour, oats, baking soda, pumpkin pie spice, and salt in a medium bowl. In a large bowl, beat butter, sugar, and brown sugar until fluffy. Add pumpkin, eggs, and ex-

tract. Mix well. Gradually add flour mixture. Add nuts and chocolate chips.

Pre-heat oven to 350 degrees. Drop 1/4 cup dough onto a parchment-covered baking sheet. Spread into a pumpkin shape about 1/4 inch thick. Continue until all dough is used.

Bake for 14–16 minutes, until firm and golden brown. Cool on baking sheets for 2 minutes and then remove to wire racks.

Decorate with icing when cool, if desired. Vee uses orange icing to outline the pumpkin ribs and green icing for the stem and leaves.

Makes 40 cookies.

Dear Reader,

I hope you enjoyed Julia Snowden's latest adventure in Busman's Harbor, Maine, as told in *Scared Off*. If this story was your first introduction to Julia, her family and friends, there are nine mystery novels, starting with *Clammed Up*. There are three additional novella collections, which also include stories by Leslie Meier and Lee Hollis, *Eggnog Murder*, *Yule Log Murder*, and *Haunted House Murder*. There are also two books in my Jane Darrowfield mystery series: *Jane Darrowfield, Professional Busybody*, and *Jane Darrowfield and the Madwoman Next Door*.

It doesn't happen often, but I got to write this tale of mayhem and murder in the season in which it is set. The lead-up to Halloween in 2020 was a decidedly scary time as parents debated whether trick-or-treating was safe. If their wild party had broken out this year, Page, Vanessa, and Talia would have been in even bigger trouble.

I hope that, as you read this story in a future I can barely imagine, you are preparing for hordes of children dressed in costumes to come to your door and then donning your own costume to go out to a party. If not, I wish for you a glass of warm cider, a plate of Vee's delicious pumpkin cookies, and a good book.

Sincerely,

Barbara Ross
Portland, Maine

I'm always happy to hear from readers. You can reach me at barbaraross@maineclambakemysteries.com, or find me via my website at www.barbararossauthor.com, on Twitter @barbross, on Facebook www.facebook.com/barbaraann ross, on Pinterest www.pinterest.com/barbaraannross and on Instagram @maineclambake. You can also follow me on Goodreads at https://www.goodreads.com/author/show/ 6550635.Barbara_Ross and on BookBub at https://www. bookbub.com/authors/barbara-ross.